FIND MY WAY DOWN TO YOU

Also by Julian Winters

-For Young Adults-

Running with Lions

How to Be Remy Cameron

The Summer of Everything

Right Where I Left You

As You Walk On By

Prince of the Palisades

-For Adults-

I Think They Love You

Last First Kiss

FIND MY WAY DOWN TO YOU

JULIAN WINTERS

VIKING

VIKING
An imprint of Penguin Random House LLC
1745 Broadway, New York, NY 10019
penguinrandomhouse.com

Edited by Dana Leydig
Text set in Baskerville

Library of Congress Cataloging-in-Publication Data is available.

First published in the United States of America by Viking, 2026

Manufactured in the United States of America
BVG

ISBN 9780593624456
1st Printing

The authorized representative in the EU for product safety and compliance is Penguin Random House Ireland, Morrison Chambers, 32 Nassau Street, Dublin D02 YH68, Ireland, https://eu-contact.penguin.ie.

For my nephew, Julian—
thank you for making me unafraid
to carry on.

I miss you
every day,
every minute,
every breath.

There is no end

To what a living world

Will demand of you.

—Octavia E. Butler,
Parable of the Sower

In vita sumus.

In morte vivimus.

In life we exist.

In death we live.

Prologue

The Before

FOR AS LONG as stories have been told, Death has never made promises nor compromises, bargains nor deals.

It is a rule I follow, without question or exception.

Yet . . . here I am. Back in a place I should not be. At least, not this soon.

The halls are bright and drenched in a familiar sourness: ammonia and decay and unrest.

I stand in the doorway to one of the many rooms. Behind me, nurses in pastel scrubs and doctors with long, remorseful expressions pass as if nothing is out of the ordinary. They cannot see me. Not unless I choose for them to.

I do not.

Machines beep in the distance. They are an underscore to the voice that cuts through my ears, sharp as a scythe. I hear him in my head. The boy I came here for earlier. His last request.

Please.

Over time, I have grown accustomed to the pleas of mortals. Their crying and begging. The fullness of their anger and sadness and regret. Their selfish *wants.* But this boy was different. His request was rare.

Somehow, he plucked the right chord that made me listen.

Please. Just this one thing.

I shake away the last dregs of his words to watch another boy inside the room.

Artificial light casts a harsh halo around him. Ivory pours through his curls like a river of starlight. His hunched body is curved like one side of a lyre.

He stands over a bed. Over a corpse.

A sling binds his left arm to his chest. His free hand trembles as it touches cold skin. Flecks of garnet cover his white shirt. Blood, mostly but not all his.

A soft chant streams from his lips. Three words—an apology. They are only interrupted by fractured breaths.

I am never here for this part. For the aching. For the goodbye.

I watch as the boy with starlight in his hair and tears on his round cheeks finally lifts his chin. *He is like any other mortal*, I tell myself. But when his umber gaze focuses in my direction, I freeze, startled, confused.

It is as if he sees something in the doorway. No, *someone.*

But that is not possible.

His stare is unwavering, unblinking. A deer finally aware it is being watched. His breathing slows as my muscles tense. We are motionless for more breaths than I choose to count. Gradually, his head droops and he cries once more for the cold corpse beneath his fingers.

My shoulders relax until a new voice emerges in my head.

Her voice.

I listen to her call. It is time to leave. This is not my only stop tonight.

It never is.

Before I can walk away, my eyes are drawn to him again. The boy who is barely holding on. Exhaustion turns his whimpers to silence. His quivering body to a stillness like oceans beneath the moon. I wait to see if he will look my way one last time.

He does not.

But I find myself lingering in that doorway a moment longer. Staring as an ending eventually becomes his beginning.

1

Nearly Two Years Later

I BARELY HAVE one foot through the door before I hear, "You're late."

It's Max.

She breezes past me. A stack of dirty plates is balanced in her hands. I look at the time on my phone.

Sixteen minutes late, to be exact. A new record.

I wish that was funny. That I had a reason to laugh. I didn't mean to be late, *again*. To stay in bed after two different alarms went off, curled in on myself, staring into the blurry edges of nothingness. Waiting for the tide to recede.

It's been almost two years, and I still haven't learned how to stop it from happening on my own yet. I'm not sure I ever will.

"You'll never get promoted like this," Max teases from behind the front counter.

I flash a weak smile. "From busboy to cashier is considered a promotion?"

"Not with that attitude!" someone calls from the kitchen. Junie, no doubt.

Max shakes her head. "Napkins are restocked. Shakers refilled," she tells me. "I reset tables three, four, and eight. I also—"

"Cleaned the restrooms?" I chance with little hope.

Her lips twist into a smirk. "Even I have limits, August."

As I pass her, Max adds, "And I'm taking a cut of your tips. Compensation for all this extra labor."

I shrug. Whatever. I don't have the strength to care. Besides, Max is the only reason I have this job. The only reason I managed to survive the last two years of high school with minimal incidents.

I owe her more than the sad tips I take home every week.

On my way through the pizzeria kitchen, I say, "I'm gonna be late on rent. Again."

"I'm shocked," she deadpans.

My feet drag as I go.

The employee restroom is tucked in a corner of a slender hall. Just beyond my boss's office. I stride by with my head down, but Angela is nowhere in sight.

Behind the locked door, I strip off my wrinkled T-shirt. I replace it with a loose heather gray VIVA CATALINA'S shirt from my bag. In the water-speckled mirror, my reflection taunts me.

Mussed auburn curls rest against my forehead like tightly

wound ribbons. The warped lighting washes out my mellow brown skin. Faint dark circles sit under my eyes like bruises. I never get enough sleep. My cheeks seem thinner too, my jaw too long.

Most days, I almost don't recognize myself.

I don't see August Clarke anymore.

Just a shadow of who I used to be.

Before the accident, I remind myself. As if I needed it.

The scents of fresh dough and earthy basil hit me the moment I'm back in the kitchen. My stomach growls. I forgot to eat before catching the bus. It's not the first time.

"'Sup, August!" Junie calls in his infectious, surfer-like drawl.

I wave half-heartedly to him and Tonia as they work on new pies. From there, I move on autopilot. It's the same routine: clear tables, gather dishes, clean the customer restrooms.

Dad would love that. Knowing I'm using my gap year to refill toilet paper dispensers. That I'm working at a pizzeria instead of being a freshman in college.

Fall quarter at UC Santa Barbara started this week. That's where I'm supposed to be. That was the plan.

Our plan.

But even after struggling to fill out the application and pretending the acceptance decision mattered, I knew I couldn't do it without him.

Without London.

When I emerge from cleaning the toilets, a melodic pop

song is playing overhead. Something from the eighties. Viva Catalina's music taste matches its decor: nostalgic. From the classic red gingham covering the plush booths and stools to the art on the walls. Not the kind of place eighteen-year-olds like me and Max would go voluntarily.

Which is why I like it. I never run into old classmates. Kids who know what happened sophomore year.

"Order sixteen! Double pepperoni to go for Dana!" Max calls out.

I slide behind the counter to fold napkins around clean silverware next to her. "What *is* this?" I point to the speakers.

She snorts. "Not a fan?"

"No."

"Well, Angela loves this stuff."

I try not to grimace. "Does she *hate* the customers?"

Max rolls her eyes. She's unfairly pretty. Silky, straight raven black hair scooped up into a bun on her head. Warm beige skin with hints of rose in her cheeks. She has her mom's heart-shaped face and her dad's delicate bone structure.

"No one cares but you," she comments.

The pizzeria is slow for a Thursday in late September. At the far corner booth, someone sits, head bowed. A group of thirtysomethings share a pie outside on the patio. The regulars gather at the bar: Miranda, crunching on a salad; Howard, piling grated Parmesan on his cheese slice; Hal, peeling off his ball cap, sweat dripping off his pale white skin as he orders his usual. But Max is right.

No one seems to care about the music. Only me.

I feel an itch in my palm. A want to scrawl lyrics on a blank page. To write something different, better. I quickly shut that feeling down. Who would I show it to, anyway?

"Hey." Max nudges me. She's a generous five foot six. But I'm six one. The height difference means her pointy elbow collides with my lower ribs. "Can you run an order to table nine?"

"The corner booth?" I look up from the same fork-and-knife duo I've folded and refolded three times now. "Why can't you?"

"I'm busy."

My eyes narrow. "With what?"

She holds up her phone like that's an answer. "I'm texting a girl. We met at orientation. I think she likes me."

"How can you tell?" I ask.

Max gives me an incredulous glare. She once told me she gives off clear sapphic vibes. I laughed until I was breathless. It's another of the many reasons I love her. There is no greater gift in the world than having a friend as queer as you.

"I need a better excuse than that," I say.

She ponders. "Best friend law?"

I've known Maxine Cho since ninth grade. Back when she fearlessly dumped her jug of ice water on a trio of boys who called me Sideshow Bob and tossed my books across the hallway floor. She didn't even flinch after they sneered at her. There was a spark in her brown eyes, as vibrant as lightning.

I knew in that moment we'd be best friends.

Since then, she's always had my back. Even at my worst, Max has been there. It's still not enough to convince me to do her job for her.

"A valid but overused reason," I say. "I have things to do."

She grabs my elbow before I can walk away. Her grin is like a hurricane. "It'll be worth it."

Discreetly, she gestures to the corner booth, where a boy sits alone. His chin is lowered. From this distance, his features are slightly shadowed, but—

"He's cute, right?" Max whispers.

I don't answer. At the end of the bar, Hal coughs roughly. He rotates his left arm in a small circle above his head. Sweat dampens his shirt. Tonia drops off a glass of water and fresh napkins for him.

Max's elbow digs into my ribs again. "Well?"

"Well, what?"

She exhales as her phone pings. "Just take him his order. He's into you."

The comment surprises me. Absently, my thumb traces the ink stained on the inside of my left forearm—a daffodil. Then, purposefully, my hand reaches for the threaded bracelet around my wrist. Blue twined around yellow. I never take it off.

It was a gift. Now a reminder.

Max notices. Her eyes soften with sympathy. I avert my gaze before that look turns into something worse:

Pity.

Without thinking, I focus on the corner booth again.

Early golden-hour light filters through the large window. It glints against the boy's dark hair. A crown of flames. He studies every movement around the pizzeria: A family of four walking in. Junie tossing mushrooms on a new pizza. Hal mopping his face dry.

I don't recognize him. He's not a regular. Santa Barbara is made up of more college students than locals. Streams of tourists who come and go. People who never leave their mark.

But something stirs in my belly, as if I *should* know his face.

"Auggie," Max tries. Her voice drips with that tone I hate. The unspoken *you can't live like this forever; you need to try again.*

It's a conversation I dance away from at every opportunity. Because I don't know how to have it. Even after all this time.

I wish there was a way for me to tell her—to tell everyone—that I can't move on as easily as they did. As if that night never happened. As if they've made their peace with the past.

So instead, I say, "You don't even know if he's into guys."

Max scoffs. "He's stared at you at least ten times since you got here."

That sounds like a lie. But heat still prickles my face.

Max slides a warm plate into my hands while reading the order ticket attached to it. "His name's Cary."

The intense sweetness of pineapples rises into my nose. I frown at the slice of pizza. It's not even Hawaiian with ham . . . only pineapples.

Who orders that?

When I hesitate, Max gives me a "polite" shove. A scowl

threatens to darken my face. But it's not worth it. Max has already returned to focusing on her phone. This is no longer her problem.

An impatient throat clears.

I almost drop the plate. How did I get to table nine so quickly?

Up close, this boy's beauty is unnerving. His features are like the carved marble of statues in the art galleries Max loves. High cheekbones, a long straight nose, lips shaped in a delicate bow. His dark brown hair reminds me of damp soil after a storm. It's slicked away from his face, a single curl resting against his forehead.

He looks around my age, yet somehow older. It's hard to describe. Like he's seen the world in ways I haven't.

A bored expression blooms over his face.

"Is that mine?" His voice is rich and deep. He has an accent I can't place. Foreign but strangely familiar.

"Y-yes," I stammer.

His eyes are black as the sea underneath a moonless sky. They're hard to look away from.

I clear my throat, pretending to read the ticket. "Cary?"

One of his eyebrows flexes. There's a sharp contrast between his all-black clothing and pale gold skin. His gaze drifts from the plate to the open space in front of him.

Oh, right.

I slide the pizza onto the table. "Here you go."

Then, to my own surprise, I don't walk away. Curiously, I say, "Only . . . pineapple?"

Cary flicks open a napkin. He doesn't answer.

That's my cue to get back to work. But I don't. "It's not a bad choice," I tell him. "I prefer my pizza sweet *and* spicy."

"I did not ask."

The suddenness of his cold tone pierces me. An arrow ripping through skin.

My head tilts. "Sorry, what?"

"I did not ask," Cary repeats with that same curtness, "what you like."

Embarrassment burns across my cheeks. I shift on my heels. The urge to leave grows. So does something else under my skin. An annoyance that's slowly building from a smolder to a flame.

During training, Angela laid out her rules.

The first: *While they're in Viva Catalina's, the customer is* always *right.*

From the moment I started here in June, I've respected that rule. I've never broken it. But with Cary . . . it's hard not to. His cruel, downturned mouth. The blade-sharpness of his glare, like he's searching for a weakness.

My life has been split in half since that incident two years ago. Divided into the promising August of Before and the ashes of August After. Who I was then—hopeful and logical and tethered—isn't who I am now.

Now I'm impulsive. Reckless with my decisions.

Most days, I keep it bottled up. I ignore the clawing beneath my skin.

But not today.

I lean down, lowering my voice. "For someone who has such a sweet tooth, you sure are salty." His finely shaped jaw tenses. I don't allow him room to retort. "Next time, add some pepperoni and jalapeños. It might make your personality a little more . . . original."

Once the words break free, guilt spreads like blood from an open wound. I shouldn't have said that. He's a customer. It was too far. It wasn't me.

The *old me*, I mean.

Angela's going to fire me. An apology fumbles around my throat.

I stop myself when Cary's eyes flash. Gold spilled over black ink. At least, it looks that way. Maybe my humiliation is playing tricks on my mind.

"You assume there will be a next time," Cary finally says. His fingers curl into fists on the table.

I open my mouth.

"You can go now," he says with a dull, uncaring voice.

His eyes—*black, they're black*—look past me. As if I'm not there.

Invisible.

Whatever I planned to say fades as the music overhead comes into focus. I recognize the song. I haven't heard it in forever. On purpose. But it streams through my ears, clear as water.

The lyrics slam into me like the other car that night: *Gonna leave this world for a while.*

A wave rises in my stomach. It swells fast. Fills my lungs. My vision blurs like morning condensation on a window. I'm drowning, and once again, those lyrics are the last words I hear before everything falls apart.

"Auggie?"

Distantly, I hear Max's voice under the tide. Almost as loud as Tom Petty's singing. The voice that haunts my nightmares.

"I need air," I gasp out.

My feet carry me past her. She tries to follow.

"Alone," I snap, unintentionally. "Give me a minute. I'm fine."

I'm not.

I never am in these moments. But admitting that out loud is too risky.

A tear slices hotly over my cheek. I stumble through the kitchen. Past Angela's closed office door.

My shoulder slams through the pizzeria's back door. I ignore the throb it leaves behind. All I want is for the music to stop.

The door swings shut behind me, snuffing out the noise. Fresh air doesn't come fast enough. I cough as rot creeps into the back of my throat. Ripe trash and filth.

My wet eyes trail over my surroundings. I'm in the alley

behind the restaurant. A thin passage between buildings.

The wave continues to push against my skin. It screams for release. For me to open the gates. I refuse. It'll be too much.

I'll never be able to stop it.

Bile sits sour on my tongue. Wincing, I swallow it down.

It happened so long ago. I should be past this by now, I remind myself.

Stray tears fall on my lips. Salt on my tongue. I'm too scared to close my eyes. To see it all again against the backs of my lids. After another long breath, I cycle through the tips I've learned from watching online videos about how to handle situations like this.

I brace my back against the nearest wall. The bricks are sun-warmed under my fingertips.

What do you see? one of the videos asked.

A blue sky bruised pink and crimson. Like the sun refuses to go down without a fight.

Next, I focus on what I can hear. Cars honk in the distance. Halogen lights flicker on. The tiny splash from a cat crossing over a growing puddle. A pipe must've burst recently.

Then, footsteps. Nearby.

Movement crosses my periphery. Through the unshed tears blurring my vision, I recognize the shape of a person. Someone emerges from behind a dumpster.

His face wakes a sharp gasp from my lungs.

Cary.

"*You*" scrapes out of my tight throat.

He's frozen, startled. The alley's shadows crawl hungrily toward him.

"What—"

The word hasn't even skimmed my lips before Cary's gone. Like a ghost.

"—the fuck," I finish while staring at the spot where Cary *should be.*

But he's not.

My gaze roams past the dumpster. There's a boot on the ground. Cinderella's forgotten shoe.

Cold sweat snakes down the back of my neck. I struggle to walk on steady legs. My shallow breaths fight for a consistent rhythm. All the effort is useless after I step around the puddle.

What I find makes me jump:

Lifeless eyes stare back at me. Blue and dull as old denim. A mouth cracked open as if it struggled for a last breath. Or tried to shout for help. The body is propped against the brick wall like a discarded marionette.

This isn't a random stranger lying dead in an alley.

It's . . . Hal.

2

HAL'S CORPSE ISN'T the first I've seen up close.

The memory always starts like this:

The sharp scent of antiseptics burns the inside of my nose. Thick, salty tears fill my throat. Underneath my fingertips, there's no pulse. Only ice-cold skin. He lies motionless on the table.

Dead.

His body is spared the cuts I suffered. The scars that took months to fade. But a river of dried blood snakes from his temple to his collarbone.

Traumatic brain injury, the doctors whisper. Their voices are like thin breezes. Nearly silent compared to the ache thundering in me.

Helpless, I stare at him. Blue lips that once held contagious smiles. Sunlit tan skin now pale as milk. His eyes are shut, but

I remember how green they were, like aloe. Under the LED panel lights, shards of glass glitter in his wavy brown hair.

He was smart. Funny. He stole attention from every room. He held me like nothing could rip us apart. He was everything.

He was . . . mine.

And in the flash of a traffic light changing. The press of my foot against the accelerator. In a blink, the suddenness of another car smashing into ours, London Sanders became a *was* instead of an *is*.

Outside the hospital room, my parents wait with his. They give me a moment, for a goodbye. But my splintered voice can only say this:

I'm so sorry.

Over and over.

Those words change nothing. They don't silence the howlingly loud guilt inside me. They don't bring him back.

I was sixteen when I stood over my first dead body.

I'm eighteen when a detective questions me about the second one.

"Mr. Clarke?"

The sterile hospital room fades. So does London's body. My shaking hands clutch at empty air, desperate to hold on to him a little longer.

I'm back in the alley behind Viva Catalina's. The stench of rancid trash clogs my throat again. Yellow tape ropes a barrier around the area. Red and blue lights from a SBPD patrol vehicle cast weird shapes along the brick wall in front of me.

I focus on the ground. Hal's corpse is gone. Crime scene markers map out where he was. They tell the story of what the police *think* happened. No one truly knows, not even me.

"You were saying?"

Detective Rosado looks as if she would rather be anywhere but in a fetid alley behind a pizzeria at 5:53 p.m. on a Thursday.

"I—" It hurts to swallow. "What now?"

Rosado sighs. "You said you saw someone else here." She consults her notes. "Another boy? Cary?"

A shiver ripples through my muscles. I refuse to blink. If I do, his face will be there. Sculpted stone. Shimmering eyes.

An impatient knot forms on Rosado's light brown forehead. "Cary as in . . . Grant? Like the actor?"

Max sidles up to me. "More like Elwes. From *The Princess Bride*."

It's one of her favorite movies. Her warmth is welcoming. She eyes Rosado, her lips curling with obvious intrigue. The detective is at least a decade older than us. That's never stopped Max before.

Rosado doesn't return the interest. "And this Cary? You saw him—"

Max half turns to me. "What happened with him?"

I recognize her curious expression. "It's not what you think."

"But *you* thought he was hot, right?"

Rosado pinches the bridge of her nose, annoyed. "Sorry, am I hearing this right? You were flirting with the *potential suspect*?"

"I wasn't," I insist.

Despite Max's hopes, I have no interest in Cary. How could anyone? He's as cold as the Pacific just after sunrise.

He's also a murderer. At least, it looks that way.

"Auggie, I don't think it was him," Max says. "He was still sitting at his table when you—" She bites her lip. But I know what that pause means. What she's trying to hide from me.

Pity dressed as sympathy.

My eyebrows knit. "I saw—"

Rosado cuts me off with a raised hand. Her partner, a short and stocky white man, approaches. He whispers in her ear.

"We have another witness," Rosado announces. "The manager from the coffeehouse next door. He said he saw Mr. Clarke having a panic attack?"

My mouth goes impossibly dry.

Rosado's eyes scan me for a second longer before she moves on. "He didn't see anyone else. Just Mr. Clarke. And the body."

Panic flares under my rib cage. A cornered beast trying to escape. I'm familiar with the potent stare she gives me. There was a dead white man left in an alley. The only other person around was a young Black boy.

I've heard this story before. I know how it ends.

On instinct, my fingers reach for the threaded bracelet around my wrist. I pull hard. My breaths sync to the mild sting.

"I didn't—"

"You're not a suspect, kid," Rosado interrupts.

I flinch at her tone. It's how most adults talk to teens. As if we are always being dramatic. Every thought and feeling and experience we have is an overreaction.

The officer on the night of the accident spoke to me the same way.

It wasn't your fault, kid.

How does he know? He wasn't in the car. Was it supposed to be comforting? Nothing about what he said made me feel any better about my boyfriend, my first love, being dead.

"We spoke with the other customers and staff inside Viva Catalina's," Rosado continues. "Mr. Connely showed no signs earlier."

"No signs of what?" Max asks, startling me.

I forgot she was there.

"A heart attack," Rosado says flatly.

"A heart attack?" I rasp out, confused.

"That's what SB Cottage Hospital's emergency docs believe. They're running tests. We'll know in a few hours."

Rosado pockets her notepad. End of discussion. Case closed.

But it can't be.

"I'll be in touch if we have more questions," she says, like she's read my thoughts. Before she turns away, her eyes study me one last time. "Are you sure you saw someone else, Mr. Clarke?"

Yes, I want to scream.

Cary was right here. Where Detective Rosado is standing now. I saw him . . . didn't I?

Grief does weird things to the brain chemistry. My dad said this a few months after the accident. He works at the hospital. As a pediatric nurse. He was the first person at my side that night when the ambulance brought us to the trauma center.

Sometimes, I think I see him. London. In the corners of crowded rooms. Walking down a street. A shadow moving along the walls, shaped like him, with his broad shoulders and long, narrow torso.

It will pass, Dad promised. It hasn't yet.

I know what I saw in this alley. And I know Detective Rosado will never believe me.

"Mr. Clarke?" she repeats.

I look away. "Maybe not."

Angela closes the pizzeria early.

"Out of respect," she says, frowning at the stool Hal loved to sit on. "We lost one of our own today."

Hal was a Viva Catalina's lifer. He came by every afternoon for the last fifteen years. At least, that's what the staff says. I didn't know him that well. I knew his order, the well-worn, frayed-brim hat he took off every time he greeted someone.

But I didn't know he was in his late forties. That he had no partner, no children. Not until Angela tells me.

I stare at the hardwood floor, ashamed. Sad.

Who will mourn him? How will they react when they find

out he died in an alley behind a pizzeria? Who will cry at his funeral?

My vision hazes as a memory comes into focus. A church's tall wooden doors. My trembling hand reaching to open them. The swift recoil of my arm when I thought about what was waiting for me on the other side.

"Okay?" Angela asks, squeezing my shoulder.

As the image disappears, I nod. I'm fine. I have to be.

I can't bear one more look like the one Detective Rosado gave me.

I used to get it all the time. From teachers. Our neighbors. Anyone who knew what happened to London. Who he *was* and who I *am*.

The boy who survived.

Angela tells us to close up and go home. When she returns to her office, we shift into motion. Cleaning and putting things away.

While wiping down tables, I absently walk to table nine. The corner booth. A plate waits in the center, an untouched pizza crust the only thing left on it.

Cary was here *when I ran outside*, I remind myself.

"You missed a spot."

Max leans over my shoulder while I scrub furiously. As if I can wipe Cary's sharp face from my memory. The spark of gold in his black eyes—an ember flickering in the shadows—when he saw me in the alley.

"You could help," I grunt.

"I am."

"How?"

"By reminding you that cleaning is an avoidance tactic," she says frankly.

"Excuse me," I say, turning, "but I don't remember signing up for a session with Dr. Cho."

Her face darkens.

Max hates being compared to her parents. Specifically, her mom, one of Southern California's most sought-after therapists. She's longing for Max to follow in her footsteps. Max is majoring in art history at Santa Barbara State. Because she loves art, but also out of pure spite.

"That was rude," she gripes.

"Sorry," I say, genuine.

"You need to talk about it."

"No, I don't." Frustration eddies in my blood again. "I need to finish cleaning. So I don't get fired. So I can pay *rent*."

When her mouth twists sourly, I grin. She can't argue against that point. She can, however, knock over a saltshaker before walking away. I welcome her pettiness. Anything to steady the ebb and flow of my thoughts.

"We should go out," Junie suggests, predictably. An early night for him is just before the sun rises from the ocean. "Let's get drinks. In honor of Hal!"

Tonia shakes their head. "Please. You just want to get wasted."

"You know me too well!"

Junípero Cruz is sunshine poured into a human body. He's all smiles and jokes. Lit up with the kind of energy I used to have.

"You in, Maxie?" he says.

Max meets my eyes. There's a question waiting in hers: *Are you in?*

We both know the answer.

Junie swings an arm around her shoulders. "Come on, you have to. For Hal."

Tonia groans from the kitchen. "Please stop using a dead man's name as an excuse for your debauchery."

Junie grins relentlessly at Max. "Fine," she sighs out. "But not too late. I have Intro to World Art at eight a.m."

"Gross."

Max watches me. "Auggie?"

My fingers itch to grab my bracelet. Or drum against the air to the rhythm of my wild heartbeat.

I can always tell when you're anxious, London used to say. *You do that thing with your hands. Like you're composing a song.*

I'd tell him he was wrong. But he wasn't. He rarely was about me.

"If we both go"—I pause to clear my throat—"who will feed Diana?"

Max's lips pucker. She's unconvinced.

"Next time, right?" Junie says. He knows how this goes too.

Whenever the staff invites me out, I always say *next time.*

Next time I'll go bowling. Next time I'll come to the beach. Next time I'll be there.

The truth is, I won't. Letting new people in is dangerous. It's the allure of a glowing fire that'll burn when you get too close. A cold, empty darkness when that flame finally dies out.

That's how it felt after London. How it always feels.

"Next time," I whisper as Max, Junie, and Tonia walk out the door.

After another thirty minutes, I leave too. Not before cleaning the restrooms again. Angela thanks me with a large box of left-over pizza.

I take my time walking to the bus stop.

It's long after sunset. State Street Promenade stretches like an artery through downtown Santa Barbara. Ten blocks of Spanish Revival architecture. Red clay tile roofs and ornate wrought iron and stucco walls white as teeth. At this hour, everything is warm and gold, like light poured through a honeycomb.

My favorite time of day.

One by one, shops are closing. Sugar and salt hang heavy on the breeze. From the mouths of an Irish pub and a British one just across the street, people stumble drunkenly onto the sidewalks, their bellies full, laughter echoing. Sharp spices from Max's favorite Indian kitchen gather in my nose, heating the back of my throat.

I smile fondly.

This is the city I grew up with. Tucked between the shadows

of the Santa Ynez Mountains and the sleepy Pacific. I'm at home among the insomniacs and stay-up-until-sunrise types. I never feel strange. Or out of place.

Here, being invisible is easy. There's too much to look at. No one notices the boy going through the motions.

Holding on by the barest thread.

The night exhales noises from every direction. I listen closely.

Since I was little, I've loved to hum. Pull random tunes from thin air. By the time I turned thirteen, my dad decided to enroll me in piano lessons. I took them for a year, but I didn't enjoy it as much as when I'd sit down to write lyrics to the songs in my head. There was something about a blank page that drew my attention more than learning scales or memorizing chords or playing "Heart and Soul."

I can still kind of read sheet music, identify basic notes, but I prefer to turn the constant looping melodies I hear in my head into my own songs.

At least, I used to.

I'd only ever share my lyrics with four people: my parents, Max, and London.

You should major in music, London would say with tender enthusiasm.

Now I squeeze my fingers into a fist. I silence the tune circling my brain before it becomes a tide of more memories I don't want to face.

On my left, the door of a gelato shop swings open. A boy emerges. He's backlit by the shop's amber light. For a second, I think it's London. Tall and wiry.

But when the boy steps onto the sidewalk, streetlamps illuminating him, I realize it's not London. This boy is dressed in all black, head to toe, instead of in a navy hoodie with loose board shorts and slides with socks. His tar-black hair falls gracelessly over his brow instead of in beachy waves swept off his face. He's pasty white, unlike London, whose skin always drank in the sun.

It's not him. It *never* will be again.

I was just imagining it. Just like everyone thinks I imagined Cary in the alley. How could he have gotten there that fast? And what was he doing? Did he try to help Hal or just watch him die?

"You okay, man?"

I flinch at the not-London boy's question.

"Y-yeah," I stammer. "I'm good."

His plain brown eyes roam over me. "Do I know you?" He looks a year or two older than me. Did he go to my high school? Does he know what happened?

"No," I whisper.

Before he can say anything else, I jog away.

On the bus, I pop in my earbuds. My head leans against the cool window as my phone loads up Netflix. I do my best to lose myself in a paranormal comedy series.

Did my grief make me see Cary in the alley, the same way I see London everywhere too?

"Fuck," I mutter.

An elderly woman in front of me jerks around to squint, annoyed.

I half apologize with a thin smile.

Max and I share a third-floor apartment. It used to be her sister Vivienne's. Since most of its students are local, SB State doesn't have any on-campus living restrictions for freshmen. Max's parents had no issues with her moving into the two-bedroom that's not far from campus. I can't say the same for mine.

High school wasn't the only echo chamber I was desperate to escape after graduation. It was my house too.

Memories were embedded into the rooms and halls. A tomb of moments spent with London that ate at me daily.

But I couldn't tell my parents that. They were fine.

They didn't remember the lemon-bright mug in our cupboard London used to slurp coffee from. That the designer sunglasses on the living room bookcase were his. Or his favorite hoodie still hanging in my closet. His lip balm on my bathroom sink. The subtle scent of honey and chocolate that lingers in my room.

They didn't sleep in the bed where we kissed and talked and planned.

Their world was changed but continued to spin. Mine was shattered, broken pieces cutting into me every day.

The minute Max asked me to move in with her, I collected what I needed. Left the rest in a house that didn't quite feel like mine anymore.

Inside our apartment, I reheat the leftover pizza. Diana's nowhere in sight. Still, I leave an open tin of wet cat food for her.

When I walk into my bedroom, I leave the lights off. A secondhand mattress sits on the floor. No frame or headboard. I found it online. Max complained endlessly while helping me carry it up three flights of stairs.

Silvery beams pour through my half-cracked blinds. The walls are bare. No Polaroids of trips to the beach. No notebooks filled with my lyrics, mostly about him, cover the floor. No extra pair of sandals next to my sneakers. The room smells more of dust and emptiness than anything else.

There's not a single trace of August from Before.

I'm halfway through my second slice of pizza when a familiar head nudges my door open. Diana slinks inside. In the slices of moonlight, her black fur shimmers. She's an American shorthair, a rescue. Max decided we needed her a week after moving in.

Under Diana's big, expressive gold eyes is a patch of white fur. It's shaped like a crescent moon tipped on its back.

We have to name her Diana, Max demanded that first day.

"Goddess of the moon," I say now, smiling in the dark while tossing her a pepperoni.

She sniffs, then eats it.

After, she climbs onto a pile of clothes I need to wash in a corner of the room. She turns away from me. Rules were established between us when she first arrived. We both prefer to be ignored by the world. Unless food is involved, in her case.

Within seconds, she's asleep.

Hot adrenaline surges in my blood as my phone starts to vibrate. I'm afraid to look at the screen. What if it's Detective Rosado? What if she found more information on Cary? Or worse, she's decided I *am* a suspect in Hal's death?

Instead, it's a message from Max. A photo of her squeezed between a grinning Junie and Tonia. The image is poorly lit from whatever bar they managed to sneak Max into.

Miss you, it says underneath.

I search for words that are good enough to reply with. None come to me. I simply like the photo, then lock my phone.

Exhaustion weighs against my body. Quietly, I hope for nothingness rather than dreams and nightmares.

Every night is the same. Stardusted scenes of London's warm face. Our first kiss. His hand in mine, then ripped away. The waking terror of the crash splintering my sleep like the windshield of London's dad's car after impact.

Next comes the shouting. I can never tell from who. The paramedics or the emergency room doctors or me.

But it always comes, constant and full.

I trace my fingers over the blue-and-yellow bracelet.

"I'm so sorry," I whisper to the threads.

My eyes grow heavy. I wonder if, instead of London, I'll see Hal tonight. Dead in an alley. Or a boy with gold-flecked black eyes. With sharp features on a marble-smooth face and a cruel mouth.

I stare at the wall, counting my heartbeats. When sleep finally arrives, Cary is all I see dancing in the shadows.

The Before

"IT'LL BE FUN!"

I hesitate. We're at the entrance of a winding driveway. The sun is golden and fading. Warm light washes over London's face, his green eyes, the depth of his smile. Noises shake me from my stare.

Even from here, the loud music is jarring.

Parties aren't my favorite thing. Neither are unnecessarily large crowds. But London insisted we come.

"It's our first high school party," he said days ago, like he'd won a golden ticket. Unlocked a door that was previously hidden from us. But I don't want to open it.

I don't want to walk inside.

My eyes bounce from London's grin to the sprawling ranch-style house at the end of the driveway. It belongs to the

Ackermans. Ryan, a senior, is hosting the party while his parents are out of town. His younger brother, Troy, has classes with London. He invited us.

Well, he invited *London.* I don't really know Troy. But Ryan is one of the assholes who called me Sideshow Bob in the hallway last September. The day Max saved me.

She's not with us. I wish she was.

Nerves creep up my shoulders. My fingers twitch at my sides. London looks down and I stop, squeezing my hands into fists.

His smile lights up again. It loosens my chest. Something about being around him always makes me comfortable.

A couple of older girls pass us, giggling. One looks over her shoulder to stare at London. He doesn't notice. His eyes are locked on me. Pride stirs in my stomach.

"Come on. It's just a party," he says. "Besides, it'll be great practice. For college."

"*College?*" I laugh. "We're barely fifteen!"

His lips curl into a weird smile. I don't know how to describe it. But it's my favorite thing about him.

"It's never too early to plan," London insists. "Haven't you thought about it?"

"No."

"At all?"

I shake my head.

He groans disappointedly. London's a planner. He once

told me that every Sunday, he organizes his outfits for school. *For the entire week.* That's not me. I roll out of bed and put on whatever is least wrinkled.

London glances toward the house, then back to me. "What are you worried about? Your clothes?"

My gaze lowers. "What's wrong with my fit?"

"Nothing." London presses a hand to my white T-shirt. His fingers spread over my chest. I wonder if he can feel how erratic my heartbeat is. "I just don't get why one party has you so nervous."

"I don't know. I just am."

After I hear the words out loud, they seem . . . silly. Shouldn't I have a stronger answer? A real reason to not want to be here?

My fingers dance by my sides.

London's mouth quirks. "Okay. Hold on." He digs into the back pocket of his shorts. When his hand opens, there's a woven bracelet resting delicately on his palm. Braided threads of blue and yellow.

"Our favorite colors," London points out.

I blink, surprised.

He steps forward. "I made it for you. It was supposed to be a six-month anniversary gift."

We've been dating since October. He asked me a month after we first met at Pride Club.

I can't stop staring.

"You made this?" My voice is raspy, too in awe to work properly.

"Yeah. I watched a couple of YouTube videos on how to."

He shrugs, as if it's nothing. I smile at his modesty. He's so smart. Half the time, I don't think he even knows it. He's going to get into whatever college he applies to.

"Here." London ties the bracelet around my wrist. Then he tugs on it to make sure it doesn't slip off before standing back. "Now you can look at it whenever you get nervous. That way you don't—" He mimics what I do with my hands when I'm anxious. The way they dance in the air like I'm playing piano again. Composing a song in my head.

Heat stings my cheeks. London almost looks like he's mocking me. But he's beaming, so that can't be true.

"Thanks," I whisper. "I didn't get you anything."

Amusement lights his face. A newborn sun. "You can later."

I squint at him. "Did you make me something because you spent all the money your parents gave you on these ridiculous threads?"

I flick the collar of his diamond-patterned button-down.

He gasps. "What? No."

"Who are you trying to impress, London Sanders?"

"Nobody!"

I tug on the belt loop of his khakis, provoking. His hands shoot out to tickle my ribs. A laugh springs out of me, so loud it forces a bird in a nearby oak tree to take flight.

"I did it, you asshole," London says, grinning, breathless, "because I love you."

We both pause, frozen. The world goes silent. All but the

ocean meeting the shore, the roaring heartbeat in my ears, and his words floating away on the breeze.

Panic tenses his jaw. He's never said that before.

Neither have I.

London swallows. His face flushes pink as coral. "I mean—"

I surge forward and kiss him. His stammering stops. He kisses me back. Over time, we've gotten better at this. Still not perfect, but better.

Between noses bumping and teeth clinking, I whisper, "I love you."

It falls from my lips without thinking. Without considering the weight and boldness those words carry. Because his weird smile is pointed at me. Because he gave me this bracelet. Because, secretly, I've wanted to say it first, day after day, but I was too nervous to.

"August, I love you," he repeats.

His voice is like honey, full and warm.

I'm helpless to the hot bloom of my heart unfolding beneath my ribs.

As he leads me up the driveway, London grips my hand. Firm and secure. It stays like that the whole night.

I want it to stay like that forever.

3

MORNINGS ARE HARD.

I'm not sure what time it is. I don't have the energy to search for my phone. All I do is watch the day chase shadows off my ceiling.

Shafts of sunlight scatter across my face. I forgot to shut the blinds. My eyes are scratchy, raw like sandpaper. Sleep didn't come fast enough last night. It didn't hold me under either.

I'm still caught in a dream. In the sticky web of a memory. The ache of it is soft, tender like a newly formed bruise.

Something vibrates on the mattress. Eventually, I kick away my blanket. My phone screen is painfully bright with a notification—a new message in my family's group chat.

> Dad
>
> GOOD MORNING FAMILY!!! 😄

Mom

Morning started almost four hours ago.

I've been up at the greenhouse since dawn.

Dad

Auggie are you up? Thinking about your plan? 🤔

Frustration flickers like a flame in my chest. I'm not sure whether it's from my dad's dramatic love of emojis while texting or his final question. I pinch the bridge of my nose, calculating a calm response.

My mom answers for me.

Mom

Cooper, it's too early for that.

We both love you, son. Come visit soon.

She always knows what to say. And when to say nothing at all. I wish I was more like her. Or that I had my dad's impenetrable resolve to never get stuck in a moment for too long. Life as a nurse gave him that.

Suddenly, a harsh image blurs my vision.

Empty blue eyes. Hal's crumpled body against the brick wall.

My pulse leaps. I stare at my phone, waiting for one of my parents to comment about what happened yesterday. The message never comes.

I search through the local news headlines. A single article about an incident around State Street Promenade pops up. No mention of Hal specifically, or even Viva Catalina's. Santa Barbara is more concerned about a festival happening near West Beach this weekend than a dead man found in an alley.

It's as if it never happened. But it *did.* I was there.

So was . . .

I change my search topic. The results populate with hundreds of different Carys, but none of them are a boy with hair dark as wet earth, a face made of stone. I switch over to social media. It's a place I rarely go anymore. I don't want to accidentally stumble upon an old photo of London on one of my former classmates' profiles.

Again, I find nothing about Cary.

Defeat sits like an anchor on my chest. "I *saw* him," I whisper to myself.

It wasn't a dream. Or a hallucination. He was there. Then gone before I could blink, like . . . *magic?*

Beyond my cracked bedroom door, I hear cabinets being aggressively shut. Max swears. It's the one thing that finally yanks me from the murky depths of my thoughts and out of bed.

When I walk into the kitchen, Max announces, "It's trying to kill me!"

I smile at the offending object. "It's an espresso machine." Vivienne left it for us.

"That refuses to make my coffee right," Max snarls.

"Are you pressing the right button?"

"Of course I am."

"And the coffee button is . . . ?"

Max's hand winds in an exaggerated circle around the compact and gleaming machine. "One of those," she huffs.

With practiced ease, I swap her mug filled with watery brown sludge for a clean one. I slip a new coffee pod into the brewing chamber. Max squints as I press the button she clearly missed.

The machine hums quietly before a slow, steady brown stream fills Max's cup.

"I hate you," Max whispers, snatching up her mug.

We settle in the living room.

Our apartment is modestly decorated. Vivienne lived here throughout college, then for her graduate program too. You can't tell because of how new everything looks, from the clean, geometric-patterned area rug to the spotless kitchen appliances. We sit on the unblemished cream sofa.

Max claims her sister was like that growing up as well. *Vivienne* stays *in places, but she never* lives *there*, she told me.

Now Vivienne's in Seoul. She works in advertising, a profession her parents approve of. Max hasn't said it, but I'm convinced the Chos are paying half our rent to bribe her into pursuing a career of *their* choosing.

Diana leaps onto the coffee table. She sniffs around. The moment Max reaches out to pet her, she springs away.

Max hisses after her.

I stare disapprovingly.

"Sorry." She sips. "I'm a little cranky without my morning caffeine."

"Cranky is your default," I say. "With or without coffee."

"Have you ever been out until one a.m. with a guy who drinks like a fish, then had to sit through an art lecture at eight in the morning?"

"I can't say I have."

"It's brutal." Max takes another long slurp. Her eyes focus on me. There's a carefully calculated look on her face that I recognize.

"I'm fine," I say.

"But you—"

"I'm fine," I repeat, defensively.

Steam from Max's mug billows in a mist thin enough that it can't hide her concern. "Auggie, you had a panic attack."

"And I said I'm—"

"It's been so long since that's happened," she says, as if I wasn't speaking.

That you know of, I don't say.

I remember the last one she was there for. The day of London's funeral. When I stood in front of the church's doors. When my body trembled like a leaf clinging to a branch as autumn's winds swept in. When I could not make my feet, heavy as stone, move to enter.

He is in there, I said through the hot ache of my tears, my raw throat.

My parents didn't understand my hesitation. It was my last chance to see him. But that's not how I wanted to say goodbye. To a corpse in a casket made up to look like the boy I loved. That's not how *we* were supposed to end.

Max didn't need an explanation. She slotted into my side, like we were one. I couldn't breathe, so she did for both of us. She guided me back to the car. She never made me go inside.

There have been other moments since. I never tell her about those.

I hated that she saw me like that at the funeral, so weak. I hate that it happened again yesterday.

"It was nothing." For emphasis, I force my mouth into a wide grin.

Doubt pulls at Max's features. "What are you doing later?"

"Picked up Kennedy's afternoon shift," I say.

I need the money. The distraction too. Work keeps me busy. It prevents me from staring at the shadows, hoping that London will come back.

Miracles are for people who believe in wishes on birthday candles and throwing coins in a fountain. I don't believe in either.

"Is Angela even opening today?" Max checks her phone.

I shrug. "I'd assume so."

If there's one thing I've learned about death, it's that the world doesn't stop for it. Especially not businesses.

"Okay, what about *after* your shift?" Max asks.

"Why?"

"We're going to a party," she says. "On campus."

Absently, my fingers reach for the threaded bracelet on my wrist. A memory tries to pull me under. I scramble to find words to remind Max why I *can't* go to UC Santa Barbara's campus. Why I've avoided it for so long.

After reading my face, she hastily amends, "*SB State* campus. It's a dorm party."

My breath finds a normal rhythm. "Max," I start, uninterested.

"We have to go. Lake will be there."

A bright pink blush fills the apples of her cheeks.

"What kind of name is Lake, anyway?" I say with a sigh.

"Says the boy named *August*." Her lips purse. "I really like her. We have a cosmic connection."

I roll my eyes. Leave it to Maxine Cho to have a crush-bordering-on-marriage a week into college.

"Auggie—" She places her mug on the coffee table. Her body twists to face me. "It's *one* party."

"It's never one with you."

"After yesterday, we need this. *You* need this."

Max smiles innocently. I could say no just like I did last night when Junie invited me out. I could spend another night curled in my bed, watching my blank walls as one day ends only for another to rip me off my feet like the tide.

But I can't let her go alone. Max hasn't spent much time on campus. Besides Lake, who else would she know? What if something happens? She's all I have other than my parents.

I exhale a long-suffering breath. "Okay. But we're not staying long."

She nods. "Two hours."

"One."

Her lips slope downward. "One? That's not enough time to get Lake a drink, flirt with her, map out our future together—"

"Make it enough."

I stand. My shift starts soon. I still need to shower and catch the bus.

On the way to my bedroom, I yell, "One hour, Max, that's all!"

Santa Barbara State is a sprawling campus. Not near the size of UC Santa Barbara. But it's just as nice.

The property line stretches from the edge of Shoreline Drive where the ocean growls to a few miles shy of downtown. Milk-white buildings with tiled roofs as red as tongues pop up everywhere. Palm trees and thick-trunked eucalyptuses rise from the grounds.

I follow Max past the library. Along the winding path of academic centers. We cross the footbridge high above Loma Alta Drive toward the west campus, where the dorms are.

Noises hit me before we reach the second floor. Voices straining above the music's hammering bass. The clink of beer bottles. Laughter echoing off the walls.

The smell is next. A cloud of sour sweat and citrus-sharp alcohol and cast-off furniture no one has ever bothered to clean.

"Don't make that face," Max warns.

"What face?"

"We're here to have a good time, Auggie."

"No. *You're* here to talk to a girl," I remind her.

"Which is a good time," she says airily, smiling over her shoulder. "And if *I'm* having a good time, then you are too."

"That's not true," I counter.

"It is if you believe it!"

The dorm is one of those suites. Two bedrooms are opposite each other, doors thrown open with students spilling out. The living room is overcrowded with people. I'm not sure how anyone else will fit inside. Somehow, we do.

The lights are off. Strips of blinking LEDs on the ceiling illuminate all the faces. They look alien under the blue-and-green glow. In a corner, a group of girls talk with drinks in hand. I notice the one in the middle—short, curvy, and muscled, hair bright like afternoon sun.

Without Max telling me, I know who she is.

Max waves at Lake. Her next destination is obvious.

I grab her wrist before she can drift too far away. "Phone and location on at all times."

She grins, as if expecting this part. As if it's as comforting to her as it is for me. "Answer every text," she says, nodding.

"Pick up every call."

"Check in every thirty minutes."

"Don't go home with strangers," I recite. A wry smile hooks

my mouth. "Especially not with girls named Lake."

Max wiggles free of my grip. In the harsh flashing colors, her eyes go tender. "Do you want to come with me? Or I can stay here."

She bites her lip. On the margins of her expression, I see concern. She's worried I won't be okay without her.

"What?" I pretend to not be annoyed. "And be the third wheel to your hookup? No thanks."

She elbows me. "I was being nice."

I lean down to say, "You failed. Now go. I might vomit if I have to watch Lake stare at you like she wants to eat your face a second longer."

Even in the room's shadows, pink pops warmly against Max's cheeks.

"Every thirty minutes," she repeats.

"Every thirty minutes," I parrot.

Max drifts off. I squeeze through the knot of bodies in the other direction.

There isn't much more room in the kitchenette. People rotate in and out. Some for beers. Others wrench open the refrigerator, faces washed out by the bright interior light. Awkwardly, I claim a space in the corner.

I never went through the party phase my classmates did. I wasn't interested. Or, well, I wasn't comfortable enough, even in spaces I knew and felt safe. Between us, London was the social one. The shameless extrovert.

He moved through rooms like the sun, always drawing

attention. Always leaving a hint of his warmth behind.

He would fit in here. He wouldn't be pressed to a wall, avoiding eye contact with all passersby. London wouldn't wince at the boring music. Or flinch at something crashing to the floor. The sharp pierce of laughter that follows.

"Here."

I look up, startled.

A boy leans against the counter. He's long and wiry. His thick black hair shines like a crow's feathers, ending at his collarbone. In his fingers is a plastic shot glass. He extends it toward me.

Violently blue liquid sloshes over the sides.

"You look like you could use it," he says.

I inspect the tiny cup, then him again.

He looks older than me, but only slightly. His delicate features—both his defined cheekbones and angular jaw—stand out against russet brown skin. South Asian, I think. He raises a thick eyebrow at me. The shot glass too.

"I'm not a drinker," I tell him.

"More for me." He tips his head back. Downs the liquid without spilling.

I watch greens and blues dance across the thin gold necklace he wears. The charm at the end is twin coiled snakes and . . . wings?

He places the empty cup on the counter. There's a neat row of them. At least five. But he doesn't seem drunk. He gestures elegantly toward the stack of cans next to the glasses.

"Bubbly water?"

"No," I say. "But thanks."

"Suit yourself." He crosses his arms, studying me. The attention warms my face. "I don't know you," he says.

I let out a short laugh. Mostly out of gratitude. I half expected this party to be filled with familiar faces. Former classmates who knew my history. So far, everyone's been a stranger.

Including this boy.

"I don't know you either," I say, not cruelly. Just a fact.

He smirks. "Are you new?"

"New to Santa Barbara?" I tilt my head. "I've been here my whole life. But I'm not an SBS freshman. *Yet.* Just visiting with—"

"No." He flaps a hand to stop me. His eyes brighten. They're light brown, almost amber in the room's weird glow. "New to this party."

"Oh." I swallow. "I came with a friend."

My eyes flit to the corner. Max is pressed into Lake's side, talking animatedly with her friends. Lake's hand is low on Max's back, her smile high on her cheeks.

"A friend," the boy repeats.

When I turn back to him, he has a fresh shot cup tipped to his mouth. His grin widens behind the plastic.

"You don't look like you want to be here."

He doesn't say it meanly. Instead, his voice is a warm, curious note above the cacophony of music and talking. Something about his loose posture makes me relax.

"Is it obvious?" I comb fingers through my curls, smiling guiltily. Sweat dampens my scalp and forehead.

The boy shrugs. "Only to me."

I don't know what he means by that. He doesn't explain. With an intense grin, he says, "Where else would you prefer to be?"

For whatever reason, I consider his question. He watches me, waiting. As if he already knows the answer I plan to give isn't the real one.

My eyes catch on something in the hallway just outside the dorm's open door. Someone striding past the room instead of into it. Even in profile, his face stops me from saying anything else. In the chaotic lights, he's a sharp shadow. His name fills my throat like a choking smoke.

Cary.

He walks with purpose around the sea of bodies trying to enter. His bored expression says this party is the last place he'd want to be.

But he's not alone.

Following close behind is a tall girl with pale white skin. Long hair flows down her back like an obsidian river. Her hand grips his.

Without thinking, my eyes leap back to him.

His head turns, as if he feels my stare. Our eyes meet. A chill slithers down my spine. There's a hint of surprise in Cary's face, like yesterday. The disbelief quickly dies, replaced by hard eyes, his arrow-shaped jaw straining against his skin.

Before my next breath, he disappears. The girl does too.

For a moment, I'm frozen. Shocked. Anger burns that feeling away. He knows what happened to Hal. And I want answers.

Now.

"Leaving so soon?"

The not-drunk boy inspects me, another drink hovering just shy of his amused lips. I forgot about him. I forgot what we were even talking about. My brain can only focus on one thing:

He's leaving.

"I have to go," I say, my voice tight with urgency.

One corner of his mouth goes higher. "Found the place you want to be?"

I don't respond. Who was that girl and what was she doing with *Cary*?

I'll never find out standing here.

"Sorry, it was nice to meet you," I say in a rush, already shoving my way into the hallway and down the stairs.

The night's air wraps around me like a fist. This close to the sea, the draft is strong. I can taste the salt in my throat as I look left and right.

No one's here. Only a wide green campus that I know very little about.

It's a maze with its identical palm trees and ivory buildings. I turn in circles. Suddenly, I can't remember which way we walked earlier. And there's nothing to indicate what direction Cary went. Not a single footprint in the lush grass.

Where is he?

I run, fast and determined. My feet pound against the stone walkways. I cross through an empty quad. Past the library lit orange by streetlamps. My eyes search hastily around.

A buzzing noise loops in my head. I ignore it, just like I ignore how my lungs swell and shrink too quickly. The exhausting ache that climbs up my legs.

Nightfall reshapes the campus until I'm not sure if I'm farther or closer to where I started.

Finally, I stop in another quad. A large fountain sits at the center. Sweat drips down my brow as I walk around it. My heaving chest fills with disappointment.

He's gone. *Again.*

In the middle of the stone fountain is a sculpted warrior on a pedestal. A Trojan, Santa Barbara State's mascot. Water leaps in clear streams from the well surrounding him. It falls back down in a splashing melody. Beneath that, I hear the buzzing again, loud, incessant.

It's my phone.

"*Where* are *you?*" Max yells the moment I answer.

"I don't know." I turn in another circle. "Nearby? I think I see a cafeteria."

"Why'd you leave?" Her voice is a mix of fury and frustration and fear.

"I saw him."

"Saw who?"

"Cary." His name is like sand in my mouth, coarse and

unwanted. "He's on campus. I need to find him and—"

"God, August," Max groans, the last syllable breaking wetly. "I don't have time for this."

My back stiffens. "What's wrong?"

"Th-there's—" She pauses to clear her throat. "There's a dead girl. In one of the dorms down the hall from the party. Someone *found* her. Everyone's freaking out. We don't know what happened."

With every word, my heart races.

I'm dizzy. Max is still talking. I hear her, but distantly.

"I don't even know who she is," she is saying, breaths as shallow as mine. "I've seen her before . . . I think? She's so tall and pale. Always wears her hair down—"

"Does she have black hair?" I ask.

Max sniffs. "Yeah, why?"

I flop down on the edge of the fountain. *The girl walking through the hall with Cary*. But how could she be back in the dorms already? Did they ever leave? Did I . . . imagine everything?

My eyes dip to the water. I blink, confused.

In the ripples I see them: Cary and the girl. They're upside down, and not on campus anymore. Somewhere different, stranger.

The moon is half-full, throwing a soft silvery glow on the water's surface. Maybe it's a trick of the light. Except, no, they're there, talking. Oblivious of me watching.

"*August?* Are you still there?"

I pull my phone from my ear. My free hand trembles as I reach for the water. "It's not possible," I whisper.

Cold creeps up my skin as my fingers break the surface. The image doesn't fade. It buckles and re-forms. I sink my wrist into the water. I wait for whatever I'm seeing to just be an aftereffect of my grief.

Instead, I feel a light grip, like getting your feet caught in the wet sand. Then a stronger tug. I try to lurch back, but my arm can't escape. It's as if the water wants me, refusing to let go until it wins. And it does.

Before I can scream for help, I'm dragged into the fountain.

Under, under, deep into the darkness.

4

THE WATER WELCOMED me, warm and flowing. Slipped across my body as gentle as fingers. Embraced me like we knew each other. I was submerged but not drowning. Then it spit me out, fast and abruptly, a bad taste in its mouth.

Now I'm on my hands and knees, coughing. My skin is feverish, but inside, ice runs like an aching stream through my blood. Heaviness weighs on my muscles.

Yet, I am . . . completely dry.

Like I was never in the fountain.

Bile stirs in my belly. Between my curled hands, something soft and grainy slips over my palms. *Sand.*

Slowly, my eyes blink open. How did I get to the beach?

No. This isn't the deep brown sand of Leadbetter Beach. It's salt white. Instead of an indigo sea, the water is black as a starless sky. It sings almost the same—long and sweet as it rolls closer, but there's an undercurrent of something else in it.

Something *wrong*.

This isn't Santa Barbara.

This isn't home.

Panting, I push to my feet. A warm breeze thick with scents of brine and sugar tickles the back of my neck. I look up. The sky is a vast canvas of pink swimming through purple. Like the edge of sunset without a sun anywhere in sight.

In the distance, beyond the endless water, something glints. The shape is hard to make out. It's tall and sharp. A blade puncturing the sky, spilling all its colors like blood.

I want to inch closer for a better view.

My feet don't make it far.

A hand grabs my shoulder. Harsh fingers pinch into tendons. I stumble back, sand flying from beneath my shoes. Fear and adrenaline spike through my body. Another hand grips my shirt, whipping me around.

I'm met with a snarling mouth and dark eyes fringed with gold.

"*How* did you get here?"

It's Cary, teeth fully bared. He pulls carelessly at my collar, almost tearing the soft cotton.

"Where—" My throat tightens. "*Where* am I?"

"Answer my question."

His breath is hot against my face. In this strange light, his beauty almost equals his wrath. My attempt to wrestle away is useless. He's stronger. With ease, he drags me back.

"Answer me," he says again, his voice a low growl.

"Where the fuck am I, Cary?" I spit back.

The margins of his face jump. He's shocked by my own angry sneer. The way I call him by his name. His hold on me loosens a bit. I take advantage.

I latch a hand onto his narrow hip. The other grasps a fistful of his black shirt. I plant my feet, twisting to throw him off me, but he's agile and more coordinated.

We tumble into the sandy shore. I land half on top of him. Instinct tells me to flee, but my limbs are still heavy.

Cary kicks and rolls. Within a second, I'm on my back, Cary scowling over me. His hands pin my wrists against soft sand, knees bracketing my thrashing hips.

"Get . . . off," I huff.

"Tell me," he barks. "How did you get here?"

"Where is *here*?"

Through the slits of his eyes, the gold expands, nearly swallowing every inch of rich blackness I can see.

He repeats, darkly, hands gripping tighter, "Tell me now, and no harm will come to you."

My arms ache from exertion. From fighting to escape. It's useless. His body is pressed against mine. I manage to choke out a response before the pain gets any worse.

"I followed you," I gasp, breathless, confused. "On campus. There was a fountain and I saw you with—" A surge of panic electrifies me. "Where's the girl?"

"Girl . . ."

"The girl! From SB State. She was with you."

Again, surprise smooths the cold edges from his expression. "It is not possible," he says quietly. "You could not . . ."

"Well, I did!"

I flail harder, but that doesn't work either. Even stunned, Cary is in control. Exhaustion holds me beneath him. A prisoner. His next victim.

"Are you going to kill me?" I ask, a tremor in my throat. "Like you did Hal."

He blinks, thick eyelashes beating. "Who?"

"Hal! The man in the alley. Behind the pizzeria," I elaborate. "You were there. I saw you."

I watch the small knot in his throat move as he swallows, the motion hypnotic like a metronome. He studies me. I can't read his expression. Something flashes through his eyes when they stray to my arm trapped behind his hand. With every second of his silence, my resolve grows.

Cary lowers his head. Loose curls fall around his temples. Roughly, he repeats, "It is not possible."

"I saw you," I say, defiant.

Frustration casts a shadow across his face. A storm threatening to unleash. It never arrives.

Not far away, a voice says, "Well. This is interesting."

My head turns. Three people walk up the shore. Two of them are dressed sharply: all-black suits, gold embellishments on their taut shoulders and cuffs, a spiky white flower on their chests. They move like soldiers, cadence synchronized. Gleaming swords in their hands.

My breath hitches, loud and panicked. Until the third person comes into focus.

"You," I strain.

"You," he says back, beaming. The boy from the party.

"H-how?"

Amusement crinkles his expression. "When I asked where you preferred to be, I didn't expect *this* to be your answer."

I blink, dazed and lost.

His eyes sweep over me, then Cary. Specifically: *Cary on top of me.*

"Then again," he says, the corners of his mouth so high, dimples appear, "I did not expect to find you—*our sweet ferrier*—in this position."

Cary sighs, exasperated. "It is not what you think, Henri."

"And what am I thinking?"

"Excuse me," I grunt out. "What the hell is going on?" I buck like a wild animal trying to escape a cage. "Also, you can get off me. Like *now*."

Cary does, though far slower than I'd like.

On my feet, I brush sand off my clothes and out of my hair. "You still haven't answered my question." I turn to Cary. "What *is* this place?"

The boy from the party—Henri—lowers his eyebrows. He looks at Cary. "He doesn't know?"

"No," Cary says, flatly. "He claims to have followed me—"

"I did," I protest.

"Right . . ." Henri scoffs in disbelief. "Lovely. I can't wait to see his face when he hears this."

Cary's eyes widen. "He knows already?"

Henri nods, his smile shrinking. "I have orders to bring him the mortal."

"Who?" I demand, stomping forward. The light flickering off the point of the guards' swords stops me in my tracks. I inhale shakily. "Wait . . . mortal?"

"Wow." Henri *almost* contains his laughter. "You truly have no idea, do you?"

I bite my lip, then shake my head.

"Precious."

Like earlier, Henri's tone isn't cruel. Or mocking. He surveys me like I'm a puzzle he's trying to fit together. Sighing, he tilts his head at Cary. Waving his hand theatrically at the rolling black sea, he says, "If you will."

Annoyance sparks in Cary's eyes. At least I'm not the only one he looks at that way. He walks away from us.

Into the water.

The waves slosh against his ankles, up to his calves. My breaths catch in my throat.

Kneeling, Cary plunges one hand in the sea. A second passes before I see light spreading beneath the dark surface. It pools around him. The singing tide quiets as Cary says something, low and soft. Then the water rises higher.

No, *he* rises.

I startle backward. A nearly transparent bridge lifts from the dancing ocean. It stretches all the way to the onyx structure in the distance.

My heart sits plump in my throat. "What the—"

"Show-off!" Henri yells, dimples pronounced by his grin.

Unamused, Cary shakes droplets from his fingers. "Shall we?"

I balk. "I-I'm not," I stammer, all my nerves lit like wildfire. "I'm not going with you."

He turns his back to me. "Fine, then stay."

"Trust me," Henri says, surprising me by his closeness. His smile isn't as comforting anymore, but, for some reason, it doesn't bother me either. "You don't want to stick around here. There's good reason to follow him."

His eyes peer behind me. "*Many* good reasons."

That's when I hear it. *Them.* The scratchy chorus of moans and pleas that weren't there before.

Past the two guards, I see bodies, gray and haunting, shifting up the beach. In our direction. Their blue mouths are cracked open, calling, begging. Wide arms stretched toward us.

"They might be slow," Henri calls, "but they are determined!"

Prickly coldness rushes up my skin. I don't wait for another warning. I run onto the bridge.

When I finally catch up, I say, "What are they?"

"Shades," Henri says, openly, honestly.

Cary gives him a long glare.

I rub my arms, unable to shake off the chill from seeing them. "Are they dead?"

"They are *souls*," Cary corrects. As if I should know that. As if any of this makes sense. Of course, he doesn't bother offering any explanations.

We follow him across the long bridge. "Careful," Henri warns in a mock-whisper, "you don't want to offend the ferrier."

An indignant frown slides across Cary's pink mouth.

"What are you, anyway?" I say, too fast to think through my words.

Cary spins around. "*What* am I?" he snaps. "I am not a *thing*, mortal."

"We," Henri says in a melodic, cautious voice, "are Deathless."

"Come again?"

"Deathless," Henri repeats cheerily while Cary grumbles, "He does not deserve to know."

I bristle. I've never been in a fistfight, but punching Cary is suddenly very high on my priorities. Instead, I half turn to Henri. "I don't understand."

Cary snorts, a first.

Henri, however, beams like a starburst. He rests a friendly hand on my shoulder as we continue walking.

"We are known by many names in many regions and cultures and languages," he says, grandly, like a tour guide reciting why the *Mona Lisa* appears to be smirking. "We prefer Deathless. Guardians and lords of Aides."

That last word slides beautifully off his tongue: *Ay-deez*.

"Lords," Cary says mockingly.

Henri presses a hand to his chest, offended. "What? It sounds elegant. Regal."

"Arrogant and incorrect."

"According to whom?" Henri asks.

"The books," Cary says under his breath.

Henri waves him off. This clearly isn't the first time they've had this argument.

My heart skips as I parse through their conversation. I whisper, "Wait . . . Aides?"

Henri nods.

My feet slow. Am I dreaming? No, I can't be. Sleep these days feels like drowning. And I'm walking on an almost-see-through bridge, a swaying black sea below, with people who are what? Magical? *Deathless?*

I blink at Henri. "What do Deathless . . . do?"

His keen eyes glitter. He's almost hard to look at. "Well—"

"Do not answer him," Cary interrupts. He's ahead of us by a few feet.

Henri's face wrinkles. "But he asked!"

"He is a mortal. Do not feed his curiosity."

"Hello," I say loudly in Cary's direction. "You don't have to talk around me. I'm right here, you know."

"Unfortunately."

Even with his back to me, I can tell Cary's frowning.

"We each have a role," Henri finally answers. "He is the

ferrier. A guide, if you will. He escorts souls from your realm to ours. He's also the only one who can lift the bridge that crosses the—"

"Enough," Cary snarls.

Henri tuts. To me, he whispers, "And he's also what you mortals call emo. Very brooding. Very boring."

Laughter escapes my mouth before I can silence it.

Over his shoulder, Cary's eyes narrow callously. I don't run from his glare. I stand taller, ready for another fight.

He looks away.

"What about you?" I ask Henri.

"Me?" His long fingers squeeze the charm at the end of his gold chain. "I'm a messenger. Of sorts. A guide as well."

"Like him?" I motion toward Cary. The light breeze moves through his hair, loosening curls. I try not to stare.

"Not quite."

I wait for Henri to explain. Instead, Cary says, "We are here."

Looming in front of us is a large gate. The wrought iron design reminds me of the balconies above State Street Promenade's shops. Around the vertical bars, golden vines bloom into sculpted flowers with six-pointed petals like the ones on the guards' chests. I can't remember the species' name. My mom would know.

A breath hitches in my throat. Will I ever see her again? Or my dad? Am I trapped in this place, this *underworld* forever?

I clench my fists at my sides. No, there's no time to think about that now. I need to stay vigilant.

Beyond the gates, a building reaches so high, it feels endless. Somehow, it's slender like a skyscraper and sweeping like a palace. Imposing but beautiful. Light winks off the inky surface.

The gates sway open.

I lean forward for a closer look. "What is—"

My words are cut short by Cary's stiff "Do not make any sudden movements." His warning is followed by howling. Snarls coming from multiple directions.

Instinctively, I think to run. But where to? I have no clue where I am or what this place *is*.

Fingers coil around my wrist. Cary's firm grip holds me still. Slowly, he steps in front of me. We're so close, my chest almost pressed to his spine. He positions himself between me and whatever is emerging from the billowing mist ahead.

Then I see them. A trio of Great Danes. Their fur is smoky dark. Wild eyes bluer than the Pacific stare me down. They're big, stalking closer, pointed teeth bared.

My eyes flit to Cary. Over his shoulder, his face is fearless, almost bored.

Henri yawns. "Is this really necessary?"

The dogs' barks echo like thunder.

When I refocus on them, there aren't three Danes anymore. Just one enormous hound towering over us. A three-headed monster.

"Call off your beast, ferrier." Henri flaps a dismissive hand. "We get it. He's big and scary. Protector of the realm. No one in or out. Blah, blah, blah."

The growling deepens, as if they just might rip Henri into three equal pieces.

Henri rolls his eyes, unbothered.

Cary edges forward. I'm forced to move with him. Being that he's still holding my wrist as if I'm a toddler who can't be trusted.

He drops to one knee. His other hand reaches out. "Cerby is not a *beast.* He is only doing what is asked of him."

All at once, the snarling stops. With a quiet whimper, the Dane—Cerby—bows his heads. Each nudges into Cary's touch. His tail wags vigorously until his body shrinks, then splits. He's no longer one but three Danes again, tongues lolling.

The beginning of a smile inches Cary's mouth up. Maybe. I doubt he's capable of such a thing.

He whispers something to Cerby. Three pairs of hungry blue eyes jump to me. Cerby's jaws crack, teeth visible. I don't breathe. But Cary's fingers snap and Cerby's attention immediately returns to him, happy whines escaping his mouths.

"Are we finished here?" Henri asks, pouting.

Cary ignores him. With a final scratch behind each dog's ears, he stands. Before slipping back into the mist, Cerby's heads tilt as they examine me curiously.

"He does not know you," Cary says, "but he will not harm you."

I hate how my body relaxes, trusting his words.

"Does that mean"—my gaze falls between us—"I can have my hand back now?"

Flecks of gold flare in his eyes. He unceremoniously releases my wrist. Cool air brushes the strip of skin where his fingers just were and I chase off a shiver.

Turning away, Cary says, "This way."

I drink in the building's interior. The main room flows seamlessly like a hotel lobby. Warm amber light pours from a chandelier made up of glass bobble candles. It floats overhead without wires or chain.

The walls are a deep midnight blue. With every step, the designs seem to shift. Filigreed fish swimming in an ocean. Crows with shimmery beating wings. Roses blooming from thorned vines. Stout marble columns line the walkway. Gilded accents are carved into their tops and bases.

Floral notes drift in the air, the fragrance dizzying. Intricate geometric patterns spread across the marble floor. A thick red rug stretches from the entrance to a glass desk in the middle of the room.

Someone sits behind it, clacking at a computer.

As we approach, soft music plays. I can't tell where it's coming from. It almost sounds like "Für Elise," one of the songs I could never get right on the piano, but slower, sadder. My fingers move to the melody as I try to find the notes in my head.

I've never seen or heard or *experienced* anything like this. It still feels like a dream. But it's not.

When we reach the desk, Henri says, cheerfully, "Meli!"

The girl has large eyes. One black, the other pale blue. Her hair is the same way—half pitch black, half a startling white.

She's soft-faced, young. Her cheeks flush under Henri's gaze.

"Greetings, Lord Henri."

"Ha! See!" Henri gestures toward her. "*Lord* Henri."

Cary lets out an exasperated breath. "You bribe her to call you that."

She winks, an admission.

Henri's jaw drops. "I don't bribe. I *bargain*. Something you should consider doing."

"Pointless," Cary grumbles. "I am not my brother."

"Oh, I know."

Henri grins wickedly. Annoyance cuts darkly across Cary's face. I consider asking who they're talking about, but Henri doesn't give me a chance to.

"Shall we go up?"

Just left of the desk is an elevator. Meli's two-colored eyes find me. I feel like an alien on display before she says, "He is waiting on you."

Cary strides in the direction of the elevator. I follow, not that I have a choice. The guards are close behind.

Inside, there are no buttons. No panels indicating whether we're going up or down. Thankfully, the ride is short. I'm still unknotting my stomach as the doors glide open.

Unlike the lobby, this room is wide. Walls of floor-to-ceiling windows illuminate the space from opposite sides. Light reflects off polished ebony floors. Tall vases hold slender-stemmed flowers. Their white petals are the same as the ones from the gates and on the guards.

Near the room's center is an ivory rug. It runs like spilled sugar toward a raised crimson dais. Sitting on top is a plush black throne embellished in gold.

A throat clears.

My gaze snaps to a boy. He looks a year or two younger than me. Smooth tawny skin, knife-sharp features. Thick eyebrows frame bright eyes. His black hair is cut low and even, but I can see the start of curls at the top.

He walks closer, hands folded behind his back. His tailored charcoal suit fits him well. A garland of bristly green leaves circles his head. Cypress, maybe?

When he stops just short of me, my heart crawls anxiously up my throat.

He's *beautiful.*

The guards give him a small bow.

Henri does too. "Prince Milos," he says, "this is—"

"The boy," Milos interrupts, his voice rich, his smile deep, "who has defied death."

5

THE WAVE SWELLS in me so fast, I struggle for air.

My fingers ball into tight fists. Salty tears threaten to slip past my eyelashes. Anger and sadness clash inside my chest. The full weight of my grief tugs on me, hard. It promises to drag me below.

Memories splash violently in my head.

The red stoplight. A quiet neighborhood. My hands on the steering wheel. Tom Petty's gritty voice flowing through the speakers. London's familiar, weird smile in my periphery.

Then green light. My foot on the gas. The sudden impact shattering the windshield into a million tiny stars. Sirens in the distance, not coming fast enough. London, in my arms, eyes closed, blood trailing from his temple.

Me, the only survivor.

My lungs burn as Milos's words echo in my head.

The boy who has defied death.

I slip into another memory: High school. Weeks after the accident. All the eyes still following me in the halls. Whispers chasing me from class to class. Every empty, dark room I hid in to escape.

Troy Ackerman laughing with his friends. "August must be a superhero," he sneered, "because the grim reaper can't touch him."

Now it's hard to stay upright, on my feet. I dig my blunt fingernails into my palms until the tide calms. I can't afford to have a panic attack. Not while I'm in this strange, unreal place.

When my vision clears, Milos is watching me. His eyes are the color of honey in a jar. A warm, playful smile sits on his lips.

"I'm not— I haven't . . ." Words dry up in my throat. "I haven't defied *anything*."

Milos looks at Henri, then Cary.

"You have not told him?"

"I was going to, but *someone*"—Henri elbows Cary—"stopped me."

Cary's dark eyes lock on me.

Quickly, I avert my gaze. There's something unsettling about how intense his stare is. How it takes everything inside me to forget it.

Milos waits until we're focused on each other again. "My apologies for their rudeness." His smile creeps higher. "You are the first mortal to cross over to our realm in a very, *very* long time."

"Cross over?"

He nods with an unreadable expression. "How did you get here?"

"I don't know," I say.

Milos rubs his chin. His fingers are long, elegant. Everything about him is regal. "A mortal boy who can simply walk right into Aides—"

"His name is August."

The sharp interruption comes from Cary. Suddenly, he's right by my side, shoulders squared. The way he says my name—strong like a bass note, yet soft like a chime. Every syllable pronounced. My stomach dips.

"August," Milos repeats. It sounds different coming from him. Sweeter, wrapped in fascination. His gaze skims over me, slow and steady. "As in great. Magnificent. A beautiful name to match its owner."

Heat buzzes up my neck.

Cary says, flatly, "He is just a mortal."

I bristle. What was I thinking a second ago? There's nothing soft about Cary. If he had it his way, he probably would've let Cerby chew on me like a dog treat. No remorse.

He ignores my glare to say to Milos, "He is nothing to worry about."

Milos looks less convinced. "How did he get here, then?"

"That's a fun story!" Henri says with a smirk. "He saw Cary. In the mortal world. With a new shade."

"Saw him?" Milos's lips quirk. "Is that so?"

The edges of Cary's mouth twist, but he doesn't reply.

"August followed him here," Henri answers for him.

"Incredible!" Milos's eyes barely leave me as he turns to Cary. "Out of practice, sweet brother? After all this time, your powers are finally starting to fail you?"

Brother?

I suck down a gasp and look between them. The similarities are slight. Equally tall. Thick eyebrows and delicate cheekbones. Their unnerving beauty.

Cary clears his throat. "I have no issues."

Milos lets out a small derisive laugh. "Of course not. The ferrier never fails." He concentrates on me again. "But *he* is not 'just a mortal.' "

"I'm . . . not?"

I blink, still confused on what the hell they're talking about.

Milos licks his lips. "No. You're our guest!"

He takes my hand in his. Silky skin kisses my palm. With a smooth smile, Milos says, "Welcome to Aides, August. I am Milos. Prince of the Deathless."

"And final judge of souls," Henri adds, chest puffed.

Milos looks a mix of sheepish and irritated. He's difficult to read. "That too," he admits. "I am happy you are here."

"You are?" I say slowly, cautious.

He nods.

"It is a shame he cannot stay longer" comes from somewhere else in the room.

Sighing, Milos releases my hand.

Heels click on the marble floor. Someone approaches from a far corner. Shafts of sunlight halo a girl who's all perfectly drawn lines. She's short, her hair as green as ivy and chopped into a pixie cut. She has creamy white skin, her red lips bolder than a freshly bloomed poinsettia.

She stops next to Milos. "The rules, my prince."

He exhales with a flippant expression. "Thank you for the unnecessary reminder, Aminta."

I glance around. "What rules?"

Once more, Henri swoops in with an answer: "Though it is rare, any mortal who successfully travels to Aides is only permitted to stay a short time." His brow pinches. "Technically, not at all. But—"

"*You* are welcome to visit anytime, August," Milos chimes in. He brushes his thumb over my knuckles. "As often as you like."

His grin lingers a second too long.

Face warm, I say, "Thank you?"

Aminta scrolls through a tablet in her hand. "We need to go, my prince. You have . . . appointments."

"Can they not wait?"

Aminta's eyes cut in my direction. They're a deep green like her hair, narrowed. "Unfortunately, no."

Funny, there's not a drop of remorse in her tone.

A thin smile stretches Milos's mouth. "Fine. I suppose we all have our roles." Briefly, his gaze shifts over to Cary. "I trust you know how to see him back?"

Henri steps up. "What? Our resident historian?" He pats Cary's shoulder. "Of course he does!"

Milos's eyes don't stray from his brother. Tension rolls through Cary's jaw before he nods.

"Good. Do so."

It's a command, not a request from Milos.

Cary doesn't argue.

Milos gives me a final smile. "I look forward to getting to know you more, August."

My eyes widen. Foolishly, I say, "Um, me too."

Henri doesn't bother hiding his chuckle.

I stare at Milos's back as he leads Aminta and the guards to the other side of the room. They exit through a door I can't see but hear as it clicks shut.

When my lungs finally remember how to breathe, I twist toward Henri. "Why can't you take me back?"

Smiling apologetically, Henri says, "That is beyond my abilities."

Great. Here I am, in a strange place that shouldn't *exist.* With people who are all frighteningly gorgeous and apparently have powers. And the one boy who *can* take me home looks like he'd rather eat his own face.

"Cheer up!" Henri points at Cary. "At least if he kills you, you can hang out here permanently."

His laughter echoes in the room long after he's gone.

Silence fills the air. For a beat, I keep my back to Cary, thinking. Counting the exasperated breaths he lets out. After the fourth one, I spin on my heel to face him. His detached expression is unbearable.

I bite my lip. "How do we do this?"

Instead of answering, Cary walks to the elevator. His eyes say, *I will leave without you*, when I don't immediately follow.

I don't risk calling his bluff.

He doesn't bother holding the doors for me, so I leap inside. "Thanks!" I grunt. Throwing myself against a wall, I cross my arms. "Are we going back to the beach?"

"No."

"The bridge?"

Cary stares straight ahead, silent.

"Are you always this chatty?" I huff.

"Obviously you are."

My eyes narrow into a pointed glare. His body rests peacefully against the opposite wall. Still as ice. "At least tell me where we're going," I demand.

Expectedly, he doesn't.

The elevator pauses. Its doors part and two people in black suits blink owlishly at us. Their bodies appear shimmery due to the blinding white light from the floor we've paused on.

One of them gasps, bowing. The other stammers, "*Oh.* Lord Cary. Sorry. We will wait for the next one!"

Cautiously, they back away. Their eyes never leave Cary. Like he's a viper whose fangs might show at any second.

The doors shut again.

I laugh, the noise caught in my throat. "So, Henri was right."

Cary pins me with a menacing stare. "What?"

"You *are* a lord."

His cheeks suck inward, eyebrows sloped with clear frustration. Good. At least he looks how I feel now.

The elevator descends—or ascends?—into the belly of the building. I have no idea. We exit into a room that's not the lobby from earlier, but just as extravagant.

Everything is either a deep wine or smoky charcoal. From the walls to the carpet. It doesn't seem much like a room either. More of an in-between. A wide passageway that leads from the elevator to a stream of golden light at the other end.

The walls are lined with stone statues. A sugary floral scent tickles my nose. Colorful blooms spill from open mouths and cupped hands, circling heads like the crown Milos wore. I recognize some of the flowers: roses and orchids and hyacinths. As we walk by, their petals unfold and flutter.

I marvel at them. "Do they always do that?"

Cary studies the dancing blossoms. Then his eyes land on me again. "This way."

I fight to keep up with his pace. He's only an inch or two taller, but his strides are longer, purposeful. Like he's desperate to get rid of me.

The feeling is mutual.

He guides me toward the growing light. I remember what Henri said earlier, on the bridge.

He is the ferrier. A guide, if you will.

Out of the blue, I say, "You didn't really kill Hal."

His shoulders tense, but he doesn't slow down.

"I mean," I clarify, "you're not a murderer." As if that sounds any better.

"I am not Death," he replies.

"That's . . . good to know."

I stare at my feet. Golden beams greet the tops of my sneakers, climbing up my legs. The floral fragrance intensifies as we step outside into a garden with trees that have greenish-white bark. Blooms of various shapes and sizes burst through waxy leaves. It's as beautiful as my mom's greenhouse.

How is *this* the underworld?

Somewhere farther, beyond manicured hedges, I spot the beginnings of a structure wrapped in elegant vines.

"I do not end lives." Cary tilts his head to the light. "I only go where she calls."

"She?"

"Death."

I wait for more from him. An explanation, a story. *Anything.* It never comes.

Down the twisted path, a cool breeze ruffles my curls. I notice Cary walks almost blindly, as though he's taken this trek a thousand times before.

"How often have you done this?" I ask.

"This?"

I hear the frown in his voice. He's still at least five steps ahead of me. Just under his word is a soft, steady noise.

Water.

The pebbled road beneath our feet turns to smooth sand. We come up on a bank bordered by tall, swaying grass. This place is smaller than the beach from earlier. The water is narrower. A piercing blue instead of glittered black.

Finally, Cary stops. I stomp around him until we're face-to-face. "How many times have you taken someone *back* to my world?"

The hesitation in his stare, the deep creases in his brow alarm me.

My body goes rigid. "You haven't done this before, have you?"

Dark feathery eyelashes beat like the wings of a blackbird. Cary's continued silence says a million things at once.

"You are the first."

"No, no, no." I inch back. "Are you serious?"

"Sorry to disappoint you," he says dryly. "Mortals do not suddenly appear in Aides all the time. Your kind is not meant to travel back and forth."

"Well, guess what? I'm here!"

He lets out a very disappointed exhale.

My fingers dig into my curls. "I'm not an *experiment.* What if something goes wrong? Will I be stuck here forever?"

Under his breath, Cary mutters, "I hope not."

Even his sarcasm can't dissuade my heart from racing like a captured wild animal.

I turn in a circle. "There's gotta be another way. Let's go

back to the beach. That's how I got here, right? Just—take me back that way."

Exhaustion tugs his mouth downward. "That will not work. The books say—"

"Books?" I practically screech. "You mean I'm supposed to risk getting home safely or being trapped here for however long based on something you read in a *book*?"

Unbelievable.

He levels me with a pointed glare. Flecks of gold shimmer in his eyes. Fortunately, the glow fades as quickly as it appeared.

Cary lowers his voice. "You are scared."

"What gave it away?" My hands can't stop trembling.

Sighing, he extends his hand toward me. "I will not hurt you."

I want to laugh in his face. "Did you forget what happened on the beach?"

"That was . . ." His gaze drops. Does he feel guilty? "I did not mean to react that way."

"Is that an apology?"

"You startled me," he says instead.

I snort. "I bet you're a ton of fun at surprise parties."

"We do not—"

"Forget it." I pinch the bridge of my nose. When I finally look at him, Cary's expression is as smooth as the river's surface. "Are you sure you can do this?"

"August, I will not let any harm come to you."

There it is again. The twist in my belly. Sureness moving through my blood despite everything that's happening.

I *believe* him.

"Okay," I whisper, then take his hand. His skin is cooler than Milos's was. Not as silky, but still oddly nice. His grip is as confident as it is careful. "How do we do this?"

He motions toward the water.

We move slowly. At the shoreline, Cary turns to face me. He steps backward but never trips. His eyes stay with mine. They steady me as the cool water licks at my ankles, then my shins.

The stream rocks gently.

I chew on my lip. "How far do we need to go?"

Cary continues to hold my gaze. "Not too far."

"Okay," I repeat, suddenly warm. Not from his attentive stare. Or his fingers tightening around mine. But from the river's song. A soothing serenade that hushes the pounding of my heart.

"You need to—" Cary pauses. Cautiously, he pulls on my arm. "Be closer to me."

I swallow, wary. "How much closer?"

His mouth pinches. "Much."

We're chest-deep in the water. Cary searches my face for permission. My breath comes too fast as I nod.

After a long, awkward moment, our bodies are pressed together. My hands on his shoulders. His arms around my back. The water is forced to move around us rather than between.

He smells sweet. Not like the garden's flowers. Something else. Fruit, maybe. A smell I know but can't name currently with his fingers on the small of my spine.

"Are you okay?"

The question surprises me. So does the gentleness in his voice. I stare at the single curl resting against his forehead, then ask, "What now?"

"Wait."

"For?"

The calm in his eyes is the only response I get.

I close my own. Concentrate on anything but him. Like the notes of earthy musk hanging on the breeze. From the cypress tree I saw near the shore. Absently, I hum an accompanying melody to the river's song, the music gathering in me in a way I've avoided for too long.

A whisper breaks through. "Breathe."

I do.

"Again," Cary instructs.

My next inhale is deeper, measured. The ache of fear flees my chest. His arms go tighter around me.

Suddenly, the water pulls on me like at the fountain on SBS's campus. Except this time it's tender.

"One more breath," Cary tells me.

My lungs expand. A shiver chases up my spine as the river kisses my collarbones, then my neck. Cary doesn't let go.

I keep my eyes closed as we sink and sink.

The Before

I HEAR HIM before I see him.

Feet pounding on the metal stairs. Quick, heavy breaths. His low, frustrated swear when he undoubtedly loses one of his slides and has to hop back down to get it.

I smile. For some reason, he refuses to use the elevator. Even though it's a lot less work to get here.

I'm in my favorite place: the clock tower at the top of the Santa Barbara County Courthouse.

In my favorite spot: the stone bench tucked underneath a teal-framed window.

The view is perfect. Deep blue skyline. Clouds drifting by like floating islands. The city, small and vast below. Me, far from its reach.

Here, I can think. No, *write.* Lyrics pour from my pen. I

tap my fingers on a half-finished song while waiting for him to finally appear.

After a moment, his head pops up from the stairwell. Windswept brown hair, cheeks flushed pink. Wild green eyes search until our gazes meet.

London grins. "I knew I'd find you here!"

When he bends over to kiss me, my chest swells.

It's not the first time he's done this in public. We've been together over a year. Everyone knows. But there's also no one around to see us. It's late afternoon. While the clock tower is a high-traffic tourist destination, very few people come around this time. Especially not on a random Wednesday in February.

Which is why it's my favorite time to come. Just me and my notebook and the ocean-salted breeze.

And sometimes London.

He plops onto the brick floor in front of me. Right on the painted white compass. Carelessly, he yanks off his messenger bag, fumbles with the flap, then drags a hand through his hair. He's fidgety. Almost . . . nervous.

London's never nervous.

My head tilts. "What's wrong?"

He looks up, smiling weirdly. His eyes go to my notebook. "Can I see?"

Reflexively, my hand covers the page. I always share my songs with him. Even when they're bad or silly. Not once has he laughed at me. Or offered polite critiques, like my dad, even though he knows nothing about music.

But more and more, my lyrics have been about . . . *him*.

It's not intentional. It just happens.

I clear my throat. "I'm not finished."

"So? That's never stopped you before."

Heat gathers behind my jaw. He's right. But I'm not ready for him to see these.

Squinting at him, I say, "Are you deflecting?"

London squirms a little. I laugh. He wiggles one of his slides off to toss at me, half-heartedly.

"What is it?" I ask him, serious.

He stretches out his legs. He's getting so tall now, nearly my height. That's not the only thing I notice. His shoulders are widening. Soft hairs are growing in thicker along his sun-kissed calves.

Occasionally, I have to stop myself from staring. From *wanting* to see how high the hair goes. We haven't taken things that far yet.

His mouth curves up. "I've decided where I want to go to college."

My eyes widen. "Already?"

We're only sophomores. But I shouldn't be surprised. This is London. He loves to plan. Constantly thinking ahead.

College is still two years away. I haven't considered where I'd go. *If* I'd go. My parents bring it up casually, but they know me. I like to live things day to day.

I've tried to be more like London. But I'm not on his level. Not even close.

He nods, still beaming.

"Where?" I ask through the lump in my throat.

I'm scared of his answer. He's brilliant. And he works hard. Any university would beg to have him. He could go *anywhere.*

London leans back, gesturing to his hoodie. I study it. I guess I wasn't really paying attention before. When he first arrived. I was too distracted by the sunlight against his face to care about what he's wearing.

Now I see it. The familiar navy color. Blocky yellow letters stamped across his chest.

UCSB.

My heart clenches. *"Here?"* The word struggles to make it past my tongue. "You're gonna stay here? In Santa Barbara?"

His smile splits his face. "They have a great engineering program. And aquatic biology. Mathematics too."

That's one thing London hasn't decided in advance—his major. I'm sure it's coming soon.

"That sounds great," I tell him, muting the shock still buzzing through me.

He tips his head back. Those green eyes hold me still. "You need to think about where you want to go too."

I shake my head, chuckling. "There's still time."

London frowns. "True, but not much. There's the SATs. Early admissions. Picking the right classes for junior and senior year. Application fees and financial aid—"

The more things he lists, the farther my shoulders fall. He's thought about all these things. All I've thought about is my next song. Remembering to shower. The way London's hand feels in mine and how his mouth looks right after I kiss him.

"You can't just do what you always do," London warns gently.

He means wait until the last second. Or when it feels right to me.

Swallowing, I nod. "What should I do?"

It's a question I ask him a lot lately. London always has a solution.

His smile returns, bright and dreamy. "I have an idea."

He tugs something out of his bag. Carefully, he tosses it to me. I catch it, almost knocking over my notebook.

The cotton is soft between my fingers. It's a similar shade of navy. My pulse jumps as a gasp frees itself from my mouth when I unfold the sweatshirt.

Yellow letters spell out *UCSB*.

"Come with me," London says before I can process anything. Before the impact fully settles.

He's crouched in front of me. His thumb traces the bracelet around my wrist. Our faces are inches away.

"What?" I say, breathless.

"Let's go together."

I stare into his eyes. See the want, the excitement. It's overwhelming and still so inviting.

"How—"

He cuts me off. "I have a plan."

Of course he does.

London tells me everything. The things I need to do. The steps to take. What I'll have to talk to my parents about. Then he makes me write it all down.

I do with a trembling hand.

After, with the sun steadily falling behind him, London says, "What do you think?"

It's a heavy question. One that I don't have an instant answer for. London wants me to come with him to college. He sees us being together past high school. A future.

That's what I want too.

"Well?"

I kiss him. It's the only answer that matters.

6

WARM LIGHT BEATS against my closed eyelids.

I'm halfway between a dream and waking. Drowsiness melts the margins of my thoughts. Heat trails up my skin like slow fingers. I groan, my muscles begging to stretch. Something presses repeatedly against my chest.

I blink one eye open.

Diana's big gold eyes stare back. She paws guiltlessly at my blanket.

"You're a menace," I tell her.

She meows, then hops off me, sauntering out of the room.

My room. In the apartment.

I lurch upright, instantly regretting the motion. My head spins. Pieces of last night rattle around like marbles going downhill. Santa Barbara State and pulsing blue lights and a fountain at the heart of campus. Falling . . . No, *pulled* into water.

Into another world.

I wait for the dizziness to stop before finding my phone. The battery's almost dead. The screen is dim as I read the time:

10:02 a.m.

I haven't slept this late in forever. As it is, I barely sleep at all. But, outside the fuzziness in my head, my body feels good, rested.

Noises from outside my cracked door steal my attention. Before I roll out of bed, something appears in my periphery.

White petals.

They're scattered all over my pillow and mattress. Slender, soft, oddly familiar. I've seen them before. But where? As I search through my memories, I hear Max's voice a room away:

"Would you please just *work*?"

I leave behind the mess on my bed.

In the kitchen, Max fights with the waffle maker. A thin veil of acrid smoke hangs in the air. Globs of batter dirty the counter. Two blackened, misshapen circles sit in the sink. Clearly her first failed attempts.

"Can I help?" I offer.

She spins around, a fork pointed at my chest.

I raise my hands, surrendering. "Put down the weapon, Max."

She blows out a breath to get strands of black hair out of her face. "Where were you?"

"In my room?"

"No." She slams the fork on the counter. "*Last night.* What happened to you?"

"Oh, I was—" The words feel loose in my mouth. Cottony, wrong. I do my best to rewind through yesterday, but my memories are bleary. "I was at the party. With you."

"No, you left me," Max snaps.

"I did," I say, more to myself, the images gradually coming into focus.

Those awful lights. The loud music. A boy with plastic shot glasses.

"You didn't even let me know you were leaving," Max continues. "We have *rules*, Auggie."

"I know. I'm sorry."

A mixture of anger and hurt twists her face. "Then someone found a dead girl—"

The memory hits like a crash of cymbals. "The girl," I breathe out.

Her pale skin. Long dark hair.

"No one knows what happened. Some assholes claimed she was on something. Her roommate said she'd never do that." Max shakes her head, whispering, "It's the Hal situation all over again."

A chill like water slips down my spine. I remember:

The white sand shore. A bridge lifting from a black sea. The boy with a leaf crown made of cypress. His confident touch, striking grin.

"I saw Cary. And . . ." My voice trails off. I'm trying to wade through the rush of memories.

"You saw Cary and *what*?" Max's foot taps impatiently.

My mouth opens. Nothing comes out. What am I supposed to say?

I saw Cary with the dead girl, and I followed *him? Then fell into a fountain that somehow transported me to the underworld? Oh, by the way, that's a real place. With a lot of weirdly hot, powerful people and a three-headed dog.*

No, I can't tell her about Aides. About what I saw or what happened. If I did, would she even believe me?

Max doesn't give me a chance to say anything. "Oh my god." She gasps. "I can't believe it."

"Believe what?" I ask anxiously. Does she already *know*?

Smiling, she says, "You hooked up with Cary."

The air is knocked from my lungs. "I didn't," I wheeze.

She wiggles her eyebrows. "Yes, you did! You rushed out of the party. When I called, you were clearly distracted." Her finger circles me from neck to belly. "And you're still wearing the same clothes from *last night*."

My eyes lower. She's right. I'm still in what I wore to the party. What I had on in Aides. While my outfit is wrinkled, there's no sign of sand or water.

More flashes of Aides streak across my brain:

Cary's arms wrapped around me. His sweet scent. Calm, black eyes holding my gaze as we drifted deeper and deeper.

"Nothing happened," I blurt.

"Liar," Max scolds playfully. "You're blushing! I didn't even hear you come home last night."

I wrinkle my nose. There's a gap in my memory. Between

the river and waking up in my bed. A void I can't force my way past. How did I get back to the apartment?

Max scrapes a moderately charred waffle off the griddle. She hands it to me on a plate. "I'm glad you're getting out there. Dating is good for you. *Trying* is good, Auggie."

"I didn't *try*," I argue.

I don't want to sits unsaid, an uncomfortable lump in my throat.

Before I realize it, the tide inside me churns. Tears bite at my eyes. I squeeze my free hand into a fist, forcing the grief back underwater. I hate how it's so easily triggered. How everything in my life revolves around it.

Max frowns. "I'm not pressing you," she says quietly, "but when are you really going to give people a chance again?"

I look away.

"You deserve to be happy," she adds.

I lift my chin, defiant. "Who says I'm not?"

Max kicks my shin on the way to the living room. "The fact that your only friends are me and *our cat*."

"She's great company," I say, sinking onto the sofa with her. "Unlike you."

"I can call my mom," Max offers. She searches the cushions for her phone. "You don't have to meet with her. She gives great referrals."

"I don't need one." I bite roughly into the waffle. My anger is beginning to eddy. The new version of August pushing at his cage. "I can handle this on my own, Max. I don't need help."

A shadow falls over her face. I've seen a hundred different varieties of this expression. From my parents, classmates who I used to sit with and talk to, who'd known me for years.

It's disappointment. As if turning down their solutions to fix *my grief* offends them. As if I owe them for offering a solution in the first place.

I don't need anyone to "fix" what I'm feeling. This thing I've been experiencing every day since London died. I need them to leave me alone.

For a moment, Max eyes me. Then she lets it go. "I'm going out." Her face brightens. "Meeting Lake for a brunch study date."

I blink, confused. "Who?"

"Ha-ha. You're hilarious." She tugs the strap of her bag over one shoulder. "I know you think I'm falling too quickly."

I might. If I knew who she was talking about. The exasperated edge around her mouth says I shouldn't test her with more questions.

Shrugging, I say, "Have fun."

Max pauses at the door. "Do you have plans?"

Hope lies belly-up in her voice. She's hoping I won't spend my entire morning in bed, in yesterday's clothes, gazing at my blank walls. It was my first thought.

My only one, truthfully.

"Yeah," I lie. "Of course."

I'm staring at a pile of dirt.

Well, not just dirt. *Soil.* In a garden.

My mom has left her phone lying in one of her flower beds. She video called me "out of the blue." A big part of me doesn't believe that. I think Max had something to do with it. I've been doing exactly what I told her I wouldn't: nothing.

Letting the day slowly, painfully drift away.

I study my phone screen. Ribbons of sunlight cascade through a domed glass roof. I imagine being there.

My mom's greenhouse.

The comfortably warm air. My nose filled with the fragrant perfume of orchids and violets and stargazers. Lemons hanging from a tree in the corner. Dirt beneath my nails.

The greenhouse is a family heirloom. Passed down through generations on my mom's side. I used to spend almost every day there, even though I'm not half the gardener Mom is.

Through my phone's speaker, pebbles crunch under boots.

"Sorry!" Mom appears again. Thick curls hidden beneath a colorful headscarf. Deep brown skin drinking in afternoon light. Sweat dewy on her forehead. She smiles. "I had to check on my latest obsession."

I give her a small grin. "Which is?"

"Agapanthus praecox."

"English, Mom. Please."

She studied genetics and plant biology at UC Berkeley. Sometimes, she forgets the rest of us didn't.

"African lilies," Mom clarifies. She wipes her brow.

"Sounds pretty."

"They are."

Mom walks around the greenhouse. I can see all the new blooms she's planted. Her delicate touch in every petal and leaf. She was the same way when it came to me. Careful when I was sick or when she wiped my tears after a bad day at school.

But I'm not that August anymore.

She knows that. I can see it in her expression when she looks at me.

"Are you gonna come by the house soon? To visit?"

I hesitate. In the corner of my screen, I stare at my face. The look in my eyes that says, *I wish I could* and *I miss you* and *I can't* all at once.

"Maybe," I say through the thickness in my voice.

Mom nods, but I can tell she doesn't believe me. "I have a box for you," she says. "I'll bring it by."

In her background, the scenery shifts. She's still strolling leisurely through the greenhouse. I don't hear what she says next. My eyes home in on what's behind her: a beautiful burst of tangerine petals.

Marigolds. London's favorite.

My world tips. I remember his smile whenever I'd slip one behind his ear. The envy of the sun itself. He wanted his prom boutonniere made of them. He never got it.

Instead, my mom made a wreath of marigolds for his casket.

"Auggie?"

Mom's voice cuts through the waves crashing around my

skull. I flinch. Her eyes watch me. Then she looks over her shoulder. Reality unfolds across her face.

"Oh, August."

"Mom, don't," I beg.

"The anniversary is soon."

She says it like I need the reminder. As if I'll ever forget the night it happened.

Gingerly, she asks, "Do you want to go by his grave?"

Last year, I was too shattered to do anything other than let grief consume me. My parents came to visit. Max sat with me in the dark. London's parents tried calling. I didn't answer.

What could I say to them?

My throat is raw when I say, "Yes. Will you come with me?"

Mom doesn't hesitate. "Of course, Auggie."

Later that afternoon, Mom drops off the box.

"It's just a few things," she promised. "Your favorite snacks. Things for Max. Some of your old clothes."

I almost trip over Diana when she weaves between my legs as I carry it to my bedroom. She watches as I sit on the end of my bed to peel open the flaps. Immediately, a laugh bubbles up in my chest.

There are bags of sour candy. The brands I'd demolish as a kid until my mouth was raw and puckered. Underneath that are packs of seedlings. Mom still believes I'll discover my green thumb. For Max, she's packed art books.

Next, I find a leather journal. It has a soft, rustic feel. I hold it gently. I know what Mom's hoping. That I'll use it to write new songs, find my love for music again.

Frowning, I rest it on the floor.

At the bottom of the box is a stack of neatly folded clothes. Mainly shirts I outgrew when I turned sixteen and my growth spurt hit. The last item is a thick navy hoodie.

Tension latches onto my body. Water fills my vision. Without unfolding it, I know this isn't my hoodie.

It's London's.

No, it *was* his. Death is awful like that. A constant reminder that everything it touches belongs to the past now.

My thumbs brush over the soft fabric. Like I'll still find the grainy bits of sand from our trips to Hendry's Beach there. The times he wrapped it around my shoulders on cool nights walking around downtown.

Absently, I inhale. His scent is gone. Just like him.

When my eyes close, I see him in it. The first time—after he ran up the clock tower to tell me he wanted to go to UC Santa Barbara. Before he gave me a matching sweatshirt. Asked me to come with him.

The times he'd sit at my kitchen table with his laptop. When he'd plan out our lives post–high school with confidence blazing in his green eyes, his weird smile pointed at me. He'd settled on engineering for his major. Journalism for mine.

"You can do music on the side," he suggested. "Journalism will be better for a degree. For a career."

I didn't argue. Part of me thought to, but it didn't matter. We were going to be together.

Our future was set.

Then one red light turning green took everything from me. My carelessness stole all of London's dreams from him.

I fall back on the bed. Tears trickle from the corners of my eyes. Guilt piles onto the ache in my chest. Thick, weighted, unending. My fingers dig into the hoodie.

London should be here. Starting his first year at UCSB. I should be watching him walk the campus, make new friends, become the man he was supposed to be.

If he was right here, I would—

Stop.

My eyes blink open. I'm being foolish. It doesn't matter what I *would* do. I can't change what happened. London's not coming back.

Carelessly, I toss the hoodie across my bed. The impact sends something flying into the air. Small delicate white petals. They float back down. Land on my pillow.

I stare at them, my breath catching.

You are welcome to visit anytime.

Milos's voice runs through my head, as clear as a river.

I sit up so fast, I'm lightheaded. The realization punches me hard: I've been to Aides. I've met the ferrier, who has guided every soul to the underworld.

Could Cary have met London? Guided him somewhere in Aides that he can take me to?

A dangerous feeling flickers in my stomach: *hope.*

Maybe I can see London again. Tell him everything.

That I never intended to rip away the future he was meant to have. That I would take it all back if I could. I would've said no when he convinced me to take his dad's car for a quick drive. I would've stayed outside his parents' house and talked and held him instead. I'd tell him that I didn't deserve to have this life he wanted so badly because I'm doing nothing with it.

That I still love him. That I was better with him than I'll ever be without him.

I'd tell him the one thought that follows me in my dreams and nightmares and everywhere in between:

That it should've been me that night.

Maybe Cary can give me the time Death ruthlessly stole from us. But first, I need to find the one boy I hoped to never see again.

I don't know why I think I'll find Cary in Santa Barbara. People die all over the world. He could be *anywhere.* Still, I take my chances, assuming that being an immortal Deathless means he travels to collect souls quicker than I imagine. That he'll eventually come back . . . here.

Santa Barbara Cottage Hospital.

It wasn't my first choice to search for him. But creeping around alleys or hospice centers felt too morbid. Just the idea made my skin prickle.

Now that I'm standing outside, I think maybe those weren't the worst options.

It's early morning. Rising sunlight glazes the hospital, the largest in the city. As with every other downtown building, the exterior is bone white. Well-kept plants decorate the walkways. Deep blue water dances in a wide-mouthed fountain several feet from the main doors.

I arrived twenty minutes ago, but fear has frozen me. My feet won't bring me any closer to the entrance. If I want to see London again, tell him how I feel, say goodbye, then I need to move. Or I'll always be somewhere between Before August and After August. Never whole, never at peace.

I'll never be anything more than the boy who survived.

The wind is cool against my hot face. It quiets the noise of my heart. Another minute goes by as I steel myself, build courage.

Then I hear: "August?"

I whip around, startled. It's my dad.

He walks up with a brown paper bag in hand. His scrubs are apricot orange. He loves wearing bright colors for the sick kids he tends to. It makes them happy. For some reason, it does the same for me.

"Hey, Dad," I say, low.

He tugs me into a hug. I'm taller now. It's weird no longer being the small boy who fits neatly in his arms.

"What are you doing here?" He steps back, eyes wide with panic. "Are you sick? Is it Max? Your mo—"

I cut him off. "No, no. Everyone's fine. It's nothing." My eyes flick to the hospital's automatic doors opening and closing. "I wanted to see you."

The lie tenses my shoulders. I can't tell him the real reason. That I'm looking for a boy who might be a god. He wouldn't believe me. I don't even believe myself.

Dad scratches his rust-colored beard. His blue-green eyes run over me. There's something skeptical in his stare.

"You came to see *me*?"

I nod with as much confidence as I can manage.

He grins. "Want to have breakfast?" He holds up the bag, shaking it. "Tacos! I have extras. Tabasco sauce too."

My laugh surprises me. It's deep and fond. Dad's not a fan of spicy things. But, out of habit, he always grabs handfuls of hot sauce packets. In case Mom or I are around.

Even though, lately, I never am.

Guilt roils in my belly. I follow him to a nearby wall that's a couple of feet off the ground. A massive Moreton Bay fig tree is planted on a raised bed, surrounded by smooth stone. The tree's limbs stretch wildly in all directions. Roots poke up from the soil like thick serpents.

Dad passes me a soft-shell chicken taco.

"You look tired."

I point to the heavy shadows under his eyes, his fair skin paler than usual. "Look who's talking."

"I'm supposed to be exhausted. I'm a working adult."

"So am I," I say through a bite.

"You're barely eighteen."

"Which is, legally, an adult in the state of California," I remind him.

He fans a hand between us as I add Tabasco to my taco. The scent alone is too spicy for him. "Did you get the journal I left for you?"

I blink. "That was from you?"

"Um . . . *yeah*!" He chuckles. Broken sunlight peeks through the gaps in the tree's leaves. "Remember all those songs you used to show me? The ones you thought were terrible?"

My chest warms like the earth under a cloudless sky. Shyly, I say, "Because they were, Dad."

"They weren't that bad." He chews with a thoughtful expression. "I mean, you were fourteen, Auggie. Who writes great songs that young?"

"Stevie Wonder. Adele," I list. "Taylor Swift."

"Nobodies!"

He laughs again. A deep rising bass note that sends birds soaring. I don't bother fighting the smile that inches up my mouth.

Dad opens his second taco. "Thought a new journal would give you inspiration. If you want to apply to UCSB's music department, you need some fresh material to show them. Fall quarter applications are due by the end of November."

I freeze, taco halfway to my mouth. "Dad."

"You still plan to study music, right? UCSB has—"

"Dad, *no*," I snap. My throat is tight as a fist. "I can't."

Disappointment carves its way through his furrowed brows, the hard line of his mouth. "Auggie, we had a deal. We agreed to a gap *year.* Take a breath and get a fresh perspective. Figure out your next steps."

"And I am," I argue, all my will keeping the tremble out of my voice. "But I can't go to UCSB."

"It's a great university," he says. "Your dream school."

Our dream school, I want to yell.

The frustration licks hotly against my skin. I crumple up the unfinished taco. My hunger is gone.

Dad pulls a hand through his swoopy hair. It sticks up at weird angles. "Auggie," he strains, his patience thinning. "You can't put your life on pause forever. You have to stop giving up on yourself."

"I'm not giving up," I say, unconvincing.

"This isn't the life you planned."

He's right. Because London planned it all out. From the applications to what classes we should take as freshmen to which dorm we'd live in. *Everything.* Now I can't imagine stepping one foot on that campus. I'm not even sure where to start if I did.

Life and death don't care about the plans you make. How detailed and organized they are. Most times, the future looks nothing like you imagined.

I wish I didn't learn that so young.

"Plans change," I whisper.

Dad's smartwatch lights up. "I have to finish my shift." He gathers our trash. Before he stands, he pushes my curls off my brow. Tips my head back until our eyes meet.

"I'm sorry this is hard for you," he says, gentle and sincere. "But I'll never stop wanting the best for you."

He kisses the top of my head. Like he did when I was just a kid. On those days when I couldn't get out of bed because the pain of grief was too heavy.

"I love you, Auggie."

He disappears into the hospital before I finally say, "I love you too."

I stay behind for a beat. I know what's on the other side of those automatic doors: Memories. Cold rooms filled with loud machines. Sterile beds where bodies once were. A torrent of grief ready to knock me off my feet like a flood.

But I might find something else—the ferrier of souls.

My hands grip the hem of my shirt. How many times has Cary been here? Escorted someone's soul away? Left behind a loved one to cry over a cold body? How many times has that cruel, hardened face been the one to guide someone to whatever happens after we die?

I need answers.

I need to see London.

In the distance, sirens approach. Their wail is a warning. Death is coming closer.

I can do this, I tell myself.

My pulse knocks hard under my jaw. All I have to do is take one step. Then another.

Before I can, from behind me I hear, in a taut, familiar, annoyed voice:

"Looking for me?"

7

CARY GLARES AT ME.

It's unsurprising. As is his all-black attire. The blade-sharpness of his jaw, the cut of his black eyes. That single curl resting on his forehead. Everything about him is captivating except for that cruel, flat mouth when he sighs, bored.

"Well?"

"Who says I am?" I ask, defiant.

Cary flicks one thick eyebrow up at the hospital. A quick, silent, challenging motion.

"My dad works here," I spit.

Again, he taunts me with quietness. His head cocks as if he's not convinced. Or I'm not giving him the answers he wants.

But I'm not telling him what I really want. Not yet, at least.

After a beat, Cary starts to turn away. "I do not have time for this."

I move with him, keeping us face-to-face. "How do you get here from . . . *there*?"

A knot forms between his brows. "There?"

"You know." I point downward.

"Do I?"

I groan. "Why are you so difficult?"

"Me?" He looks incredulous. "You are the one who refuses to answer my question."

"I already did," I sigh. "My dad works at the hospital. I was visiting him."

"You never come here."

That makes me pause, my mouth slanting. "How would you know?"

Something crosses his face. A little flash behind his eyes. "What do you want of me, August?"

Even in his exasperated voice, my name comes out differently. Beautifully, like a C major 7th chord. For a second, it unnerves me, but his hard eyes bring me back to my goal.

"I want to go back to Aides," I admit.

"No," he says coolly. Firmly.

"Why not?"

"It is no place for mortals." His eyes run up me. I shiver. "Especially for one like you."

"Meaning?"

"Meaning"—he steps left—"I am leaving."

"Take me with you," I all but demand.

Frustration pulls at the angles of his face. "I will not."

"Fine." I cross my arms and his eyes briefly dip to my biceps. Heat skitters across my skin. I fight it off. "Then I'll follow you."

I doubt that it's possible. He's fast, godlike. Already, I'm struggling to keep up with the way he sidesteps me. But he's the only one who can get me to London. Desperation feeds my determination.

"Where you go, I will go," I say, smiling. "I'll be like your shadow. You'll never get rid of me."

"I am sure"—he lets out a long exhale—"I am not the first who has tried."

I ignore the urge to punch him. "I want to go back."

He scoffs. "I would like to see you try."

We're only a breath apart now. Morning light falls around his face. His pink lips are full and pouty even when he's not scowling. All three buttons of his Henley are undone, exposing a long, pale gold throat, finely sculpted collarbones. He stands tall but not rigid. Comfortable in his skin.

I swallow, then look up. A warning glazes over his eyes, bright and gold. I refuse to let it break my resolve. He's not leaving here without me. I won't let him steal away my chance to see London again.

I might not be able to force him physically, but . . .

A thought comes to me. "You actually *have* to take me."

His snort is cold, humorless. "And why is that?"

"Milos invited me back. Anytime I want," I remind him. "He's the prince, right?"

Something else burns against his black irises. I'm not

sure what. It's enough for his mask of confidence to slip.

"I don't know how things work in *your* world," I say wryly, "but I'm pretty sure it means you have to do what he says."

Cary's chest puffs, fingers flexing angrily at his sides.

I grin as he sniffs. Eyes narrowed, he says, "You smell like hot sauce."

Humiliation pricks against my cheeks. I stagger back. It's enough room for Cary to finally move around me. The impulse to punch him comes back stronger than ever. If I break a few knuckles—or my entire hand—at least I'm already at the hospital.

Cary doesn't go far. "Wait here."

I look around, confused. "Right here?"

His mouth scrunches. "Is that not what you mortals say when you want someone to stay where they are?"

"Yeah, but—"

He cuts me off. "Then wait here."

"Are you coming back?"

Cary pauses to glance over his shoulder. In this glow, he's so boyish. Almost normal.

To my surprise, his voice slips into something softer. "Yes, August."

He doesn't wait for another one of my questions. I watch him walk into the hospital. To collect another soul. To escort them to Aides. Where London is.

I sway a little on my feet. I've been to the underworld. And now I'm going back.

I'm going to see London again.

It's been nearly two years. More days and hours and unending sadness than I care to remember. But I'm so close.

This has to work. And for it to happen, I need to do better at pretending to *like* Cary. Which can't be that difficult. Acting is all I do now. It's the only way I survive every single *Are you okay?* and *I'm sorry for your loss* without ripping my skin off.

Without letting After August take center stage.

"Why do you look like that?"

I jump at Cary's voice.

He's in front of me again. How long has it been? Minutes? It's as if he never left. Except, his hair looks darker, damp. The lock on his forehead is curlier.

"L-like what?" I stammer.

He examines my face. "Like you might cry."

"I don't."

Cary surprises me again with a subtle smirk.

"I'm not gonna cry," I snap quietly, then grimace. The heat in my words isn't going to help me win him over. I adjust my expression. "Sorry. That was rude."

Cary watches me a second longer.

I swallow. "Should we go?"

"Soon." The breeze carries his scent closer. A nice blend of earth, fruit, and salt. It's distracting enough that I'm unprepared for what he says next: "Why are you so eager to return?"

I bite back my instinctive response: *I need to find someone.* Instead, I say, "I want to understand."

"Understand what?"

"You know . . . *you*," I say with a shaky smile. "And your world. All of it."

His mouth flattens. "Try again."

My brain spins. *Lie, lie, lie.*

Sunlight reflects off the hospital's tall windows and draws my attention. I can't hide my frown. The words spill out like a river over rocks:

"I need to be somewhere else."

Cary continues to study my face, searching for more. I give it to him, freely.

"When I was in your world, I didn't feel any of this." I pause. The waves inside me curl higher. Refusing to let them drag me under, I avert my eyes and say, "You know, you cared a lot less about me when we were at the pizzeria."

There it is again. The small, almost unnoticeable twitch around the corners of his mouth. He folds his arms. The Henley's fabric pulls tautly around his biceps, across his chest.

"Your incessant need to talk made it easy."

"It's part of my charm."

"Oh, is that what you call it?"

I beam for him. "I'd be a lot more charming if we weren't standing outside of a *hospital*."

The longer we're here, the more my neck prickles.

Huffing out a breath, Cary reaches toward me. He takes my hand in his. It's somehow softer than I remember. Stronger too. He pulls me to the stone fountain.

I balk. "We're getting in *there*?"

"Did you not ask how I travel to my world?"

I stare at him suspiciously.

His free hand waves to the blue water, the surface rippling with the breeze. "This is how. Through water. Rivers, lakes, oceans—"

"Fountains?"

His scowl deepens. "I am the *ferrier* of souls. If the body of water is large enough, I can travel through it."

I squirm against his grip. "And there's no other way?"

He smiles brightly. "You can stay here. Leave me alone. Never return to—"

"Fuck," I hiss. "Fine, fine."

My eyes flit anxiously around the area. We're out in the open. People pass by on the sidewalk. Step outside the automatic doors to answer their phones. No one bats an eye at me or the fact that Cary has one boot already inside the fountain.

As if reading my thoughts, Cary says, "They cannot see us."

My brows wrinkle. "You I get, but what about me?"

"They cannot see, hear, or even sense *either* of us. Not while we're . . ." His voice trails off. But his dark eyes dip to our hands.

Suddenly, I'm very aware of how hard I'm squeezing his fingers.

Then I remember something: "But I saw you at the pizzeria that day. We all did," I argue, thinking over how Max knew his name and the customers who confirmed to Detective Rosado that Cary was inside when Hal died. "And I saw you in the alley," I add in a whisper. "And on campus the next night."

Even though no one else did lingers in the back of my mind.

A restless sigh leaves his lips. "Shall we go before one of us kills the other?"

I squint at him. "I thought you said you didn't kill people?"

One side of his mouth curls into a vicious grin. "No, I said I was not Death."

I smile back, just as ruthless. "Does that mean I can kill you? Do Deathless die? Seems kind of ironic to call yourselves—"

"August."

My name on his tongue is a hypnotic melody. I nod once before stepping into the water with him.

"Should I . . . ?"

Uncomfortable warmth spreads over my face before I can even fully ask him what I'm thinking. He crooks an eyebrow. Water sloshes at my feet until I'm right in front of him.

Swallowing, I say, "Do I need to be close to you? Like last time?"

Cary's head tilts. "You remember?"

"Yeah." I give him a blank stare. "Why wouldn't I?"

He eyes me quietly. "No. You do not need to be . . . close. Not for this."

My stomach unravels with relief.

"Close your eyes," Cary instructs.

I do, happily. Staring at his unreadable expression—the soft glow of sun on his gold skin—is nauseating.

"Breathe," he whispers.

I exhale. Water swirls at my ankles, tickles up my legs. I inhale. Drops spread over my forearms. It's like cool sweat from a run at dusk.

"One more breath."

I don't remember sinking. Being submerged. Only the rhythm of his voice matching my pulsing heartbeat as his thumb glides gently over the back of my hand.

I double over, hands on my knees, dry-heaving. My skin is on fire. Ice stings in my blood. And Cary stands over me, uncaring. As if this is nothing for him.

I guess it is. Since he does it all the time.

A tiny part of me wishes the bile would come up, so I could spew it all over his nice boots.

"Finished?" he asks, uninterested.

Gasping, I stand straight and drag the back of my hand across my mouth. "How do you get used to doing that?"

"I do not have a choice."

I look up curiously, hoping for more. Predictably, Cary doesn't give it. His expression is a shadow, hiding everything.

After one more swallow, I say, "Okay. I'm good."

Cary pivots to walk away. Not without letting out a quiet snort. I scowl at his back before following.

We cross the sugar-white sand. The black sea's hymns are sung in series of gentle notes. My eyes scour our surroundings for signs of those gray haunting bodies I saw last time. The ones longing to cross the bridge. But there's no one else around.

Only us.

"Where are we going?" I ask.

"To see Milos."

My feet and words fumble at the same time. "Wait, uh . . ."

Cary gives me a long side glance. "Is there a problem?"

Yes, I want to say.

I stare off at the obsidian building in the distance. Something aches in my sternum like the wrong note played. A warning. I don't believe London's in there. I can't explain it. I just know.

When my fingers begin to stir to the sea's song, Cary's eyes watch. I force myself to stop. My mind drifts to London.

Once, he whispered, *You look strange when you do that in public.* He said it with a smile. With his fingers rubbing along the bracelet he gave me until my hands stilled.

Now I tug gently on the yellow-and-blue threads. London's somewhere in this vast world I'm still unfamiliar with. Cary's the key to unlocking all its mysteries.

Pushing out a smile, I say, "Can we walk around first? I'd like to see more of Aides."

Distrust sits in the corners of his narrowed eyes.

Fuck. I need to think fast. "Come on," I say, sweetening my smile until it reaches my eyes. "Didn't Henri say it's rare for a mortal to find their way into the underworld?"

Cary answers me with a stiffer glare.

I refuse to let it dissuade me.

"Show me around. Just this once." I move a little closer to him. "After today, I might not ever come back here."

"You will not," he says sternly.

My stomach lurches. Is there enough time to find London on this one trip? I press on, unwavering. "Fine. But if this is my last time, what's it gonna hurt if you give me a small tour?"

Cary holds my gaze for a long moment, considering. I do my best to look more curious than desperate.

Finally, he says, "You are very persistent."

I shrug. "It's part of my—"

"Stubbornness," he finishes.

I flash him a toothy grin that hides my growing need to shove him right into the black ocean.

Cary spins away from me. "This way." He doesn't wait to see if I'm behind him. I'm forced to jog to catch up.

"You know, for a guide, you could be a lot friendlier!" I huff.

"And for a *guest*, you could talk less."

My jaw clicks shut. But not because of his comment. Because I'm too distracted watching him step into the inky waters, effortlessly lifting the bridge from their depths.

We walk in silence to the gates. Instead of opening them, Cary leads me to a winding path along the side. Stone steps melt into a smooth dirt path.

"Is this a secret passage?" I ask.

He sighs. "More questions? How very un-August of you."

Despite myself, I snort. "Come on. Do you really expect me to be quiet the whole time?"

"One can only dream."

When his eyes meet mine, a tiny flicker of gold snakes around his midnight irises. It disappears as we come to a large field of rich green grass. The blades list with the breeze. Tall flowers sprout from the ground. Instantly, I recognize their spiky white petals.

I lean down to sniff. Sweet like honeysuckle.

"Asphodel," Cary says.

"Where are we?"

He looks out to the cypress trees in the far distance. His mouth loosens into a rare smile. "The Meadows."

I turn to take it all in. Land unfurling infinitely. Beautiful plants I can't name dotting the terrain. Sea salt and soil and that heady scent that follows thunderstorms thick in the air. To my left, I hear a noise, something moving in the grass.

No, not something. *People.* Walking and talking and even dancing under the pinkish-purple sky.

"Are they . . . ?"

"Souls," Cary tells me.

After a moment, some stop to stare at us. At me.

My pulse rattles. "Like the ones from the beach?"

The thought of them makes me slink closer to Cary. A muted laugh vibrates in his throat. "No," he says, amused. "They are harmless. Ordinary."

I wouldn't call them *ordinary*. These souls don't have that filmy gray fog around them like the others did. Instead, they glow bluish like desert bluebells. And they look in no hurry to leave this place.

"How'd they get here?" I wonder aloud.

Hesitation shifts over Cary's expression. He still doesn't trust me. I let him study my face, openly, until his suspicion dims.

Eventually, he says, "My brother decides. Milos, the—"

"Final judge of souls," I echo what Henri said. A lump forms in my throat. "So then, he decides where every soul in Aides goes?"

Cary gives me a quick nod.

I make a note to ask more about that later. My eyes are caught on the souls not far from us. I search through the faces, but it's hard to get a clear look at everyone. There are so many. What if London is one of them?

When I try to get a better view, fingers wrap around my forearm. "Not too close," Cary warns.

"Why?"

"They have not seen a mortal since their death." His thumb skims up the daffodil tattoo on the inside of my arm. My skin buzzes. His breath ghosts along my ear as he whispers, "They might want to keep you."

I draw back until our eyes find each other. There's something teasing in his expression. That hint of a smile again.

"You're joking," I say.

"I do not joke," he replies, but not very convincingly.

"You wouldn't let them keep me," I say with a smirk. "Then you'd be stuck with me. Forever."

After a beat, Cary's fingers uncurl from around my wrist. "Yes," he says on a deep exhale. "Who would want that?"

"Definitely not me," I murmur.

Quietly, he leads me through the field. I stay close to avoid disturbing the souls. Every few steps, my hand accidentally brushes the back of his. When it does, Cary's eyes dart in my direction. Then look away.

To end our awkward silence, I say, "Do you come here a lot?"

"Sometimes." The fingers on his other hand tickle the pointy petals of asphodels as we pass. "I do not have much free time."

"Oh, right." Embarrassment warms my cheeks "Because you're the ferrier and all."

"Ferrier and all," he repeats almost wistfully.

A strange curiosity comes over me. I wonder what it's like to have to travel the entire world constantly. To always be needed. Does he ever sleep? Is there freedom to do anything other than guide souls?

By the distant look on Cary's face, I can tell he doesn't want to talk about it. I decide not to press him.

My eyes concentrate on the souls we're not far from. Blue and gossamer and *real*. So many different faces. Young and old. From every region of the world.

A few of them pause to smile at Cary. One raises a hand to wave. Cary acknowledges her with a tiny nod.

I have a thought: "Do you remember all the souls you ferry?"

There's an unexpected warmth in his voice, something like pride, when he says, "Most of them, yes. But not all."

What if he remembers London? I consider asking, then quickly stop myself. I can't seem too eager, too obvious.

Gradually, the crowd of souls grows. It's nearly impossible to see everyone. I try anyway. But none of them look like the face I want. The one I *need.*

Disappointment wells in my stomach.

I turn to Cary. "Are there any other places souls go?" This can't be all of Aides.

"There are . . ."

His eyes fix on a point beyond my head. I twist around, looking. Deeper out, a snaking river slices between this meadow and the next. Even from this distance, its vibrance is eye-catching. A glittery veil casts the land in gold.

With reverence, he says, "Elysium."

Awe coats my voice. "What is it?"

Cary's chin lifts. "Home of the exceptional. Of heroes. The selfless. Mortals who made great sacrifices for others."

The cool breeze sweeps against the back of my neck. A smile kisses my lips. "It sounds amazing."

"It is."

I stare intently at the fields of gold. Elysium. I wonder if *that* is where London is, warm, happy, and safe. "Can we go?"

"No," Cary says flatly.

My eyes widen, mouth open. He shakes his head. "I cannot take you there."

"Why not?" The question comes out strongly, aggressively.

Cary's eyebrows droop into that familiar scowl. "It is sacred. Forbidden for anyone other than the Deathless or the souls granted passage."

Anger crests in my chest. London could be just on the other side of that river, but Cary refuses to take me. For a second, I consider ignoring him. I can see a path to the other meadow. I could leave him and his ridiculous laws behind.

The rules of Aides aren't *my* rules.

One look in his inky eyes freezes me. A request instead of a demand treads the perimeter of his irises:

Do not make me do this.

I hate everything about this place. All the barriers and rules that keep me from London. I hate how much I need Cary's help to get to him. But it's the one thing that simmers the fight in me. I force out a smile.

Quietly, I say, "Okay."

The wind ruffles Cary's hair. Loose curls fall around his temples, framing him in that boyish look again. I imagine him much younger. Coming to the Meadows to sit in the grass and pluck asphodel petals, staring up at the sky. Wondering what's next.

Was he ever that way? Curious and hopeful? Or has he always been an impassive ferrier?

"How old are you?" I ask him.

A knot forms between his eyebrows. "Come again?"

"You talk like you belong in a movie where everyone wears top hats and travels by horseback and no one's ever heard of the internet."

He glowers.

I laugh so loud, more souls turn to watch.

"Time works differently here. Much slower," he explains through his teeth. "My existence has no true mortal equivalent."

"So, what—seventy thousand–ish?"

A flush colors the tops of his cheekbones. It fades quicker than it came. "Once we accept our role, we become ageless," he grits out.

My head cocks. "Accept your . . . role?"

"Enough questions."

His glare crackles with fire. I don't know why that excites me. Like maybe he's capable of an emotion other than boredom. Or annoyance. At least it's an improvement.

My mind stumbles back to my first time here. Wrestling with Cary on the beach. His hands pinning my wrists to the sand.

Him on top of me . . .

Before my thoughts have a chance to continue, Cary grunts, "We are leaving."

He stomps back the way we came.

"Wait for me!"

I start to chase after him, sparing one more glance over my shoulder. To Elysium. Longing churns restlessly in my stomach. It's like a hunger I can't ignore. A persistent ache.

Secretly, I hope London's not there. Because then I'll probably never see him again. I'm the reason he's dead. I'd never be worthy of a place like Elysium.

It's *selfish* of me to want him to be anywhere else. That doesn't make it any less true.

Turning away, I jog in Cary's direction. That ember of hope inside me grows into an inferno. I'm not giving up.

I will find London, no matter what.

8

THE MOMENT THE gates of Aides peel open, the howls come. Loud and vicious. Starved.

Once again, Cary steps in front of me. Arm extended almost protectively. His shoulders square like he's prepared for a fight.

"Stay behind me."

I do. But instead of a towering, three-headed hound with homicidal eyes and unhinged jaws, the trio of smoke gray Danes scampers from the shadows. They sniff the air, sensing more than just Cary. Their blue eyes find me before I can make myself smaller.

I suck in a quiet breath, ready for the worst.

That also never comes.

One of the Danes sits in front of me, tongue lolling. A second flops onto his back, belly up. The last climbs me until his front legs are on my shoulders.

I laugh as he licks my face.

"Enough of that," Cary growls half-heartedly, "you mongrel."

"He's adorable," I say while leaning away from more sloppy tongue action.

"He is supposed to be guarding the gates."

"Maybe he likes me?" I suggest, smirking.

Cary huffs, "Well, he would be the only one."

With a loud snap of Cary's long fingers, Cerby—all three dogs—scrambles to his side. They sit with stiff backs, heads up, awaiting orders.

"As you were."

As quickly as they came, the Danes sprint back into the shadows.

Giddily, I say, "Can I take one home?"

Cary glares at me. Underneath the narrow blackness of his gaze, I can see amusement starting to crinkle the corners of his eyes.

Inside, the lobby smells of almond, like the unturned pages of old books. Music floats down from the ceiling. I recognize it immediately. Symphony No. 5 by Beethoven, one of my favorites. I never made it far enough in my piano lessons to learn it.

This time, Meli isn't alone at the front desk.

"There you are!"

A young woman approaches. She's tall and curvy. Her deep umber skin drinks in the lobby's warm light. The gold threads in her flowy black dress shimmer. Her face is sparkly too, the glitter around her eyes and nose like constellations against the night sky.

"There *you* are," Cary says, the corners of his mouth tilting up.

She stops in front of us. From a distance, she was pretty. Up close, she burns like the heart of a star.

Without another word, she smacks Cary's chest. It's a loud *crack*. I flinch.

"What was that for?" Cary gripes, glowering.

"You were gone too long," she answers.

"Did you miss me?"

"I missed bothering you." She reaches up and tousles his hair. Cary attempts to duck away from her touch. It's too late. His curls are everywhere.

I can't help snorting, which draws her hypnotic brown eyes to me.

"Hello there."

"Hi," I say after a swallow. "I'm—"

"August," she says before I can. One side of her mouth lifts into a delighted smirk. "I know who you are."

"You do?"

She nods. She has a heart-shaped face. Long, straight black hair streams down her back.

Cary sighs. "From Henri's gossip, no doubt."

She swats him again. "Be nice."

"I am," Cary counters just as I blurt, "He is."

Our eyes meet. A flush creeps high into my cheeks. His stare is weighted, thick with a look I've never seen.

"Well. That's interesting."

My head snaps back to the woman.

"Actually, August"—she rests a hand delicately on one of Cary's stiff shoulders—"I've heard of you because of our sweet ferrier. He talks of you. Quite a bit."

I furrow my brow. There's no way Cary would ever talk about me to anyone. At least, not in a good way.

To prove my point, Cary frowns and says, "I do not."

A playful smile pulls at her lips. "Yes, you *do*. In your dr—"

"Enough, Poppy," he snaps, but with far less bite than I'm used to.

She shrugs, unaffected. "I'm Poppy," she says to me.

I wince at the shock and amazement flooding my voice as I say, "You're a Deathless."

Poppy grins, friendly, unguarded. "Of sleep and dreams."

"And nightmares," Cary grumbles.

Meli clears her throat loudly.

"Forgive his rudeness," Poppy says. She manages to elbow Cary and shake my hand simultaneously. When I breathe in, that almondy scent is richer, filling my chest.

Finally, I recognize it. "Poppy like the flower."

She winks. "A bit on the nose, innit?"

Cary's face twists. "Why are you talking like that?"

"Sorry." Poppy giggles. "I've spent too much time in the dreams of this wonderful mortal from Bradford. It's like living inside one of those British baking shows." Her expression softens. "Her time will come very soon."

Cary doesn't react. Is this the way he sees every person's death? As just another thing that happens? Simple as the sun rising and setting?

What is life to someone who will never die?

"Let's talk more about *you*, August." Poppy considers me. Her eyes gleam, almost silvery. "How does a mortal like you end up down here?"

I shrug one shoulder, still unsure.

Cary answers for me: "We do not know."

Poppy flexes an eyebrow. "Don't you, Cary?"

She says it like he's hiding something from her. But what? He's the one who brought me here this time. And the first time was . . . an accident? A side effect of him passing through the fountain?

My gaze runs over him. I try my best to read between the lines of his perfectly blank expression and fail. Cary gives me nothing.

"He's different," Poppy comments. She leans in Cary's direction with a conspiratorial grin.

"Different," he agrees, low and enigmatic. "Not in a good way."

My hands ball into fists, knuckles cracking. But it's Poppy who hits Cary for me. Square in the chest again.

I like her.

"We do not have time for you," Cary hisses, marching toward the elevator. "He cannot be here long, Poppy. You know the rules."

She exhales. "Rules, rules, rules. You're such a by-the-book wanker."

Cary pauses to shout, "And stop visiting that Bradford mortal!"

The elevator dings. Hastily, I run to join him. Over my shoulder, I give Poppy a final wave. "Nice meeting you."

"See you again soon, August." Her words come out cryptically. I wonder if she's visited me in my dreams before? Probably not.

I don't sleep long enough for dreams or nightmares. Only enough to drown in the constant waves of my grief.

The elevator doors part in time to hear the echoes of a wobbly cry:

"Your Highness, I don't belong there. *Please listen!*"

We step back into the room with the throne. In the middle of the white carpet, two guards hold a struggling woman back by her arms. She's a soul. Her body is washed out in gray. She looks older, the deep wrinkles around her eyes unable to hide wild desperation.

Her loose shirt is splattered in dark stains. In one moment, they look charcoal. Then . . . maroon?

She wails, "He was gonna kill her. My *daughter*!"

On the throne, Milos slouches, looking bored rather than princely. Like a petulant child forced to be here. His eyes are anywhere but the screaming woman. The cypress crown sits crookedly on his head.

With a lethargic sigh, he says, "So *you* killed *him*."

"I had no choice!"

The crack in her voice sends a hard shudder down my spine.

Aminta notices. She stands at the back of the room with us. In her hand is an electronic tablet. The screen glows bright blue. On it is a long list.

Names.

Her red lip curls at me. "*He* should not be here."

Cary shrugs carelessly. "Tell that to Prince Milos."

"The mortal is not on the schedule."

There's a noise at the back of Cary's throat. A laugh held back. "Should we schedule meetings with mortals now, Minta?"

She wrinkles her nose.

I glare at both of them. They're acting as if I'm not right here. Fire hisses in my bones, the sparks of After August's wrath rising to the surface. I shove him down when I hear the soul say, "Your Highness, I beg you. Don't send me *there*!"

The rawness of her plea makes my stomach drop. I half turn to Cary and whisper, "You said there are other places souls go."

He nods once, eyes straight ahead.

It's impossible to stop the stammer when it reaches my teeth: "Wh-where?"

A muscle in Cary's jaw jumps. Matching my low voice, he says, "You do not want to know."

But I do. I need to know. Where else is there besides the Meadows and Elysium? Where else can I search for London? And what other land is so terrifying that this soul is quivering, silvery tears slipping down her weathered cheeks?

"Your H—"

"Enough." Milos leans forward. His elbows rest on his thighs. Steepling his fingers, he gives the woman a long look. "Murder will not be rewarded. Or forgiven."

"P-please—"

With a listless wrist flick, the soul's words are cut off. She's frozen.

"I have decided," Milos says. "The Abyss."

In front of me, Aminta nods. Her finger swipes down the tablet's screen. I watch names scroll by. They move too quickly. A blur of letters strung together. But my eyes focus when the list finally stops.

My heart shoves its way into my throat.

She highlights a name: *Leila Avci.*

But near the bottom of the screen, I see it.

London.

I mean . . . I think I see his name? Just like I thought I saw him outside the gelato shop. Or on the bus the other week. Is this the grief again? All my anguish manifesting his name on the screen?

It doesn't matter. Aminta clicks off the list before I can confirm anything.

She taps on Leila's name, then a column with destinations pops up: the Meadows, Elysium, the Abyss.

Aminta locks the screen, but I can't shake the feeling. What if it was his name?

"It is done," she says.

Exhaling, Milos wiggles the fingers of one hand.

A shadow falls over the sugar-white carpet. It moves like a python toward Leila's frozen form. The guards back away. My pulse pounds against my temples as the black stretches up her ankles. It consumes her slowly into the inky pool of its mouth.

The last thing I see is fear etched into Leila's face. She's gone. So is the trail of blackness, dissolved like smoke into the carpet.

I breathe in sharply.

That small noise alerts Milos to my presence. His face brightens. Leaping from the throne, he claps his hands.

"You came back!"

His sudden mood change is jarring. Like he hadn't just looked apathetic while condemning a woman to—eternal horror? As if she wasn't *right there.* Where he stands now. Her begging still eddies in my head.

Milos eyes me, waiting.

I force myself to grin. "I did!"

A wily smile pulls at his mouth. "Could not stay away from me, could you?"

A fake laugh bubbles up my throat. I know what I need to do to keep him on my side. To win everyone over. "Well," I say sweetly, "I've never met a prince before."

Milos bows gracefully. "I am honored to be your first." He takes my hand, pressing a light kiss to my knuckles. "And how did you find your way back to me this time?"

I pause, swallowing. Instinct calls on me to look at Cary. Say his name. But I didn't know if, technically, he's allowed to bring a mortal here. Will he get in trouble?

Not that I'm worried about Cary being punished. It's just that—I need him.

"I brought him."

Milos's eyes cut away from me. "Did you?"

I follow his gaze to Cary. He's still as a statue. All but his jaw as he chews out, "Did you not want to see him again?"

With a sniff, Milos says, "Yes. But shame on you for abandoning your obligations to do so."

"I have not abandoned anything," Cary retorts coolly. "What about you, brother?"

Silence sits heavy between them. Gold flickers across both their eyes. I chew my lip, anxious, wondering how long it'll last.

Milos breaks first.

He smiles at me. "Never mind *how* you got here." His tone is carefree again. "The important part is you are here now."

"Mmhmm," I say, tempted to sneak a glance at Cary.

Milos squeezes my fingers. Soft, intent. "Come."

He guides me across the room. Aminta is close on our heels. When I finally look at him, Cary is farther back. Eyes averted, face stiff. But he's following us.

It's oddly comforting.

When we reach the other side of the room, Milos says, "Is Aides not beautiful?"

We're standing in front of a towering window framed in gold. Light warms my face as I look out. Milos is right. It's breathtaking. A world I couldn't begin to imagine existing days ago.

Below, flowers bracket the dusty trail Cary took me on. Where the blue river sings. Past that, rolling green hills. Groves of cypress trees. Then something darker I can't fully make out, onyx and mountain shaped.

My eyes fall back to the garden. To its left, I see pieces of that structure I noticed before. Overgrowth covers it. Tangly vines, a scattering of vibrant flowers.

Milos squeezes my hand. I almost jump, surprised.

"What do you think?"

"Incredible," I manage after another swallow.

Because it is. Even just this partial view of the underworld.

Dread stirs coldly in my belly. This place is much bigger than I thought. I need more time to roam and search.

I peek at Aminta's tablet by her side.

"August?"

My eyes fly to Milos's face. Most people would agree that he's handsome beyond words. They'd probably say the same thing about Cary, if he wasn't scowling every five seconds.

From the corner of my vision, I see him watching me. A flash of heat surges up my neck.

"You will come back again?" Milos proposes in a sweet, charming voice.

"Of course," I say, half laughing.

I don't have a choice. Not if I want to find London.

Milos's head tilts and he stares at me like I'm a rarity. A diamond in a collection of pearls. "To see *me*, yes?"

My heart thuds. Does he know my plans? Why I'm really coming back? He made that soul disappear with a wave of his hand. What else can he do?

Then I notice his gaze cheating behind me. Something clicks into place:

Milos thinks I'm here for *Cary*.

Which is absurd. Ridiculous. I have to swallow my laugh before I say, "Definitely. To see you."

Satisfied, Milos beams.

Aminta steps between us. Her cold gaze rakes over me. "They should go." She lifts her tablet. "You said we'd clear half this list today."

My stomach plummets. I can't go yet. Cary told me that time moves at a different pace here. Slower. What if that means London hasn't been judged yet?

What if he's one of the souls Milos is meeting with?

Milos glowers so Aminta says, gently, "You promised, my prince. The labyrinth is getting *full.*"

That changes Milos's mood. "Fine. If we must."

He turns back to me. His silk button-down is a deep maroon. The color brightens his skin like the edges of a fire.

"You must come back soon." His fingers coast over the back of my hand "For the celebration ball."

"Celebration . . . ball?"

He smiles, nodding.

I quirk an eyebrow. "What are you celebrating?"

Coyly, Milos replies, "You, August."

"Me?"

A blush tickles my cheeks. But Milos flaps his hand like it's nothing. "I love any reason to celebrate. Right, Minta?"

For once, Aminta looks like a rose's soft petals instead of its thorns. "Yes, my prince."

Milos draws in so close, his scent surrounds me. Charcoal and conifer. "Trust me, it will be worth it."

My head spins a little. He's *so much.* But in a way I can't seem to resist.

"Would you deny a prince?"

I hesitate. A party is the last thing I want to attend. But it's another chance to get back here. To finish what I couldn't today. Besides, when I glance over my shoulder to that spot on the white carpet where Leila was, a shiver ghosts through my muscles.

Denying Milos means I could end up like her.

"No," I finally say.

Delighted crinkles form around his eyes. "I look forward to seeing you soon, August."

A cold, inescapable quiet blooms between me and Cary.

In the elevator. Through the long room of statues and dancing flowers. Into the garden.

He doesn't utter a single word.

I'm forced to double-time my steps to keep up with him. When I'm shoulder to shoulder with him, I ask, "Is Aminta a Deathless too?"

Eyes forward, he says, curtly, "No."

"What is she?"

Milos clearly trusts her. Enough for her to always be by his side. To record the fates of souls. I need to know more about her. A way to earn her favor and get my hands on that tablet.

After Cary ignores my last question, I change tactics. "Is there something going on between her and your brother? I don't want to assume, but, like. She seems very protective of him."

His silence continues.

"And," I go on, "if she's worried I'm trying to get between them—"

Finally, Cary stops. "What happens here is none of your concern."

His eyes are as gold as a wolf's. Irritation is drawn into every precise line of his face. I stumble back, blinking.

"Did I do something wrong?"

Cary clenches his jaw. A soft breeze rustles through his hair. The ends stand up like when Poppy tousled them earlier.

I bristle. How did I let myself get used to that side of him? Or the one from the Meadows? He's still that scowling, obnoxious boy I met at the pizzeria.

"Why are you like this?"

He lifts a thick brow. "Why are you?"

I snort, exhausted from trying to be nice to him. "You're so—" I don't finish, stomping ahead of him.

His heavy footfalls follow.

"Are you going to act this way when I come back for the party?" I grumble.

"You are not coming back."

I whip around to face him. Fury races through me. "What do you mean?"

The sky frames him in burning pinks and golds. "You cannot return," he repeats, like that explains anything. Like that one statement doesn't cut me to the bone.

"Why?" I demand.

My hands shake. Every breath feels suffocatingly short. Cary can't keep me away when I'm just beginning to learn more about Aides.

When I'm closer to getting back to London.

Cary stands taller. "There are rules—"

"I don't want to hear about *rules*, Cary," I groan. "I'm coming back."

He looks down and shakes his head.

I shift on one foot, ready to walk again. "You can't stop—"

Before I finish, he says, "A mortal can only cross over five times. After that, they are forced to make a choice."

My voice goes small. "What choice?"

There's a long pause. I see the battle play out on his face: the pull of keeping the secrets of Aides hidden and the push of not wanting to lie. Every second that passes, the ache in me grows.

His mouth dips. "Remain here, for eternity. Or never return. Not until death."

The shock of his words rattles me.

"It is an unbreakable rule."

Is that *regret* in his voice? No, it couldn't be. What would the ferrier of souls—someone as frigid and unmoved as Cary—have to feel sorry for?

My pulse punches against my tonsils.

For eternity. Or never return.

I close my eyes. Of course this wasn't going to be easy. I'm in the underworld. A place like this comes with unbreakable rules. Life-or-death ones.

My ears ring. A somber note on repeat. I can't stay here forever. What about my parents? And Max? Santa Barbara has always been my home.

But is it still?

All my life, I've known the roads. The taste of the ocean breeze. The best places to watch sunsets. Now, though, every part of the city haunts me. Reminds me of London.

It's not like that in Aides. Here, I can breathe. I don't feel the pain of *what was* versus *what is.* Here, I could be with London.

I drag a hand roughly through my hair, thinking. Then it comes to me. Something Cary said minutes ago.

"You said five times?"

He nods again, squinting.

"But I've only been here twice," I say, more to myself than him. My lips are tugged into a grin. "So I can come back for the party. That'll only be the third time."

"Yes, but—"

"So I *can* come back," I repeat, resolute.

Cary rubs his forehead. "You should be careful."

"Why do you care what I do?" I laugh at his narrowed glare. "You didn't invite me. You don't even want me here. What does it matter what I do?"

Curls fall over his brow, shadowing his eyes. Icily, he says, "I do not."

"Great. Then I'll do what I want."

"Based on your history, this does not surprise me."

I cock my head. "Meaning?"

For a beat, Cary chews on his lip. Hesitance fills his expression again. He lets out a sigh. "I have seen enough to know that is what all you mortals do. Whatever you want. You treat choices like a game."

A snort tickles my nose.

I don't treat choices like a game. How can I? I've been losing ever since I *chose* to get behind the wheel of London's dad's car. When I chose to get distracted by a song playing over the speakers. By London's smile and the light turning green.

It feels like I never make the right choice.

Until now.

Closing the distance between us, I say, brightly, "I'm coming back for that party. With or without your help."

He swallows, unblinking. Silent. Good, I don't have the strength to fight with him any longer.

I'm so angry, so flustered, I don't pay attention. My foot catches on a root, and I trip.

Before I slam into the ground, there's a flash of movement. I'm caught mid-fall. An arm tight around my back. A hand cradles my head. Wide black eyes stare down into mine.

"Are you okay, August?"

I'm too startled to answer. My fingers dig into his shirt. He doesn't complain. He doesn't do anything but watch me, gaze roaming as if he's hunting for injuries. But there are none because I never hit the ground.

Cary didn't let me.

He . . . he protected me.

"I'm fine," I say between unsteady breaths. He continues to hold me in his arms like I'm featherlight. Absently, my fingers run up his arm. I feel the smooth bicep under his Henley. The strong, taut muscles.

When he looks, I yank my hand away as if burned.

"Th-thanks," I stammer.

Cary stands us up. He releases me. Light washes over his pink cheeks. Is that a blush? Noticing me staring, he turns away.

"I will bring you back," he says evenly. "If you want."

"You will?" My voice is a whisper on the breeze.

Cary nods his head once.

He keeps his back to me, concentrating on the dancing limbs of a cypress tree as if they're the most fascinating thing he's ever seen.

A knot tightens my chest. I can't explain why I suddenly want him to look at *me* that way. It's a fleeting thought I blame on the adrenaline.

When the dizziness settles, I say, "So . . . is it time for me to go home?"

Cary answers with an outstretched hand. He waits for me to take it.

I do.

When my eyes blink open, the world is fuzzy. Quiet. Darkness with hints of silver swims through my vision. Shards of moonlight cut through the half-cracked blinds over my bedroom window. It's nighttime.

I pat my shirt. I'm wearing the same one from this morning. And it's dry. I don't know why I'm surprised. Like everything that has happened is just the same dream I keep waking from over and over.

Maybe it is.

Except, something blurred sits in my periphery.

I turn my head. Flower petals. Soft and white and *there*, scattered across my pillow and mattress. Their rich honeyed scent fills my nose. But that's not the only thing I smell.

Sweetness, like ripe fruit. Heady. Lingering in the air.

Him.

My skin is cool where his arm held me. The back of my head tingles at the absence of his hand. On the tips of my fingers, I still feel the definition of his bicep, the coiled muscles.

I sigh, eyes shutting again.

I'm too exhausted to question the smile inching across my mouth as sleep drags me back under.

9

THE WEEKEND RUSH hits Viva Catalina's hard.

A continuous stream of people flows in. They spread out and fill up tables, booths, the long bar. Saturday afternoons are like this, when State Street Promenade is swarmed by families and tourists. The fleet of bored teens desperate for time with friends and away from their parents.

I haven't stopped moving since my shift started two hours ago. There's always something to do. Collect used dishes. Wipe down tables. Drop off plates of food when Max or Kennedy are overrun with orders.

It's a nice distraction. Never a moment to think. To remember it's been *days* since I was last in Aides.

I look forward to seeing you soon, August.

Milos's words echo through my head on repeat. Before Cary brought me back, he didn't mention when he'd return.

When the celebration was. Maybe it already happened. Maybe Cary lied.

Maybe he never planned to come back for me.

But then I hear the undercurrent of what he said:

I will bring you back. If you want.

I still don't know what to make of Cary. But I believe him. Honesty ran like a river in his voice. The steadiness of his face. His unflinching lips.

He *will* come back for me.

I just don't know when.

Which has me on edge. How much time do I have left before London's next on Milos's list? What if he's sent to Elysium, a place I can't go? Or worse . . . the Abyss? My organs knot painfully, remembering the way those shadows swallowed that begging soul right in front of me.

"Watch your six, Curly!"

Kennedy swerves around me with both palms propping up pizza pans.

I spin in a small circle. "Wait, where's my six again?"

Her laugh lingers as she strolls over to a large family seated at two pushed-together tables.

In the kitchen, dishes clatter. Junie and Tonia assemble pie after pie, joking and playfully shoving each other. It's impossible to hear their conversation over customer chatter and the music.

More eighties songs. At least I know this one. Fleetwood Mac's "Everywhere." I've heard it playing in the background of an online ad before. My foot taps along to the sweet harmonies as I restock the napkin dispensers.

Nearby, plastic hits the floor. A splash follows. Tiny cubes of ice slide toward the toe of my sneaker.

"Oh, Hannah, careful!"

Someone's five-year-old has knocked over an entire cup of soda. No one moves to clean it up. From the front counter, Max gives me a pitiful stare.

I tip my head back, sighing. "I'll get the mop."

Shortly after, things slow down. The pizzeria has almost emptied out. Only a smattering of customers here and there, mostly regulars.

"Order seventy-two for Thao!" Max calls over *I am the son and heir of nothing in particular.*

I slump next to her behind the front counter. Cooling sweat slips down my temple. My feet ache. Max looks just as exhausted. Junie steps out of the kitchen, towel on his shoulder.

"That was nuts."

"Unbelievable," I agree. "When's the last time we were that busy?"

Max twirls her hair into a sloppy bun high on her head. "Not since before the thing with Hal."

I blink at her. "Since the thing with who?"

"Hal," she repeats.

"Who's Hal?"

Max's eyes widen just as Junie says, "Dude, not cool," his face twisted.

I look between them, confused.

"August, don't joke around like that," Max says bitterly.

"I'm not—" The words stop cold on my tongue. I've seen that expression on Max before. And I know exactly what it means.

Who are you?

A familiar, unwelcome rawness scrapes at my chest.

The last time Max looked at me this way was not long after London died. Back then, I barely got out of bed to shower or change my clothes. All I did was sleep and cry and sleep more.

I missed almost three weeks of school. Max came to see me every day. She'd bring my class assignments, then sit with me for hours, talking even though I never had anything to say. The ache was too consuming. She didn't seem to mind.

Except, one afternoon, she came by begging me to leave my bed for some ice cream and sunshine.

I couldn't. No, I didn't *want* to.

What would ice cream fix? A strawberry sundae wouldn't bring London back. It was pointless.

Everything was.

That didn't stop Max. Her stubbornness is as tough as iron.

Finally, I rasped, *Go get fucking ice cream by yourself.*

It all came without thinking—the impulsive words. My anger. And the impact was instant.

Tears welled in Max's eyes. She didn't cry in front of me. Maybe she didn't at all. But she stared at me like she does now. Like she doesn't *know* me.

Like I'm no longer August.

Junie won't meet my eyes. "Hal was one of us. He sat right there." He points to the empty stool at the bar, then whispers, "All the time."

I stare at the red gingham pattern, fading from years of use. I try to picture all the customers who've sat there. But I can't see him.

There's a hazy, heavy fog clouding my head. Everything else about the pizzeria is crystal clear. But that stool—who sat there—isn't. I reach for memories of this Hal guy. Nothing appears.

Nausea roils in my stomach. It's probably just hunger. I skipped breakfast.

"I think—" I swallow. Try again. "I think I'll take my break now."

No one stops me.

Tonia hands me two slices of pizza with a weak smile. I nod my appreciation.

It's not until I sink low in the corner booth that I notice the pizza toppings. Pepperoni and pineapple. My throat constricts.

I nudge the plate aside.

Without meaning to, my brain leaps to Cary. That first time I saw him here in this very booth. A face like marble. Eyes like the darkest corners of the earth. A tightly kept mystery wrapped in a scowl and black clothes.

Tugging out my phone, I search his name on the internet.

The top four results are: Cary Elwes and Cary Grant, the actors. *Caryophyllaceae*, a pink flower Mom would know about. Finally, Cary, a town in North Carolina I never plan to visit.

There's no mention of the Deathless. Or the ferrier of souls.

"Of course not," I whisper before switching tactics.

My next search is *the underworld*. A Wikipedia link pops up. I've barely made it through the introduction when a voice groans behind me.

"Oh gods, no. Never trust Wikipedia."

Someone slides in opposite me.

Henri.

He grins mischievously. "August, you're one difficult mortal to find."

"Am I really?"

"No." He laughs. "But it sounded great, right? Very enigmatic. Like maybe you're more than you seem." The last sentence comes with an eyebrow raise. An unreadable glint in his brown eyes.

I bite the corner of my lower lip. "I guess?"

Henri relaxes his arms across the back of the booth. His green blazer looks velvet, expensive. The cream-colored shirt underneath is barely buttoned, exposing hints of his pale russet chest. His glinting charm.

Snakes and wings.

His smile grows. "Well? Go ahead."

"Go ahead and what?"

He rolls his eyes. Not out of annoyance. More like he finds me entertaining. "Go ahead," he repeats, "and ask me what you want to know."

"Oh." I scratch my chin. "Um . . ."

He flicks his wrist, gesturing to my phone. "I swear. Mortals will believe whatever the internet tells you." He tsks. "Did you know *anyone* can edit those entries? All you need is a username and an imagination."

I chuckle. "I mean, *some* of it is true. There are citations. Sometimes bibliographies and further reading."

"Yes, yes, yes." Another eye roll. "All collected from scholars who trust whatever some privileged, dead white man with a story and an audience said."

Well, he certainly has a point about that.

Henri leans forward. "Tell me: Is every story told about you true?"

Immediately, my thoughts slingshot to high school. *Troy Ackerman.* His square face, freckled white skin, shaggy blond hair. Those shrewd blue eyes always pointed menacingly at me. The ugly words behind his flat smile.

"No," I say with a bite.

"Exactly! So what would you like to know?"

I blurt the first thing that comes to mind: "Tell me more about the Deathless."

"So vague." He points violently toward the article still open on my phone screen. At the top is an art piece of ancient deities and monsters. Something Max would love. "We're nothing like *that*."

"Okay. Then what?"

"The basics? We're immortal, powerful, gorgeous"—he pauses to wink—"and we all have a role in mortals' journey to the next realm. Trust me, it's very boring. And there are so many of us."

I sit taller. "There are?"

"Yes," Henri says, sighing.

"Are you born a Deathless?"

"No. We are chosen." He pushes a lock of raven black hair behind his ear. "But some are born from other Deathless. The rest . . . come from elsewhere."

"Where?"

The questions keep bubbling up my throat. Fortunately, Henri doesn't appear as annoyed as Cary does after each one.

"*Elsewhere*," he says again, this time with a quiet chuckle.

"Which Deathless?"

"Did you have someone *specific* in mind?"

My cheeks catch fire. I consider lying. It's the only way to keep my plan a secret.

"Tell me, August"—Henri's mouth quirks high—"which Deathless do you really want to know more about?"

His question is a challenge dressed in his charismatic grin, a flare of dimples.

Milos's name weighs heavy on my tongue. Aminta's isn't

far behind, even though I know she's not a Deathless.

Instead, I say, "Cary."

A genuine smile unfurls on Henri's lips. Glee sets like jewels in his eyes. He rubs his chin, pretending to think. "Oh, our sweet, sullen ferrier."

A beat passes. Overhead, the music shifts to something I don't recognize.

"He is . . . complex."

"In what ways?" I inquire, a little too eager. I clear my throat, attempting to look more nonchalant.

Henri's gaze lowers back to my phone. "You won't find any truth about him on there. Out of all of us, he's the one your kind gets wrong the most."

"How so?" I ask.

There's another moment of silence. Henri's mouth twists, considering. "Okay, he certainly has that all-black, super-cryptic, not-very-talkative vibe going for him. The grim reaper energy is strong in that one."

The beginnings of a laugh scratch at my throat.

With a thoughtful head tilt, Henri adds, "But his role is very different from the rest of ours. He doesn't spend much time with mortals."

This time, I let out a loud snort.

Henri shakes his head. "That doesn't mean he doesn't understand you."

"Me?" I choke out.

"Mortals."

Oh. Obviously he meant humans in general. Not me in particular. Because there's no way Cary understands me. He's never tried to.

And I don't want him to.

Cary is simply a means to an end. He's my way to finding London. Nothing more.

"Then," I say, "him being an asshole is by choice?"

Henri drags my plate of pizza toward him. He picks off the pepperoni. "I told you—he's complex. In many ways."

"Like . . . ?"

"You know, you could ask him all these things."

I blow out a breath. "As if he'd tell me anything."

As much as I need him to. What's it gonna take for me to break through his walls?

Henri doesn't offer me any answers.

"You're right." He takes a big bite of pizza. Chewing, he says, "Enough about that boring bookworm. Shall we discuss Milos?"

A suggestive smile flashes across his mouth. Another wave of heat burns my face.

"What about him?"

"Oh, please. I see how he looks at you." Henri lifts an eyebrow. "And how you look at him. Interested?"

I stop myself before my eyes roll. Henri and Max would be great friends. They're equally terrible at matchmaking.

But I play along. For my own reasons. "He's interesting," I say.

"That's not an answer."

Shit. It's not. And by the way Henri's watching me, I wasn't very convincing either.

Thumbing my bracelet, I say, sincerely, "I'd like to get to know him better."

It's the truth. Milos could be my key to London. To giving me more time with him.

Henri takes another bite. "Is that so?"

I nod. "He invited me to his celebration ball."

"And you're coming, yes?" He drops the half-eaten slice. "You have to. And not just to keep me company. But mostly that."

"How would I even get back? Can you take me?" I do my best to hide my urgency.

"No. I was serious about that. I can't bring mortals across realms. Unless you're dead."

I shudder. "Then how will I get there?"

Deep dimples form around Henri's wide grin. "I'm sure you already know *how.*"

Great. Just the answer I didn't want: more waiting on Cary.

Henri dusts off his hands. "I need to go."

After standing, he plucks a small black card from inside his blazer. He passes it to me. "Here. In case you ever need to reach me."

I stare at the pearlized surface. When the light hits it, the card glitters. But there's nothing on it.

No name, email, or phone number.

"It's blank," I tell him.

"Is it?" Casually, he slides his hands into his pockets. "When the time comes, I'm sure you'll look a little deeper."

He leaves the pizzeria without another word.

"How do I look?"

I lift my gaze from my phone screen. Max stands in my bedroom doorway. She's wearing a tan blazer over a ribbed crop-top sweater, pleated navy skirt. Her hair's down, pin-straight and brushing her collarbones. Silver threads of night-fall seep through my window onto her pink cheeks.

My eyebrows climb my forehead. "Wow."

"I'm going for dean's list scholar who's not afraid to make out on the first date." She curtsies, smirking.

"Mission accomplished! Who's the lucky girl?"

Max frowns. "Lake."

Right, *Lake*. The girl I'm supposed to know. Except, I don't. I've tried retracing where we might've met—the pizzeria, the promenade, SBS campus—but my head's such a mess, nothing clicks.

I smile for Max. "She won't be able to resist you."

"Obviously!"

A beat passes. Max lingers in my doorway. She rolls her bottom lip between her teeth, ruining her lip gloss. There's that look in her eyes. Concern verging on pity.

Hiding the irritation in my voice, I say, "What is it?"

"Who was that boy earlier?"

"What boy?"

She sighs. "At Catalina's. The one you talked to on your break."

Oh. Henri.

Almost every part of me wants to tell her. About Aides and the Deathless and my plan to find London. But I'm still afraid she won't believe me. Or worse, she'll try to stop me?

My fingers encircle my bracelet. "No one," I say, even as guilt coils around my stomach. "Just someone I met. At that party on campus."

"Are you interested in him?"

I snort. Henri's stylish, vibrant in an uncontainable way. He's also fun to talk to. But he's not my type. Plus, he's a god or something.

"Not even a little," I say.

Max hums. It's a noise that draws my gaze to the happy pucker of her lips. "So there's still a chance for you and that Cary guy?"

I sit up, fast. Head spinning. "What? No."

"But—"

"Max, stop!"

She flinches. I haven't yelled at her like that since that day she wanted me to get ice cream. This time, I couldn't help it. Something claws under my skin, desperate to burst free. I wait until it settles beneath the surface again.

Swallowing thick saliva, I whisper, "Sorry. I didn't mean to . . . I need more time."

Max smiles dimly. "Okay." She won't make eye contact. Her gaze flits around my room. "We really need to get you some furniture."

A quiet grin flexes the corners of my mouth. "Does that mean you'll help me carry it upstairs?"

I think about the last time. All the complaining she did. How we went in without a plan of attack and immediately regretted it.

Max is obviously thinking about it too. She grimaces, then says, "Hell no. We'll hire someone."

"With what funds? My tips?"

"*My* tips," she corrects me.

I let out a low laugh. It feels like we're back to normal. Almost.

When Max's phone vibrates, she checks the screen. "I'm gonna go."

"Okay. Phone and location on at all times."

Her smile slowly widens. "Answer every text. Pick up every call—you know, that thing you didn't do last time."

"I answered!" I squawk.

"And then abandoned me for a hot guy you won't admit you like," she half mumbles.

I toss a pair of balled-up smelly socks at her. She ducks. We hear Diana's claws skittering on the floor as she chases the ball.

"Don't break curfew," I warn in a teasing voice.

"Whatever, Dad."

Max hesitates, one foot out the doorway. A bridge of silence reaches between us. With an exhale, she says, "I'm here, Auggie. I know I'm not . . ." Her voice trails off.

But I don't need her to fill in the gap.

Once more, my fingers hook around my bracelet. They tug hard. Until I no longer feel like I'm being yanked by an undertow.

"I'm here," Max repeats, quietly.

"That's the problem," I joke with a forced smile. "You're supposed to be on a date. Go. Lake's waiting."

Her nose wrinkles. She looks like she's a second away from steering the subject back the other direction. I hold my breath.

Finally, she says, "I'll be home late," with a wicked grin. "Or in the morning. You know, after we're done—"

"Maxine Cho, I don't need that mental image!"

Her laughter echoes through the apartment long after the front door slams shut.

It's another thirty minutes before I relocate to the living room sofa with a cup of instant noodles. Diana joins me. She perches on the coffee table, cleaning herself as Netflix cues up one of Max's favorite baking shows.

I sit in the dark, slurping loudly. There's a broth stain on my T-shirt. A hole in my joggers. Pizza sauce under my nails.

The annoying, unfunny British host knocks over someone's mixing bowl and the weak laugh in my chest never rises any further.

This is my Saturday night. This is *every* night. Shoving noodles into my mouth, trying not to think. Counting down the seconds until sleep comes for me. Hoping I ache a little less tomorrow.

Even after Henri's visit, I don't let myself get too anxious over the thought of Cary showing up. When he shows up. *If* he shows up.

I let my brain zone out. It's safer that way.

Next to me, my phone lights up. I start to ignore it. Probably just Mom or Dad in the group chat. But my eyes catch on the notification: a direct message to one of my rarely used social media accounts.

Curious, I tap it open.

It's from @HaruSam. Instantly, I recognize the goofy grin and denim jacket in his profile photo. He's an old classmate.

TODAY 8:11 PM

Hey August. It's Sam. sorry to slide into your dms like this.

I saw you the other night at an SBS party.

I wanted to talk to you but . . . I felt bad for not speaking since high school.

sorry about that too.

anyway found this old pic of you and london. I miss him. hope youre ok.

My hand trembles. Beneath Sam's messages is a photo. I don't know why I click to make it bigger. Why I want to see every detail.

Why I want to see . . . *us.*

We're sitting together on a ratty sofa in someone's basement. It's summer. We're fifteen. I can tell by the roundness of my cheeks and the sun streaks in his hair. I'm laughing, mouth wide, while London side-eyes me, an arm thrown around my shoulders.

He's wearing his weird smile and the navy hoodie. *UCSB* stands out in bold yellow lettering. I have on my matching sweatshirt.

The room spins. My phone falls from my hand. It knocks over what's left of my noodles. Diana leaps away, meowing. Ache spreads cold and fast through my chest.

I don't have time to stop it. The tide of grief. Its vicious grip strangles me.

When I look down, my phone screen is still lit. The photo mocks me from the floor.

In a rush, the memory pulls me under:

Sweat hangs in the air. The stench of too many teenagers

in a small dank basement. A silly, forgettable pop song thuds in my ears.

London leans close. His breath is warm against my cheek. He tells me my music is better. That one day we'll dance to one of my songs. He'll pay the DJ to play it at prom.

That never happened.

London never went to any school dances. The last suit he wore was the one his mom picked out for his funeral.

He never got to wear that hoodie on UC Santa Barbara's campus either. He never even filled out the application. Or walked across the stage for high school graduation. He never got to become all the things he told me about.

Neither did I.

But that hurt doesn't come close to the ache of knowing I never got to watch all of London's plans—the ones he worked so hard for—come true.

It's all my fault. Even if it was an accident.

I took away the life London was supposed to have.

Jolting to my feet, I pace the living room. My fingers tangle in my curls. There's a steady throb in my head I can't get away from.

What am I doing? Why am I like this? Stuck in a time loop where he's dead and I'm just . . . here. Not being the son my parents want. Or the friend Max wants.

How am I supposed to exist in a world where everything I was is gone?

I pluck at my bracelet. The threads feel loose. A guitar string ready to snap. Every instinct inside me begs to run away, leave. Disappear forever.

A heavy knock at the door startles me. My next breath comes out like the A0 note on a piano—low, deep, reverberating. Mist fills my eyes.

Another knock.

I wipe my face. My pulse hammers away. As I sink under the grief and memories, my panic rises.

One more knock.

It's enough for my brain to finally come up for air. "Max?" I call, stepping over Diana. "Did you forget your key?"

There's no answer.

I creep over to the door. For whatever reason, I ignore the peephole. My shaky hand wraps around the knob. It takes three tries to turn it. I'll never be able to explain why my heart settles so quickly when the door swings open and I see who it is:

Cary.

10

"YOU ARE CRYING."

It's not the three words I want to hear from Cary. Honestly, I don't know if I want to hear *anything* from him. But just seeing him standing in my doorway is a sudden rush of relief I'm unprepared for.

Because he's not Max. Or my parents. Or one more person expecting something from me.

He stares at me for a long moment.

I'm still coming down from the panic attack. Eventually, I drag a hand over my cheeks, feeling the wetness on my palm. I take a small step back, leaving the door wide open for him.

He doesn't walk through.

"You can come in," I say. Then I squint at him. "Wait, do I have to *invite* you in? Is that a thing? Are Deathless like vampires?"

Sighing, he breezes past me. "They wish."

I pause, blinking. "Vampires are *real*?"

He throws a glare at me over his shoulder. But the corners of his lips are rising. "Why? Are you scared?"

"The only thing I'm scared of is how many black clothes you own."

Tonight, he's in a flowing black trench and fitted pants. His pushed-back hair curls behind his ears. The cut of his V-neck is deep. His long throat and sharp collarbones are visible. So much smooth, pale gold skin.

I do my best to avert my eyes.

"Why were you crying?"

From anyone else, the tone of voice might sound like concern. But not from Cary. From him, it's an observation wrapped in a question.

I smile flimsily. "Put too much hot sauce in my ramen."

Slowly, he takes in the apartment. My knocked-over ramen cup leaking broth into the carpet. Max's mug of cold coffee on the kitchen counter. Unwashed dishes in the sink. Diana batting my balled-up dirty socks around.

Cary raises an eyebrow at me. "You like spicy things. I remember."

A blush scorches my cheeks when I realize how he knows that. Our first conversation at the pizzeria. The pizza toppings. Well, it wasn't much of a conversation. But that was his fault.

He continues looking around from his place near the sofa.

Something hits me. "*How* did you know where I live?"

"I am a Deathless."

"You're a stalker," I accuse without any heat behind my words.

"August, do you truly believe you are worth that kind of attention and effort?"

I gasp, scandalized. He gives me a blank stare. I want to punch him. Right in that pretty perfectly shaped jaw. Before I can, I hear a soft meow.

Diana has abandoned my filthy socks to strut up to Cary. For a second, I think she might swipe her claws at him. Defend my honor. Instead, she sniffs one of his boots, then rubs leisurely against his leg, *purring.*

"Traitor," I hiss at her.

Diana happily ignores me.

"She's not usually this . . . friendly," I say.

Cary lowers to one knee. He stares into Diana's enormous gold eyes. She meows again. Carefully, he scratches behind her ears. Ducking his head, Cary whispers words I can't hear to her.

She purrs again, sweetly.

"What did you say to her?" I ask.

Cary stands, avoiding my question. "I am here to escort you to Aides," he says. "For Milos's celebration."

Today has been so long, so heavy, I almost forgot about that.

He tilts his head. "Did you change your mind?"

"N-no," I blurt. "I still want to go."

I need *to go.*

The television's bluish glow cuts across the angles of his face. Moonlight reflecting off an arrowhead. "Then let us go," he says with a slight hesitance.

He turns toward the door.

"Hold on!" I look down at myself. My stained T-shirt. Bare toes wiggling on the carpet. The front door is still open, and a small breeze passes through the hole in my joggers. Shyly, I admit, "I don't really own anything to wear to a celebration."

His eyes drag over me. "Nothing?"

"Do you want to look in my closet?" I chew out.

There's that little twitch to his lips again. Almost a smirk. "Are you inviting me to your bedroom?"

Heat runs through me like a flood. He lets out a muted snort. Cary *actually* finds this funny.

"Your current attire is not a problem," he says.

God, I hate the way he talks. No, I hate that I'm growing accustomed to it. That I find it a little endearing.

I glance around the apartment. My next questions feel so silly: "How are we getting to Aides? You need water, right?"

He nods.

"Are we going to fill up the kitchen sink?" My face screws up. "Or get in the shower?"

The second I say it, a new rush of embarrassment sears my skin.

What is wrong with me?

Did I just invite the ferrier of souls—a god who's also a pain in my ass—to get in the shower with me?

When I look at him, there's a thin haze of gold around Cary's eyes. Bright as sunset. It disappears in a blink. Long, sure fingers wrap around my wrist. He's right in front of me. Unnamed sweetness pours off him.

Bending his head, he whispers into my ear, "You ask too many questions."

Aminta is waiting at the end of the bridge after we cross. The breeze off the black sea flutters against the material of her jade gown. Peacock feathers, bold and lustrous.

Cary stops in front of her. "Aminta."

She bows. "Lord Cary."

A wry smile teases my lips. I cough into my hand, "*Lord.*"

I'm expecting a glare from Cary. But it's Aminta's harsh green eyes that fall on me.

Hoping to win her over, I give her a friendly wave. I need to get my hands on that tablet tucked underneath one of her arms. "Nice to see you again!" I say.

My friendliness doesn't work.

"Prince Milos instructed me to meet you," she says to Cary, her scowl never softening. "To help get the mortal ready."

The way she says it—*the mortal*—it's like poison on her tongue. As if I'm a curse she wants to spit out.

I stop myself from bristling. Maintain my polite smile.

Cary steps closer to my side. His warmth is a surprise comfort. "I will accompany you," he says.

Aminta startles. "You will?"

"Yes. To make sure he is presentable." His mouth flattens, fingers flexing at his sides. "For my brother, of course."

I bite my lower lip.

Is that why Cary brought me? Because Milos commanded him to? For no other reason? The thought makes my insides contort. But I don't know why.

"Shall we?" Aminta leads us through the gates.

I follow a step behind Cary. The lobby's empty, quiet. Aminta's heels click loudly against the marble floors. We walk into the elevator. For a long moment, I wonder if this is all a mistake.

How can I win Aminta over? Get access to her tablet? And if I do, will I even know how to find London in there? Did I really see his name that day? Is there a map or something to help me get to where he is?

I shake the doubt from my head. I can do this.

Aminta directs us through a pair of crimson doors with ornate gold accents.

"In here."

The private chamber is lit by more floating globes. It's elegantly decorated. Two plush chairs with velvet throw pillows. Vases stuffed with tall asphodels, their white petals blooming the moment I look at them. Odd, like everything else here.

On the ceiling, a spacious blue sky is painted. Spun white clouds drift above our heads. Etched into the garnet wallpaper are golden-scaled snakes.

The far wall is made of mirrors. In front of it is a paneled privacy screen. Behind that, a suit waits on a satin gold hanger.

My mouth falls open. "Is that for me?"

I've never seen anything so stunning. It's a deep navy. The slacks are creased. A banded collar on the shirt. But it's the jacket that steals my breath—golden embroidered flowers stream from the left shoulder to the chest, down the right sleeve.

Daffodils.

When my fingers brush them, the petals shudder. I smile.

Aminta snaps her fingers. "Put it on. And be quick."

I look around, wide-eyed. There's no en suite. No secret side door with a changing room. Just the privacy screen.

"Here?"

She sighs impatiently. "Yes. We cannot have *mortals* running around Aides in their undergarments."

Cary's eyes flick over me. Fire bursts across my face. "I didn't plan to attend the ball in my boxers, thanks," I gripe.

"Good." Aminta yanks the suit off the hanger. She shoves it at my chest. "No one wants to see that. Now change."

I hold the garment close. "How do you know it'll fit?"

Her face screws up like she can't believe my audacity to ask that question. Irritation sharpens her glare. "Prince Milos has his ways."

"What does that mean?"

"It means—"

Cary steps between us. "Minta," he says, cutting off her hiss. "He is a *guest.* You can go. I will wait with him. Do not fear. I will ensure he does not wander."

She hesitates. "Are you sure?"

A flicker of warning circles Cary's eyes when he looks at me. He's silently telling me to shut up. When I do, he says, "I am."

Huffing, Aminta turns to the mirrors. She smooths out the bodice of her gown. No doubt to impress Milos. I fight the urge to make a face in the reflection. Her emerald nails tap along the tablet's screen.

My pulse quickens.

"Do not be long," she says, slicing off a glare in my direction.

After she's gone, I whisper, "Thank you."

He nods once, then motions to the privacy screen.

"You can change behind there. No one will bother you."

He walks to the other side of the room. Turns his back to me. My neck warms at the kind gesture.

As I strip out of my stained T-shirt, I ask, "What are these celebrations like?"

"Lavish. Loud. Long," Cary says dryly. "All things Milos loves."

I snort. "I'm guessing you don't?"

"Not at all. I usually avoid them."

"You do?"

"Trust me, once you have been to one, that is more than enough."

Does that mean he hates parties, like me? My fingers rest nervously on the waistband of my joggers. The screen is opaque, framed in black.

He can't see me.

Inhaling, I quickly wiggle out of the joggers. "Will Henri be there?"

"Always."

"And Poppy?"

"Oh, yes. She would not miss it." I hear a fondness in his voice, even though he's obviously trying to hide it.

I slide on the suit's slacks. Then button the shirt. The jacket melts around my body, fitting me perfectly.

"Will you stay?"

I step from around the screen. His back is still to me. I clock his look from the long coat to his black boots. Not exactly ballroom attire.

His head tips back to watch the floating clouds. "Why? Do you need more supervision?"

"I can handle myself."

"Can you? History says otherwise."

I let out a loud breath. "Why are you trying to ruin this for me?"

"I—" Whatever Cary is about to say fades as he finally turns around.

Our eyes meet.

He stares at me like—I wish I knew. It's not the same way Milos does. Or how London used to. This is different. Cary watches me with a reverence that pulls a blush into my cheeks and twines strangely around my belly.

Shyly, I take my eyes off him. In the mirrored wall, my fingers tiptoe over the jacket's flowers. The precise lines of the silhouette. Warmth tingles against my skin. Soft, silky, alive.

Magic.

"This is the first time I've worn anything this nice."

I fiddle with the lapels. They look crooked. Or maybe it's my posture.

Cary inches closer. With a sure, strong grip, he rotates me toward him. His hands bat mine away from the suit and I almost jerk back. He smooths the material. A poised and calm touch unlike my own nervous fidgeting.

Immediately, the jacket responds, the petals shivering with relief. "There," he says. "You—it looks great."

The tops of his cheeks flush.

"Sorry," I mumble. "I haven't had a suit on since—" My voice cuts out.

In the empty space, two words sit sourly on my tongue: *his funeral.*

Cary considers me like he already knows what I almost said.

My head spins. Was he there when the accident happened?

And afterward? Did he come to the hospital? Did he find London's soul in the morgue?

When did Cary take him away from me?

All the questions eddy through me. Building into a whirlpool I'm scared to get lost in.

But it's Cary's eyes that rescue me. There's a surprising tenderness in them. An unspoken *you don't have to say it* that I'm grateful for.

"I've never been to a ball before," I tell him. "Or any formal dance."

The tide in my chest is replaced by a tiny fire. A memory catching like flint.

I skipped prom. Junior and senior year. I couldn't even stomach helping Max dress shop for either of them. My mom did her best to encourage me. She promised to buy me a suit and drive me and even wait outside in case it was too much.

Anything to get me out of bed.

"It's a once-in-a-lifetime thing," she swore.

It was. One of many I was supposed to experience with London.

That night, I locked myself in my bedroom. Watched horror movies for hours. It was better to be scared of fake monsters than the real ones living inside my head.

I blink away from the memory.

Cary continues to wordlessly study me.

"What kind of dancing happens at these things? Waltzing?

Some weird, fancy tango?" I laugh nervously. "Should I watch some instructional videos—"

"Your hand."

I blanch. "My what?"

"August," Cary says, patient in a way I've never seen him. "Give me your hand."

That's when I notice his own. Outstretched and lifted. Waiting on me.

I shake my head, then say, "Are you serious?"

He flexes an eyebrow. A definitive *yes* in his eyes. His hand never drops, suspended in midair.

Exhaling dramatically, I slide my palm against his. He guides my other hand to his shoulder. Then his fingers rest lightly on the small of my back.

"There's no music," I tell him.

"Of course there is." His head bends. A rich sweetness wafts off him. His lips brush my ear. "Just listen."

All I hear is the knock of my heart against a bone cage. My stilted inhales. His slow, steady exhales. But when I truly focus, clear notes cut through the noise. Outside, the sea sings.

"Follow my lead," Cary instructs.

He steps left. I sway with him. Backward, to the right, forward. Another step, then repeat. We turn in tiny easy circles to the rhythm in the distance.

Cary moves like the ocean. Natural, fluid.

I rock like a ship in a storm.

"Wow," he breathes out. "You were right."

I furrow my brows. "About what?"

The fringes of his mouth lift. "This is your first time. You are . . . What would Henri say? Tragic?" He pretends to think. "A hot mess?"

Mortified, my eyes start to lower. His fingers tighten on my back. The move pushes me closer to him.

Softly, he commands, "Do not look down."

Despite the flare in my stomach when our hips brush, I half growl, "I'm just trying to keep up with you."

"I will not let you fall, August."

My heart skips. His eyes are pools of the richest onyx. I plunge into them, leaping without questioning their depths.

Cary is true to his word. When I trip on his foot, his firm hand on my spine steadies me. He redirects our rhythm. Holds my gaze until the anxiety flees my shoulders. Until I barely notice we're chest to chest.

The lulling sea guides us. His muscles are loose under my hand. My back arches below his fingers.

Face hot, I stammer, "H-how did you learn to dance like this?"

There it is again. The quirk to his lips. His almost smile, the one I don't mind as much anymore.

"From watching you." My eyes bulge, so he quickly adds, "Watching *mortals*."

His cheeks glow pink again.

"Do you spend a lot of time in my world?" I ask.

"Only as needed. It is my role, after all."

Something goes cold in my gut. An unexpected sadness. Is that all Cary knows? Being the ferrier? A guide who sees so little of us, other than in death?

His gaze shifts away from mine. He looks over my shoulder, his face smoothing in thought. "Sometimes, I am there before it all ends. I see their last moments. I do not linger like a *stalker*."

I roll my eyes, even though he can't see.

"But I watch," he whispers. "And wait for their time to run out."

"That's it?"

He lifts a single eyebrow.

"I mean . . ." My palm is sweaty against his coat. "Do you ever just go to be around us?"

"There is no time, August," he says stiffly. "And why would I?"

A frustrated exhale leaves my nose. "To see that we're fun? Or loving? More than just, I don't know. Whatever you see us as. Maybe you wouldn't hate us so much."

His thumb shifts in the hollow of my hip bone. A knot forms between his eyebrows. "I do not hate you."

I laugh breathily. "You mean mortals, right?"

Our steps slow. Eventually, he releases my hand. The sea's lullaby fades as Cary moves away from me.

"We should go. Milos is expecting you."

He's standoffish again. Nothing more than a hard jaw, rigid shoulders, distant eyes. Anger flickers hotly in me. For a few minutes—for a single dance—I thought he was different.

But he's still just the ferrier.

"Sure. Let's go."

Before I can reach the door, Cary's fingers circle my wrist. "Be careful with what you say at the ball," he tells me. "Do not reveal too much."

I scowl. "Why should I listen to you?"

Beneath his cold stare, there's a hint of something I wish I could name. "This is not your world," he says. "Trust me."

"Trust *you*?" I blow out an incredulous breath. "The guy who keeps everything tight to the vest?"

Cary's nostrils flare, but he says nothing.

"What? Am I just a shiny toy to them?" I ask.

To you rushes toward my lips, but I hold it in.

His eyes trace my face. "Some will think you are a marvel. Others will believe you strange and fascinating. A puzzle to solve." His gaze stops at my mouth. "And some will think you are something else."

My pulse is a heavy bass note in my ears. Cary lets go of my wrist. A muscle in his jaw ticks.

For some reason, my fingers itch to touch it. To feel it under my skin. Just once.

"What else?" I say on a quiet breath.

His eyes find my face one last time, but his lips stay pressed together. He sweeps past me. His honeyed scent sticks to the back of my throat, his warmth a ghost haunting my skin.

The door shuts and silence blankets the room.

All I hear is my heart pounding wildly in my chest.

11

WHEN I WALK into the hallway, I'm startled to find Cary waiting. He leans against a wall. Quiet as midnight.

"Wear this."

A rose gold masquerade mask dangles from his fingers. The cool metal is lightweight in my palm. Elegant flowers decorate most of it. I recognize them—more daffodils. Etched along the mask's edges are musical notes.

I hold it up for Cary. "Really?"

His shoulder rises for a half-hearted shrug. "I told you. My brother loves drama."

Cautiously, I slip the mask on, tying the silky ribbon behind my curls.

Cary eyes me. His jaw moves like he wants to say something else. He doesn't.

We follow floating globes of light through the serpentine

hall. This place is a maze. Locked doors and shadowed corners. I want to ask Cary about all of it. Except, he's back to being a silent, broody dick.

I should be used to it by now. I shouldn't be so frustrated. So . . . confused by him.

One moment, he's straightening my suit, strong hands resting gently on my chest. Turning me in slow circles as he teaches me to dance. Ink black eyes never leaving my face. Confidently drawing me closer to him. Warm breaths near my cheek.

Then he's like ice again. A lake frozen by winter's touch.

Inside the elevator, Cary's fingers flex at his sides. Those fingers were on me. Gripping my hand. Teasing along the dip in my spine. I shut my eyes, grimacing.

Cary's an unwanted distraction. I have no time for him.

Another minute passes before the doors yawn open. I gasp, my eyes unable to pick one place to look.

The grand ballroom is massive. Guests are everywhere. In gowns and suits or a combination of both. Extravagant masks on their faces. Laughter sails above bouncing symphonic music.

I step inside. White marble floors gleam like pearls. The brocade wallpaper is stamped with silver filigree designs: keys and flowers and crescent moons.

To my left, a grand piano plays on its own. The keys depress, untouched. My own fingers wiggle as I try to follow every note and chord. On my right, crimson petals drift down from the air, evaporating before ever contacting the ground. Servers in burgundy clothes move around me with glasses on gold trays.

I inhale a mix of fresh fruit and earthy dark chocolate. Flutes of red liquid are handed out. Tiny seeds sit at the bottom like glimmering rubies.

The entire scene is stitched from magic found in storybooks. Sewn together by the promises of dreams. A tapestry of myths and lore.

And I'm standing here in the middle of it.

"August!"

The cry comes behind me. I turn, searching. It's not Cary. He's disappeared in the sway of bodies. Instead, I find Henri.

Matching dimples outline his grin. He saunters up in a suit so colorful and bright, I'm forced to blink.

He tugs me into a hug. "Finally! This soiree was so boring without you."

I laugh. "I doubt that."

Behind his feathered gold mask, his eyes roll. "Fine. But *I* was bored and lonely. A devastatingly handsome messenger among unworthy conversation partners."

"I'm so sorry," I say dryly, smiling.

He steps back to inspect me. "Impressive!" A blush flows from my temples down to my neck. "Someone obviously thinks highly of you."

My eyes flit around. I don't see Milos anywhere. Absently, I thumb the daffodils on my jacket. I remember Cary's hands there. The petals quiver like they remember too.

"Come, come," Henri cheers. He hooks an arm with mine.

I falter. "Where are we going?"

"You said you wanted to know more about the Deathless."

I did. But everyone in the room is overwhelming. Power radiates off them in effortless waves. My natural urge to be invisible, to be a shadow among them, leaves my skin damp with sweat. Henri clucks his tongue.

"No time to be shy. They won't bite." He pauses. "Well, *some* of them won't."

I groan as he tugs on me.

Henri spins us around a girl dressed in nothing but plump jewels and a mask of diamonds. Next to her, someone with copper skin is covered in tattoos that move.

Meli waves at me. Her two-tone dress is a collision of long silk and wild shreds. I smile her way.

"Careful," Henri singsongs. "She'll give you nightmares."

He never gives me a moment to ask questions. We keep moving. Gasps break out as Poppy struts across the floor. Her black gown is threaded with crystals, a collection of changing constellations. Woven through her lace mask are red flowers.

Poppies.

Near the piano, a raven-haired woman wears a chic black suit and a starburst crown. Her pale skin silver like a full moon. "Cate," Henri says offhandedly, "Deathless of the crossroads."

My nose wrinkles. "And her name's *Cate*?"

Holding a finger to his lips, he whispers, "Don't call her that to her faces."

When I look again, there's three heads instead of one. Like Cerby. I blink and she's normal again.

“Shit,” I hiss.

“Mmhmm.” Henri points to three people standing not far away. “Deathless of vengeance. Triplets.”

He nods at each one: Alek with cropped blond hair against bronze skin, frosted eyes behind a wolf mask, and a fiery suit; Megan, blood dripping from the eyeholes of her mask, sharp talon rings gripping the flowy fabric of her lilac dress; Tish, the tallest, has a horned mask, their indigo tux studded in opals to form a winged beast.

“Never play poker with any of them,” Henri warns. “They’re mean and they cheat.”

As we walk, I feel their stony gazes follow me.

Henri names more guests. So many, I lose count. Some are Deathless. Others, he doesn’t give a title.

From corner to corner, curious eyes are drawn to a beautiful girl with ivory hair and fair green skin. A collection of white leaves makes up her mask. Her iridescent dress shimmers.

“Leu,” Henri says, awed.

“Is she a Deathless?”

“No. But Milos is fond of her.” He grimaces. “Never tell Aminta I said that.”

I nod, reminding myself to find her.

“Though Milos might have a new favorite.” Henri’s wicked smirk is pointed at me. I duck my head. “Well?”

“Well, what?”

He laughs. “Do you like him?”

I don't know *him*, I want to say. That would shatter the illusion of why I'm here. I trust Henri. More than anyone else in this room. But is that enough to share my secret with him?

A server pauses in front of us. Henri grins, swiping two flutes from his tray. When I look closer, I recognize the boy. From outside the elevator my first time here. That same white shimmer surrounds him, but it's not the lighting this time.

It's *him*. He's glowing.

With a bow, the server scurries away.

"He's a—" I start.

"Soul," Henri fills in. He gestures around. "They all are."

My eyes dart around. Despite their burgundy uniforms, every server illuminates like the sun reflecting off Santa Ynez's snowcapped peaks. There's at least two dozen of them.

Henri reads the confusion on my face. After a sip, he says, "Souls arrive here constantly. Sometimes hundreds in a blink of the eye. It's a chore to keep track of them. Milos does his best. And Aminta helps."

The tablet, my brain screams.

I grip the drink Henri hands me, mouth dry.

Frowning, he notes, "Not every soul *likes* their next destination."

I think back to Leila, the woman in the throne room. Clothes stained in blood. Her cries, begging.

My gaze follows a server carrying a tray of glazed tarts. "So how do they end up here? Like this?"

"*Occasionally*," Henri says in a lowered voice, "Milos bargains with them. They work in Aides. Help maintain everything. It's like a fresh start."

In a shadowed corner, a soul cleans up a mess made by rowdy guests. Light brown hair falls over his shimmery face. My pulse spikes. For a brief second, I think it's London. When his chin lifts, I see that it's not.

I bite the inside of my cheek and push the disappointment away.

Henri sips from his flute. "Eventually, they're brought before Milos again. For a reevaluation. He sends them to the Meadows. Or Elysium. Or they stay here—"

His eyes stray to another corner, where Aminta watches the room closely.

"—and become part of us," he finishes.

"You mean, Leu? And Aminta? They were . . ."

He nods slowly. "More than just them."

I almost choke on my next breath. Aminta was a soul. She was *mortal* once, like me.

Henri clinks his glass to mine. "Anyway. Back to Milos—smash or pass?"

I take a small sip from my flute to avoid answering him. The heady scent hits my nose immediately. It's almost recognizable. "What is this?"

"No worries! It's not alcohol."

He remembered what I said at that party. I smile around

another sip. It's equal parts sugary and tart. The seeds tingle against my lips.

"Pomegranate," Henri offers. "Now, about Milos . . ."

I keep drinking.

Over the lip of my glass, I search frantically around the ballroom. My eyes track every soul. Their glowing faces. A wild hope starts beating in my chest again. One of them could be *him*.

Another burst of awed voices breaks my concentration. The crowd parts. Milos slinks through the open space.

His cypress crown catches the light. Instead of a mask, sparkling gold paint streaks around his eyes. His formfitting suit is currant red. The jacket's hem flows out into a floor-length cape. It's as if he's being followed by a river of blood.

Wide-eyed guests gape at his beauty.

I do too.

He ignores the calls from the people he passes. Drifts by an earnest Aminta. He doesn't stop until he reaches me, smiling smoothly.

"You came."

"You invited me," I say hoarsely.

His eyes gleam. "I do not expect everyone to accept my invitations."

Behind me, Henri coughs. A wrinkle forms between Milos's neatly manicured eyebrows. Henri whispers, "Sorry."

I chew on my grin. "Does that mean I'm not the only one you asked to show up for this?"

Milos steps closer to touch the back of my empty hand. His fingers are gentle but assured. "No one else matters."

Over his shoulder, I watch Aminta stomp away.

"Would you like to dance?"

Before I have time to consider, Henri plucks the glass from me. With very little subtlety, he nudges me forward. But I didn't need him to.

There's no way I'm missing this opportunity.

"Absolutely," I say brightly.

Milos leads me to the center of the ballroom. Whispers break out. They're muted by the rise of music. I try to remember what I learned from Cary. Then instantly regret thinking about him.

Nervously, I rest my hand on Milos's shoulder. It's the first time I notice the embroidered details on his suit. A mazelike pattern of swirls. With a wry smile, he coaxes me closer. Flush against his body.

In the ballroom light, his eyes are vivid brown. Like the shore at dawn.

"Shall we?"

Milos dances with grace and control. I'm still wobbly, uncertain with every step. But he doesn't mock me. His smile curves high, and he looks nothing like the boy I saw sentencing a soul to the Abyss.

After stepping on his foot, I blurt, "Sorry. I'm not good at this."

His fingers dig into my hip. "I can teach you."

I consider telling him his brother already tried. I'm sure he'd love that.

Leaning closer, Milos says, "Or you can tell me what you *are* good at." The flickering fire in his eyes makes my skin flush.

"Cleaning restrooms?" I tease. When his eyebrows slope, I shake my head. "Never mind. It's a joke. A bad one."

I watch as a faint laugh bobbles in his throat. His thumb rubs along my knuckles. "What else?"

With a weak shrug, I say, "I used to do music. I wrote songs. Played a little piano."

I'm surprised by how quickly the words leave my tongue.

Milos hums. "And you stopped?"

"Yeah, um." My eyes drop guiltily to our feet. I hear Cary's voice in my head: *Do not look down.* I jerk my head up. "It was just for fun. It wasn't serious."

Now London's in my head: *Journalism will be better for a degree.*

Milos twirls us in a steady circle. I manage to not trip on his cape as my thoughts continue to tailspin.

My eyes catch on someone by a table. A server with broad shoulders and a narrow waist collects empty glasses. It's still not London. But the sight jars something in me. My attention flits back to Milos.

"How do you decide where souls go?"

His expression shifts, dimming.

Quickly, I say, "Sorry, I'm curious. I don't mean to be rude."

"You are not." He smiles smally. "Very few people ask such questions."

I nod, waiting.

"There is a process. Rules. Books to consult." He sighs, like this is the most tedious thing ever. As if deciding how someone spends their eternity after death is as mindless as doing a load of laundry. "I let them tell me about their lives as mortals. What they wanted. What they did with their time."

"And then?"

A smirk ticks along his lips. "My turn to ask a question."

I force myself to relax, even while my frustration grows. There's only one way to get the answers I want. I need to play Milos's game.

"What do you want to know?"

"Tell me about your parents."

My brow knits. "They're not very interesting."

"I doubt that."

I snort loudly. "No, seriously. My dad is a pediatric nurse. My mom works with plants. It runs in the family. My grandfather, his mom. They all loved plants and gardening."

There's a subtle curl to his mouth. "Is that so?"

I ignore his question for one of my own: "What about the souls in here?"

He grips my hip tighter. "What about them?"

"You're giving them a second chance, right?"

"A second chance," he echoes.

"Is it true that you choose some of them to become more than just souls?"

Like Aminta? I almost ask. *Do you remember each of them? Please tell me you do. Tell me you've seen London.*

"Someone has been very chatty." Milos's pointed gaze moves in Henri's direction. Clumsily, I pivot until I'm in his eyeline again.

I grin. "That's so kind of you. To give them another chance."

He licks his lips. "Is it?"

"I want to know more about you." The lie comes out sweetly, but it leaves a bitterness in the back of my throat.

The hand on my waist moves silkily to my lower back. Milos's fingertips dip even lower. "My turn." His electric stare crackles in my bones. "Where you are from . . . what is it like?"

"Santa Barbara?"

"No. The mortal realm."

Suddenly, I trip a little. With a firm hand, Milos holds me upright. It's not like when Cary did it in the garden. There's no gentleness in his touch or flicker of concern in his gaze. Milos does it like he was preventing himself from falling instead of protecting me.

Flustered, I say, "You've never been?"

For some reason, I assumed all the Deathless have.

Milos frowns. "My brother did not tell you?"

I shake my head.

Leaning closer, Milos says, warm breath against my cheek, "I am unable to cross over to your realm like the other Deathless."

"Why?"

His eyes grow smaller. Darker. "I am the final judge. Aides's prince. I am bound to the throne. I must be here, always."

"Always," I repeat in a whisper.

He searches the ballroom like he's hunting for someone. Through his teeth, he grits, "It was not my choice. But it is who I am."

Trying to process everything makes my head dizzy. There's too much information. And still not enough answers.

"So, you can't ever leave?"

His mouth smooths back into a smile. "There is one way."

I look at him expectantly.

He spins us. The room becomes a blur. Dripping stars and falling petals and hypnotic scents. I'm lightheaded. Milos hauls me in until it feels like my body's melting against his.

Against my ear, he says, "You look beautiful tonight."

A flush burns against my cheeks. "Thanks to you." My hand slides down to the wing of his shoulder blade. "I love my suit."

"I am glad." His lips trail lightly down my jaw.

"Nice touch with the flowers," I comment.

He eases back a fraction to look in my eyes. "That was . . . someone else's suggestion."

"Someone else?"

The music falls away. I scan around. Everyone is watching us. Aminta with her heavy scowl. Poppy, arms crossed, curiosity shaping her features. Henri, beaming, two half-finished glasses raised. Unfamiliar faces studying me like I'm . . . a marvel.

Strange and fascinating.

A puzzle to solve.

Or something else.

Clinging to the shadows of the room, I see him.

Cary, with his flat mouth. His unblinking eyes. His expression unreadable.

Abruptly, I stop dancing. Free myself from Milos's hands. "Sorry," I say, tugging at my suffocating collar, "I need some fresh air."

Deep, confused lines wrinkle Milos's forehead. "You are leaving me?"

"Thank you for everything." I bow like an awkward amateur.

Then, without another word, I run for the elevator.

12

THE ELEVATOR HATES ME.

After I'm behind its closed doors, I look for buttons. A way to tell it what floor I want to go to. Not that I know. But this is the first chance I've had to explore Aides alone. To search for London.

I have to try something.

Except, the elevator is moving on its own. Without me doing anything.

"Please." I stare up at the domed ceiling. As if someone is listening. As if someone is sitting in an office somewhere, controlling the elevator's every action. Or maybe the elevator itself is alive with magic. "Please take me where I want to go."

I'm met with silence.

Leaning against one of the brass walls, I tug on my bracelet. My lightheadedness has faded. I still feel off. Out of place. I force myself to concentrate on why I'm really here.

London, London, London, I think until the elevator dings.

My heart is knocking against my throat when the doors slide open. I let out a hopeful breath and step off.

Into the long room of statues and flowers.

"Seriously?"

I spin to face the elevator, scowling. The doors immediately close, caring very little for my frustration.

As I walk, blooms in rich colors open. Coral roses and orchids as blue as sapphires. I trail my fingers along their petals. Nectar fills my lungs. A calmness falls over me.

The marble statues are aged. Limbs broken off, faces weathered. Still, it's as if they're watching me. They don't resemble anyone Henri pointed out in the ballroom. In the room's center, two women stand—one in carved robes with a crown of asphodels, the other holding a bouquet of daffodils.

I wonder who they are. Other Deathless? Souls Milos has trapped here?

A shudder vibrates between my shoulder blades.

What he said turns in my head. He can never leave Aides. Why would he want to? This place is dripping in power, in certainty. He never has to worry about someone he loves dying.

Stepping into the gardens, I tug off my mask and leave it behind. I hear soft whispering water from the nearby lake. Cypress leaves ruffled by the breeze.

In my periphery, something moves. First from my left. Then my right, behind me. My breaths falter as heavy footfalls come from all around. I twist and turn before I see who's followed me.

"It's only you."

Cerby scampers over. The Danes yip as I crouch down. I scratch behind their ears, laughing as their rough tongues lick my cheeks.

"Are you supposed to be here?" I ask.

Three pairs of frost blue eyes ask me the same thing.

I grin. "Let's keep that secret between us."

Cold wet noses bump my chin, heavy breaths dampening my neck. I take it as a sign of approval. A moment later, Cerby darts away. My eyes snag on the structure beyond the hedges. I wander for a closer look.

It's some sort of maze. Stone hidden beneath a tangle of vines and wild purple flowers with red threads—saffron crocus. My mom grows them occasionally.

At the mouth of the maze is an engraved plaque. My thumb rubs over the unfamiliar language. Heat hums against my skin as I touch every letter.

I walk inside.

Lush flowers are scattered along the tall walls. Above, the vines arc to form a canopy. Light bursts through the gaps in glossy green leaves. Heady spices hang in the air. Shrubs shaped like mythical animals and beasts line the long corridor.

Every turn and narrow passageway look the same. Green, lavish. Endless.

Around a corner, I find a mirror against one of the walls.

Gilded thorns form the frame. From a distance, the glass is fogged like ice on a window. But up close, the reflection slowly ripples into focus.

It's . . . me. But not as I looked at the ball.

I'm paler, washed out. A sling holds my left arm in place. My suit is replaced by joggers and a white T-shirt spattered in crimson dots. Tiny red jewels of blood shine from cuts on my face.

I know this version of me. From the accident.

My breath hitches, harsh and echoing. Underneath that, the crunch of gravel in the distance. My head snaps in the direction I came. Did Cerby come after me? The wind exhales a long groan.

No, not the wind. *Voices.*

The maze seems closer, darker. The buzz in my ears builds like a swarm of bees.

"What are you doing in here?"

Heart thudding, I spin around. Propped against one of the walls, Cary stares at me.

"Fuck," I hiss, hand to my chest. "Don't scare me like that."

His eyes narrow. "You cannot just stroll around Aides."

I sniff. "Yeah, so you've told me."

"Yet you did so anyway."

"I needed to get away from"—I flap my hand in the direction I think the ballroom is—"*there.*"

"Did something happen?"

There's a quiet flash of concern in his eyes. I'm not sure if it's real. Like the reflection I saw of myself a minute ago. When I look at the mirror now, the glass has smoked over again.

"What *is* this place?" I ask.

Cary pushes smoothly off the wall. "Milos's labyrinth. Somewhere you do not belong."

I wrap my arms around myself, forcing the image of bloodied August from my head.

"Tell me what happened inside," he requests.

My throat burns with frustration and anxiety. I glare at him. "Why do you care, Cary? You left me alone at the ball—"

"Henri was with you."

"—and you didn't invite me here in the first place," I continue. "Nothing I do matters to you." I hate the disappointed noise my voice makes on that last word. Middle C struck on an out-of-tune piano.

He scans my face. "Did you drink something?"

I roll my eyes. "It was just pomegranate juice."

Cary lets out a breath. "Nothing is *just* here, August. Not for mortals."

His words settle like bricks in my stomach. Is that why I'm sweaty, fighting every second for focus? Is that why I couldn't shut my mouth anytime Milos asked me a question? I did it to get more information out of him. But also, I felt . . . compelled to answer him.

"Shit," I whisper.

Cary frowns back at me and I finally take him in.

He's not wearing the same coat and boots from earlier.

Light twinkles over the silvery details around the shoulders and chest of his onyx suit jacket. Constellations, like Poppy's dress. The shirt underneath is only halfway buttoned. I glimpse the definition in his pale gold chest.

Is that where he disappeared to? To change his outfit? Why and for who?

"We should go." He grabs my wrist.

I let him pull me.

Backtracking through the maze takes us longer than it should. Every few feet, Cary stops, then starts again. As if he's lost. I stumble behind like a dazed child.

Once we reach the entrance, I feel the full heat of his fingers on my skin. I need him off. Before it's the only thing I can think about.

"You can stop touching me now," I growl out.

He whirls around, glowering. His grip loosens. I snatch my arm away.

"Why did you come here?" he asks. "What are you looking for?"

Panic flares in my chest. Does he know about London?

Cary's expression hardens even more. He nearly spits, "Do you want my brother? Do you prefer him?"

"Prefer him to what?" The surprise in my voice is undisguisable.

He steps closer. I back into the labyrinth's wall. Gold blisters in his eyes as he snarls, "Be honest with me, August. You want a prince, is that it? Someone with a crown? A throne? A permanent place? Is he enough for you?" His questions come so fast, so sharp. "Do you *want* him?"

"No!"

"Then what?" He pins me with his stare. "What do you want, August?"

This time, my name on his tongue is like thunder in a storm. The cry of an ocean. His breath is hot against my face. I smell him—sugar and salt and rich earth. His expression is twisted, half angry, half something else.

I want to run away from him. I want to punch him.

I *hate* him. Who he is—Death's obedient scowling minion.

I hate how . . .

How my body reacts to his nearness. Ache and need coiled around my muscles. I hate that my eyes can't look away from him. The hard lines of his jaw, defined cheeks. The wrinkles in his forehead that match the ripples of a sea.

I hate that his stiffness comes with gentleness too. While teaching me to dance. When he caught me before I fell. Stood between me and Cerby or anyone else who might be a threat. The second he found me inside that maze.

Most of all, I hate the knot in my belly when he doesn't back down. When he lets me push in. His pink, plush mouth curved downward in annoyance.

And in this moment, I hate how much I want to kiss him.

So I do.

I half expect Cary to yank away, disgusted. But he doesn't. He presses his mouth to mine, clumsy and awkward. There's a tentativeness in his kiss. Uncertainty I'm familiar with.

My lips draw away. Only a small distance. Breathless, I whisper, "Is this your first kiss?"

His body tenses against mine. "Yes."

"Oh. Okay."

I try to think of a better response. Words collect in my head, going nowhere.

Cary surges forward again. His fingers grip my waist. I angle my head. Open his mouth with my tongue. He tastes honeyed and tart, like a fruit.

Pomegranate, but not the drink Henri gave me. Raw, unaltered.

And I want *more.*

My excited fingers drag through his hair. Freeing his soft curls. My other hand flattens against the small of his back, like he did to me as we danced, until we're pressed together. I can feel him against the inside of my thigh.

Moremoremore.

I direct the rhythm of our kiss. He's like a blank page. My lips are the ink, shifting and shaping lyrics to his mouth. His breaths sing. I can't stop chasing that noise.

But I'm forced to.

"Well, well."

Mortification seizes me and I flinch backward. My head knocks against stone. The throb reverberates until I almost don't see where the voice originates from.

Eventually, she comes into focus.

Poppy stands a few feet away. And she's not alone. Thankfully, it's not guards or another Deathless or Milos by her side. Only the Danes, tongues lolling. I'm really starting to question *who* exactly Cerby is guarding.

Dangling from Poppy's fingers is a rose gold mask. "You dropped this."

A flush springs into my cheeks.

My gaze flicks to Cary. He's wide-eyed, quiet. Yet there's a subtle twitch to the corners of his swollen mouth that tells me he's not angry. Embarrassed, yes. Not disappointed, though.

Poppy saunters to his side. "I have to say, I'm quite surprised by this."

"You are?" I say around a swallow.

"No," she deadpans. Her fingers comb through Cary's hair. "This is a new look."

"Stop it," he mumbles, cheeks bright.

I hold in a laugh.

The ferrier of souls, a heartless Deathless, *blushing.* Because of what my hands did to his hair. Because he clearly enjoyed kissing me.

My chest puffs out.

"We'll be having a talk about this later," she says to Cary. "But not now. The prince sent me to check on his honored guest."

Fear snaps my spine straight.

"Don't worry. I won't say a word," Poppy says with a sly smile, and my posture slowly loosens.

Cary chews on his lip. I read the swirl of mild nervousness and a hint of shyness and soft relief in his eyes. He looks almost . . . human.

"Maybe it's time you return August to the mortal realm?" Poppy suggests. "He's been here longer than he should."

Worry streams through my blood. I don't have my phone. No way of contacting Max or my parents. Have they noticed? Panicked?

I pull at my curls. "How long? Will anyone back home know?"

"I told you," Cary says gently, "time works differently here. A lot slower. You have nothing to fear. No one will know."

"Go," Poppy says. "I'll make up a story for Milos."

Cary nods. "Thanks, Poppy."

She flicks his nose. "I want details, sweet ferrier." Her stare trails over me one more time. "All of them."

Over her shoulder, she blows me a kiss, gold glitter from her lipstick floating on the wind. "Goodbye, August!"

We walk toward the lake in silence, but the aftermath of our kiss flickers like a flame catching sparks anytime our hands brush. It's weirdly confusing how light my body feels. The waves inside me quieted.

Cary's mouth is pursed as if a thousand words are trying to push their way out. I want to hear every single one.

On the lake's shore, I stop him. "When will I see you again?"

His eyebrows lower. "Again?"

I nod, hopeful in ways I shouldn't be.

A long beat passes between us. I recognize the pinched corners of his eyes. The hesitation pulling at his jaw.

"You can't," I whisper, sour disappointment gathering in my throat like bile.

"I only have moments, August," he replies. "I cannot—" He looks away.

"Then give me that," I say, too wired and overwhelmed by today to be ashamed. To give up this fight.

The lake sings softly. Light dances off its gentle waves and reflects onto Cary's face. His mouth slips into a smile, gorgeous as sunrise.

"Has anyone ever said how stubborn you are?"

"Many," I grin out. "Give me a moment, Lord Cary."

He laughs. It's the noise of morning birds. The music of fairy tales.

"Fine, fine. I will try. For you, August."

I wake up in a haze. Sheets tangled around my legs. Moonlight dusts the room a pale ivory.

My bedroom. I'm back home.

When I blink, there's fuzziness behind my eyes. A thin fog I can't quite see through. I stretch lazily, not sure where my phone is. What time it is. A draft teases along my belly from where my T-shirt has ridden up.

Shocked, my eyes look down.

I'm not wearing a suit anymore. Only a ramen-stained

T-shirt and boxers. On my next inhale, I smell them:

Flower petals.

I was in Aides. I was with Milos at the ball. I was with Cary, before and after.

My lips tingle. We kissed.

A smile spreads across my face before I can stop it. Something else shifts in me too. It's a wildfire under my skin. Carelessly, it spreads. I'm not sure how to put it out.

Well, I am.

My bedroom door is shut. I can't hear any noises on the other side. Maybe Max hasn't come home yet. Still, I move quietly. I let my hand slide down my stomach.

My fingers skid over my hip bone, into my waistband. Then lower.

Flames rise swift and hot in my cheeks. It's been so long since I did this. Since I *wanted* to. So long since I thought about another boy in this way. But the images come without any effort.

The light across his smooth face. Pale gold skin against a black suit. His hair caught between my fingers. The muscles in his back arching under my palm. Our bodies crushed together, mouths dancing.

His sugary taste on my tongue. Nervous urgency in his kiss.

It plays over and over behind my eyelids. My heart races against my throat. The tide rises faster than I expected, filling and taking me.

I go, willingly.

It's a different kind of drowning.

The Before

I FEEL . . . DIFFERENT.

Of course I do. I'm exhausted and euphoric at the same time. My body's sore too. Muscles slowly readjusting. Sweat cools on my skin as my breaths even out into a steady rhythm.

The difference is more than just physical. Something else has changed inside me. I can't explain it. Minutes pass before I even have a name for it:

Fearlessness.

Like I could leap off the steep cliffs of Shoreline Park. Plunge into the rolling waves of the Pacific.

Like the thing I just did was awkward and exciting and brave.

All I want is to soak this moment in. Stare up at London's bedroom ceiling. Let my brain wander.

What else has changed? How does it feel? How does he *feel?*

The empty spot on the bed next to me is still warm. Seconds after we finished, London waddled into his bathroom. It was cute to watch. But now I miss him. Even though his scent lingers on his pillows and his UCSB hoodie hangs over his desk chair and every inch of this room is organized in a way that is purely London . . .

I want the *real* thing.

And I don't wait long.

The bathroom door creaks open. Bare feet pad on the hardwood floor. He pinches my still-naked hip.

Standing over me with tousled hair and his smile weirder than ever, London says, "Get up."

My brow furrows. "Where am I going?"

Dread curdles in my stomach. It claws at my thoughts. Is he kicking me out? Was that it? We had sex and now . . . he doesn't want me around?

It took a while for us to reach this step. From brief kisses to deeper ones. From not jumping every time his hand touched my thigh. From not blushing whenever either of us got a boner while making out. From me wanting in silence to telling him I was ready.

We're sixteen. We've been dating almost two years. Should this have happened sooner?

Why did I wait this long?

London's green eyes crinkle. "Well—"

He reaches for his phone. The playlist he made is still going. Harry Styles fades as London flops onto the bed. He opens the

Notes app. A pretyped checklist pops up.

"First, a shower would be good," he narrates. "Then hydrate. After, we'll change clothes"—he points to two sets of neatly folded clothes on his dresser that I didn't notice before—"and head downstairs for a movie and some grub."

Laughing, I hide his screen with my hand. "London, come on."

"Umm, I'm not finished."

"You're serious?"

The thick knot between his eyebrows says he is.

I soften my expression. "What's the rush?"

It's just after nightfall. On weekends, my parents give me a later curfew. His parents are out of town until tomorrow evening.

Napa Valley. One of their rekindle-the-romance getaways, he explained this morning. *They're probably getting divorced after I start UCSB.*

He said it so casually. Not for the first time. In the past, he's always shrugged it off, changing subjects. Like he doesn't care. But I've seen the tension around his eyes every time he brings it up.

He never wants to talk about it, so I don't press him.

"Can't we stay in your bed?" My fingers trace the hair on his thigh.

He raises his phone. "But what about my list?"

"We can do all of that too. Just later."

"Why not now?"

"Because" is all I offer.

His eyes narrow, like it's not enough. And I wish I could just say it:

Because I want you to hold me. Because I don't want everything to be a list. Or a plan. Because I don't know if you liked what we did as much as me. Because I love you even more now.

But that glowing bravery is turning into a dim-flickering ember with every second that ticks by.

I stare at him, fighting a frown. This moment changed me. Has it not done the same for him?

Swallowing, I whisper, "London—"

He silences me with a thumb to my lower lip. It's swollen, bitten raw. From the nerves and then the minutes of pain and then from bliss.

His smile is like sunshine. Bright, clear, luminous. "August, I planned this all out for us."

He did. It's obvious now.

Inviting me over an hour before sunset. Leading me upstairs. The low lighting in his bedroom. Marigold petals on the floor. Curated playlist softly humming in the background.

Kissing me—slow and purposeful—until I wasn't trembling when our clothes came off. He bought the condoms. Asked all the right questions before. And during. He set the tone and pivoted when I was clumsy and uncertain, and soothed the strangeness of what we were doing until I felt confident enough to meet his eyes.

London did everything to make tonight perfect. And I feel

bad for wanting more from him. For wanting to just . . . go with my feelings.

"Sorry," I whisper.

"No, it's my fault. I should've told you about my plans. I was just—I wanted every minute of our first time to be perfect," he says with a shyness that stings.

"It was, London." I kiss his shoulder. "This is great!"

It's everything I wanted, right?

Silence wedges between us. I watch him bite the inside of his cheek, thinking. Summer-streaked hair falls across his jaw. Pale light glosses his tanned chest. A fine dusting of dark hair starts from under his navel, dipping into his boxers.

He has changed, physically. But what else?

Finally, he beams. The face of the boy I love. "It was great." He kisses my cheek, then turns back to his phone screen. "I'm glad we're on the same page, August. And we can skip around the list. Wanna start with food and a movie?"

I nod. Ignore the small disappointment still churning in my belly. There will be other times to lie around in his bed—or mine—staring up at the ceiling, just existing.

There will be so many more moments between London and me.

13

DROPLETS OF WATER are still sliding down my bare shoulder as I walk to my room. The hot water didn't last as long as I wanted. Max probably used it all when she came home from class. At least I had time to wash my hair.

A fluffy burgundy towel hangs over my head, covering my face. I need to dry and detangle my curls. And put on some real clothes, quickly. My shift at the pizzeria starts in an hour. I still have to make it to the bus stop.

Fortunately, I know this apartment like my favorite song. I don't need to see to—

"Shit!"

My foot catches on something in the doorway to my bedroom. I yelp, stumbling forward. The mattress catches me before I sprain an ankle. I bounce, then flip over. Panic burns in my throat. What if I just kicked Diana?

Ripping the towel away, I sit up. Look around. Morning light burns bright in the room. Relief eases my pulse when I find Diana lounging, unharmed, on my pile of dirty clothes in the corner. Something else tripped me.

I see it. On the floor near the door. Wrinkled and navy and breath-stealing.

London's UCSB hoodie.

Guilt hits me so hard, so mercilessly, I almost fall off my bed.

How could I forget so easily? I went to the underworld for a reason last night. Not dancing at a masquerade ball. Or kissing a boy against a garden wall.

I went to get more information out of the Deathless. Sweet-talk Aminta and Milos. Get closer to Cary . . . *for London*. He's still somewhere in Aides and I was supposed to be focused on finding him.

How could I let one Deathless—one silly kiss change that?

Swearing, I hide my face in my hands. In my head, I count backward from ten. I swallow down a scream. I do every trick I can think of before a panic attack comes. Before I give up.

There's still time, I try to remind myself. Even if I'm not sure that's true.

After a few deep breaths, I refocus. I'm not going to let this eat at my insides, gnaw on my bones. All I need is a better plan. To get back to Aides.

I can't let anything else get in the way.

"The next time I say I'm signing up for a History of Western Civilization course," Max says, groaning dramatically, "throw me in the ocean. Burn all my cute cardigans. Hide every drop of caffeine in our apartment!"

I look up at the blue sky. "You could've majored in something else."

"Like what?"

My eyebrows wiggle wickedly. "Psychology."

Max smacks my arm. "No one asked you."

We're at Shoreline Park. On one of the wide lawns. I lie on my back in the grass, hands tucked behind my head. Late morning sun warms my face. Max sits on a blanket with a thick textbook in her lap, her coffee cup nearby.

Other students are scattered around us. They work on their laptops, scroll through their phones. The wind carries delighted screams from a children's playground not far away. Dogs pull their owners along the walking path toward the harbor. Tourists snap cliffside photos of the area.

Brine and seaweed scent the early October air. I hold it in my lungs. Breathe out every thought about how different it is from Aides. Or how it's been a week since I was last there. How I've been impatiently waiting for Cary to come back.

And he hasn't. What if he never does?

Max slams her book shut. "I knew I should've signed up for that Witchcraft, Science, and Religion course."

"You would've hated it too," I comment.

"Not as much as this." She checks her phone, then sighs. "My shift starts soon."

"Weekend tips are the best tips," I remind her.

She downs her coffee in one gulp. "Like you'd know. How did you get a Saturday off anyway?"

I'm not sure. I didn't even realize I had the day off until Junie mentioned it last night while we locked up. A fog sits on the fringes of my brain. I can see all the most important parts of my life clearly. But small details hide beneath a cloud.

Almost . . . invisible.

I shrug at Max. "Luck, I guess?"

She snorts. "With you? Highly unlikely."

"Whatever. I bet you're not like this with—" It takes a second before a name comes to me. "Lake." It feels funny on my tongue.

Standing, Max slings her bag over one shoulder. She shakes out the blanket with a tiny frown. "We . . . didn't work out."

My jaw drops. "I'm sorry."

It's her turn to shrug. "I'm already over it." The way her teeth pull on her lower lip says differently. But this is Max. Things never bother her for long.

She loops her hair into a messy bun. "What are you doing with the rest of your day?"

"I don't know."

Certainly not pacing around our apartment for the sixth straight day, hoping the ferrier of souls shows up so I can trick him into letting me see my dead boyfriend sits unsaid at the back of my throat.

Instead, I say, "Maybe go see my mom?"

She called again the other day. I feel bad. I haven't visited her or my dad despite their efforts.

"Do you want a ride?" Max offers.

I shake my head, grass tickling the back of my neck. "I'll take the bus."

She gives me a look. We both know what it means. I'm still uneasy in cars. Public transportation is significantly safer. It's a proven statistic.

"Fine," Max relents. "Dinner, later?"

"Only if you're paying. I'm still short on rent."

"You're a terrible roommate, Auggie."

"But a great best friend," I call as she walks away.

Max replies with a middle finger and a smirk over her shoulder.

I settle back into the grass, one arm thrown over my eyes. There aren't many trees on the lawns. Most of them border the fenced-in cliffsides. Overhead, the shrieks of gulls echo. Cars cruise down Shoreline Drive.

But it feels like it's just me in the world. Me and my intrusive thoughts.

I'm not alone for long. A shadow falls over me.

"Is this what you consider fun? Wow. I am disappointed."

Surprise and something unruly thud in my chest at the sound of his voice.

I lower my arm. In the bright sun, all of Cary's angles are softened. Light halos him. Gold against all the black he's wearing. His mouth curves into a half smirk as I drink him in.

"You're here," I breathe.

He looks around as if he's shocked himself. "Well, someone promised me this world could be . . . fun. I still have my doubts."

My nose wrinkles. "I said *humans* could be fun. And I didn't promise."

He rolls his eyes. He's wearing another Henley. The buttons are undone. I'm taunted by the flash of strong collarbones, his muscled chest. I avert my gaze to that one curly lock drooping over his forehead.

Cary's eyebrows tilt up. "Are you calling me a liar?"

"No." I grin. "But just because you're ageless doesn't mean your memory is."

A muted laugh wobbles in his throat. It's a weird thing to get used to. Cary thinking I'm amusing. But it's cute too, the way he tries to hide it with half-hearted scowls and straightening his shoulders.

My eyes drop away from his face to something in his left hand. "What's that?"

"Oh." That flicker of shyness I saw in his eyes after we kissed is back. His fingers tighten on a white paper bag. He looks between it and me. It's as if he's deciding something.

I sit up. "Is it for me?"

He nods.

Unexpected heat climbs up my neck. I'm not sure what to

say, how to react. Cary got something. For me. I stand, dusting blades of grass off my shorts.

"What is it?" I ask curiously.

Cary passes me the bag. He pretends to be uninterested as I peel it open, but I can feel his eyes on me. In the corner of my vision, I see his smile when I pull out a cookie from the best bakery on State Street Promenade. In all of Santa Barbara, actually.

I gape at him.

He shrugs. "Sometimes, having a sweet tooth is not so bad."

His face brightens while my cheeks burn even hotter remembering what I said to him at the pizzeria the first time I saw him.

"Stop staring at me like that," he says. "It is not a big deal."

But it *is*. Somehow, he picked out my favorite flavor—strawberry cheesecake. It's pink and thick like two cookies smashed together. When I take a bite, the soft, chewy warmth makes me moan.

He clears his throat. "Everyone deserves something sweet." The corners of his lips glide up. "Even annoying, stubborn bad dancers like you."

A comeback crawls up my throat, but my mouth is too full of cookie to say anything. Instead, I glare at him. Though, it's very unconvincing since I'm grinning too.

I can't believe he did this. That he thought of me. Curiously, I want to know how he paid for the cookie. Do Deathless carry money? Did he steal it? But I'm too caught up in how pleased he looks as I finish in three more bites.

Swallowing, I say, "How can I prove humans are way funner than you think?"

He waves a hand around. "It is your world, August. You tell me."

I pause, debating. When I came up with this idea, I hadn't really considered how to entertain the ferrier of souls. What convincing him he's wrong about us—about *me*—would look like.

Cary eyes me as if he can tell that I'm struggling.

I decide against overthinking. After all, I don't know how long I have with him. I need every minute I have to win him over.

Find a way back to Aides.

"Come with me."

Cary walks by my side, silently. It's not as uncomfortable as it used to be. I'm starting to understand him better. I'd mistaken his quietness for coldness. But it's not. He's taking in every little detail, processing. Forming his own understanding.

I point out all the parts I love about Shoreline. The spindly trees I climbed as a kid. Every flower Mom would name for me: yellow *Glebionis coronaria* and blue-orange *Strelitzia.* Crown daisies and birds of paradise.

At the pastel blue telescope, I let him look through the eyepiece as I list off the things he sees: The coastline. Channel Islands. Whales breaking through the ocean's glimmering surface.

He listens as I talk about the spot on the pavement where I skinned my knee bloody attempting to skateboard. The stretch of grass I'd lie in to trace the shapes of drifting clouds. So many small pieces of my world made bigger when laid out before me.

And for some odd reason, I want him to know about it all.

"This way."

He laughs under his breath at the way I mimic him as he took me around Aides.

Through a torii gate, we walk down Shoreline Steps, a narrow wooden stairwell built along the steep cliffside. I pause two flights before the wood turns to sand and surf. The ocean's song is pronounced here. A constant roar as waves slap the shore.

Cary leans against the railing with me, shoulder to shoulder. To my disbelief, he speaks first:

"This is your favorite place."

It's not a question. I turn my head. He's illuminated by the sun, watching and waiting for a response.

I pivot and say, "Why do you talk like that?"

"Like what?"

"I don't know." I shrug. "Old-fashioned? You don't sound like Poppy or Henri."

The breeze sweeps through his hair. He combs it back. I want to stop him, leave him messy and imperfect.

"They get to spend more time around mortals." His eyes soften. "I only have moments."

I pin my bottom lip between my teeth. The way he said

it . . . I almost feel sorry for him. "But you're here now," I tell him. "This is longer than a moment, right?"

He smiles. It doesn't reach his eyes. "Definitely. Thankfully, there are other Deathless besides me who collect souls."

My mind drifts to the conversations I've had. Things I've heard.

"Henri," I say. "And Poppy."

Cary nods. "And others. But I am the only one who can take souls across the bridge. That is my gift." The faraway look in his eyes tells me it's a curse too.

I nudge his shoulder, a grin teasing my mouth. "I guess you don't get to have a lot of conversations with people before they die."

His lips twitch. "Or after. Who wants to chat with the boy taking you to the afterlife, anyway?"

"Me," I say lowly.

My hand brushes the back of his wrist. I'm not sure whether I'm trying to convince him or if it's for another reason.

Below us, a dog barks as its owner tosses a ball across the beach. My eyes flit back to the water. But my fingers skim absently over his smooth knuckles.

"I used to come here to think."

I keep my gaze away from the wooden bench inches from us. The one I'd sit on for hours while skipping school.

"To be alone," Cary prompts.

My throat tightens, so I nod for him.

Grief is easier alone. No one can ask how you're doing. Or

recite some pretty but worthless quote they read online about healing. They can't apologize for your pain. For the ache that comes without you even thinking about it.

Words rarely make grief better. Sometimes, they hurt more.

Here, I didn't have to hear the whispers from my classmates. Or the one-note speeches teachers gave me like they were reading from a handbook. No more *sorry for your loss* from strangers. Sad, pitying smiles like any of them knew what I was feeling.

Here, it was just me and the sea.

Here, I could miss London without the weight of everyone else's grief piled on top of me.

The breeze picks up. Sea spray mists the cliff walls. I taste it on my lips, salty ocean water. Except, when I blink, I realize it's not.

Warm trails wet my cheeks. Fat tears sit on my upper lip.

I almost wipe them away, embarrassed, but Cary's flipped his hand over. He tangles his fingers around mine. When I turn my head, his gaze is on the whitecapped waves as they roll.

He's giving me the peace to hurt while reminding me he's right here.

"You came here a lot to escape," he says. Again, not a question.

"Yeah."

"Then"—his eyes finally meet mine—"what *is* your favorite place, August?"

A tiny grin flexes my mouth.

We ride the 4 bus to downtown Santa Barbara.

Cary's eyes shift around the entire time. From the gray-haired white woman rifling through the dozen shopping bags piled next to her to the young brown-skinned boy spinning a soccer ball on one finger while bopping his head to huge wireless headphones. The Black woman with beautiful purple locs reading a battered copy of *Beasts of Prey* on our left.

He whispers, "Why is that mortal yelling?"

At the front of the bus, a finance bro has been shouting into his phone for nearly twenty minutes.

"Makes him feel accomplished?" I offer.

Cary scowls. "I hope Poppy haunts his dreams."

I laugh the rest of the ride.

Santa Barbara County Courthouse is like a castle in the middle of downtown. It's large and eye-catching. White as snow with red tile roofs. We follow a flagstone path toward the Great Arch. Past the Spirit of the Ocean Fountain, nude sandstone-carved figures holding the tail of a fish spitting a steady stream of water into a clear blue pool.

The old creaky elevator takes us to the rooftop. My breath still catches when I step out onto the clock tower's viewing deck. From all sides, Santa Barbara stretches unendingly. A panoramic look at the mountains and islands and city.

My city.

I walk over the compass painted on the brick floor to reach one side of the tower. My elbows lean on the wrought iron railing. Below, a couple poses for wedding photos in the wide sunken garden. The bride's dress is stunning against a backdrop of tangerine birds of paradise. Palm trees sway in the breeze.

I shiver. Heat radiates off Cary as he joins me.

After a beat, I say, "When I was younger, my mom would bring me up here after school." I point at a building, a smudge of white against green nearly two miles away. "She'd tell me about all the kids like me my dad was taking care of at the hospital."

My fingers tense around the railing.

"She did it so I wouldn't miss him when he worked long shifts," I manage. "But I still did."

Cary watches the city, but I can tell he's listening.

"When I turned thirteen, I started coming up here on my own," I say. "Not to look at the hospital anymore."

"Why?"

My thumb rubs across my blue-and-yellow bracelet. I hesitate. "To write songs."

"You really love music."

I smile. "How can you tell?"

"You are always humming." Sunlight outlines his profile as he studies the sea. "When we are in the water together."

"I am?"

The beginnings of a grin push his cheeks higher. Warmth spills into my face when he catches me staring.

"I did love it," I admit. "Music."

I shift around to gesture at the wide ledge sitting under

the teal-framed window. "I'd write over there for hours. Silly songs with shitty lyrics. I thought I was gonna be the next Ed Sheeran."

A scratchy laugh sneaks past my lips.

He eyes me. "But you quit."

Guilt aches under my ribs.

Cary crosses the tower to sit on the ledge. His long fingers drum the spot next to him. He gives me an expectant look.

Sighing, I oblige.

The moment I'm seated, memories pour through me like an open fire hydrant:

Huddling on this ledge. The countless notebooks in my lap. Page after page of songs as lyrics leaked from my pen until my fingertips were dyed blue or black.

"Tell me why you stopped," Cary requests.

Our eyes meet. His are the deepest black. Not the dread of shadows but the endless possibility of night. The curiosity behind his lashes is almost childlike, a look I never get anymore. Everyone else wants to know things about me so they can pick them apart and decide whether I've earned the way I feel.

Before I can say anything, footsteps and voices rise from the stairwell. It's one of the courthouse's guided tours.

Immediately, I tense.

Cary grabs my hand, then whispers, "They cannot see or hear you."

Soon, the tower is teeming with tourists. The awe in their

voices echoes. They take photos from the railings. Ask the guide a million questions. But no one looks our way.

We're invisible, like that day outside the hospital.

I look down. Cary's threaded our fingers together. He gives a small encouraging squeeze.

I tell myself what I'm about to do is for London. Cary is my only link to Aides. My way back to him. Being coy hasn't worked before. Neither has being demanding.

It's time I try something else. The truth.

I don't *want* to talk about this. But I need to.

"Someone close to me died," I confess, still looking down. My sneaker scuffs the floor. "He meant a lot to me. I would show him all my songs. Sometimes, I'd sing them too."

Cary's mouth goes a little higher. "You sing?"

Fire swarms through my cheeks. "Badly."

"That sounds like a lie."

"You don't have to believe it for it to be true."

A mom and daughter pass us. The little girl has braided pigtails and a gap-toothed grin that rivals her mom's.

Cary's featherlight touch on the inside of my forearm draws my eyes. His index finger traces my tattoo. He follows the lines of every petal until a shiver ripples under my skin.

"Daffodils are my favorite," I say.

"This is a narcissus."

"I'm a what?"

He laughs quietly while outlining the thin stem. "No, the *flower* is a narcissus."

I blink at him, lost.

Another memory catches me in a sticky web: the day I got the tattoo. It was right after graduation. I was desperate to feel *something* other than the constant ache in my chest. The waves tugging me under.

Max came with me. We flipped through a thick book of designs. I found this flower on the last page. A random sketch by the tattoo artist. I can't explain it, but . . . the flower called to me.

A whispered *I will help you.*

It was silly then. Silly now. But I knew.

In the leather chair, I listened to the needle's incessant buzz. Savored its sharp bite against my skin. For a few hours, I was distracted by a different kind of pain.

"It is sacred," Cary tells me.

I almost guffaw. His serious expression halts me. "To you," I say, gently pulling my arm away.

The docent is reciting the final lines of her speech. The tour is wrapping up.

"Did you stop writing when he died?" Cary asks.

"Before," I say.

"Why?"

I exhale. "We were supposed to go to college together. I was gonna study music. One day, he told me to study journalism instead. Music wasn't something I should build a future around."

"And you listened?"

"He wasn't wrong." My fingers drag through my curls. "It's just that—I was sixteen. And not a very good planner. I'm *still* not very good. I listened because he always had the right solution. He knew what was best for me."

I pick at the threads of my bracelet. Think of every time London told me one of his plans. For himself. For *us*. All the times he told me to get serious and stop dreaming.

He was right. Wasn't he?

"He *was* wrong."

Cary's words hit like a slap. The tourists descend the stairwell, and I yank free of his hand. I stand, glaring at him.

"You don't know him," I spit.

"Of course not," he agrees. "But I know you let one mortal's opinion change who you are."

Anger thunders in me, loud and reverberating. It's the sound of After August pounding on his cage. Demanding to be let out.

"He wasn't just 'one mortal'!" I snap. *He was everything.*

Cary gets to his feet. "August, I am—"

"You have no clue what it means to be one of us," I cut in. "All you do is guide souls. How could you possibly understand what losing him did to me?"

I hate how my voice breaks.

I hate it. I hate it. *I hate it.*

"You're a *Deathless*," I say venomously. "You don't have to care about anything else."

His face hardens. Mouth tight, narrowed eyes flecked in

gold. For a long time, he's quiet. The breeze changes direction. His scent fills my nose, a sugared contrast to his sour expression.

Suddenly, he stretches his hand in my direction, palm up. "Come with me."

I flinch back. "Come with you?" A humorless snort jolts me. "Is this a joke?"

"No."

"Go with you *where*?"

Is he taking me back to Aides? To Milos? Is Cary powerful enough to end my life and banish me to the Abyss?

In a blink, the lines around his mouth turn soft. The golden wrath has faded from his eyes. "Time for me to show you what it really means to be the ferrier."

14

RANCID BILE SWIRLS in my throat, choking me.

I double over, hands on my knees, swallowing. The stinging taste makes my eyes water. My legs shake. This is nothing like traveling to Aides. It's disorienting in a way I wasn't prepared for.

"Breathe," Cary instructs.

Much easier said than done.

I cough, then force myself to take long breaths in through my nose. A minute passes before the spinning stops. When I raise my head, the world comes into clear focus.

We're not in Santa Barbara. Or the underworld.

Nightfall coats the sky black. A city spills out before me. The roads are lined with long rows of buildings. Pubs and shops that shift from brick to white to vibrant blue. A red double-decker bus passes.

"Where are we?"

Casually, Cary says, "Soho. London."

"London?"

My muscles tense again. How could Cary bring me here? To the city London was named after. But the longer I stare at him, the more I realize he doesn't know. The concern in his eyes tells me he wouldn't be that cruel if he did.

"Are you okay?" he asks.

"Yeah, uh . . . Am I *allowed* to be here? I don't even have a passport."

"No need to worry. We will not be here long."

Above the din of music and laughter and drunken shouts, a siren blares in the distance.

"Come," he says. "We are late."

Down side streets, I take in windows lit by neon signs. Union Jacks flutter above awnings. Lanterns paint the faces we pass amber. Twice, I almost lose track of Cary. He moves easily through crowds like he belongs here.

I clearly don't.

At an intersection, the mass of bodies thickens. Bright blue lights flicker on a yellow ambulance. Cary's hand finds mine.

"Do not let go," he says, then pulls me through the stream.

Near the front, officers shout to keep people away. Phones are pointed at a scene just beyond them. A section of the street is taped off. Paramedics whisper to each other. But Cary doesn't lead us in that direction.

Instead, we walk to the shadows of a darkened bookstore. He lets go of my hand. "Stay here."

"But—"

Before I can finish, he's gone. He approaches a boy sitting outside a café several feet away.

"Did you see that?" The boy blinks at Cary, mirth gleaming in his brown eyes. He's around my age, beige skin and thick black hair. A sharp nose to match his long jaw. "I've never landed that trick in my life. It was sick!"

Cary kneels to his height. "Was it?"

The boy nods eagerly. "I wish my mates could've seen it."

"They left you, Hasan," Cary says gently.

"They—" Hasan pauses, rubbing the back of his head. He frowns as his eyes roam around. "Yeah, I guess they did. We'd had a couple of pints, and they dared me to do this unbelievable trick and . . ." His words trail off.

Then Hasan truly looks at Cary. "Wait, you know my name?"

Cary's lips ease into a smile. "I do. Do you know who I am?"

Biting my lip, I watch reality sink in. It hollows Hasan's gaze. "Yeah," he croaks, frowning. "I think I do."

"And you know why I am here?"

Hasan's focus jumps to the street, where a skateboard lies snapped in half. A pale white woman sobs outside her car. Officers attempt to console her. Blood stains the road garnet. Paramedics zip up a body bag.

"That's not me, is it?"

My chest tightens at Hasan's broken voice. The way his knee bounces anxiously.

I want to run away. I can't watch this. Can't handle how hard my heart is throbbing in my throat as Hasan puts it all together.

But Cary maintains a steady smile. He carefully grabs Hasan's hand like he did mine. "It is time," he says.

Hasan sucks in a long breath like he wasn't afforded that chance before the car slammed into him. "Mate, I'm only *eighteen*. I just started uni. I was gonna do so many things," he rants. "This isn't fair."

"I know," Cary agrees. "But you lived. That is a lot. And now it is time."

Chin lowered, Hasan whispers, "I'm scared."

Cary tilts his head until Hasan looks him in the eyes. "I know that too." His thumb rubs over Hasan's knuckles. "I will walk with you. I will not leave like your friends. Okay?"

A minute ticks by before Hasan's shoulders relax. Cary helps him to his feet. That's when I see it. The slight glimmer surrounding Hasan's body. A thin veil of ivory.

Squeezing his hand, Cary says, "Come on. There are so many things left for you to do."

Over his shoulder, he meets my eyes. "Wait here. I will not be long."

I nod, unsure of what else to do.

As Cary leads Hasan into the shadows of another street, I hug myself. It's a cool night. October in Soho is different from Santa Barbara. There's a bite to the air. The noises around me grow loud again, but all I hear is Hasan's voice in my head.

I was gonna do so many things.

He was only eighteen. My age. Two years older than London was when he died.

How is that enough time to do anything with your life? How does Death decide that is all he gets?

A hand touches the back of my shoulder. I jump, then jerk around.

It's Cary.

"Shit," I hiss, clutching my chest.

His eyebrows rise. "Are you cold?"

"Yeah, well." I rub my bare arms. I'm still in a T-shirt and shorts. "I didn't plan on going overseas when I got dressed this morning. Next time I'll check the weather."

"Oh, you assume there will be a next time?"

I shrug.

He hums, inching forward. His palms are warm, soothing along my biceps and forearms. Soon, his hands slide back into mine. "We are not done yet."

As we leave, I watch the ambulance drive away. "Is Hasan okay?"

Cary smiles. "He will be."

Our next destination leaves me reeling just as much as Soho.

"Deep breath," Cary says again, standing over me.

The moment I do, I gag. A sharp chemical odor burns my nose. I know this smell. And the overwhelmingly bright LED lights over my head. The eerie stillness of the hallway.

"We're in a hospital," I choke out.

"In Tokyo."

"Japan?" I don't know why I'm surprised.

I force myself to trail behind him. Even though my knees are weak, my hands trembling. We pass room after room. I never look inside.

At the end of the hall, a little girl sits on the shiny floor. She can't be older than ten. Her hospital gown is pastel pink. Spread around her are stuffed animals—a floppy bear, a hugged-soft duck, a one-eyed bunny.

"Stay," Cary starts, but I quickly cut in with "I know, I know."

His fingers drag along the back of my hand. For a second, he looks like he doesn't want to leave me behind. But he does.

I lean against the wall, observing.

Cary sits, crisscrossing his legs. He smiles widely. The girl pushes the bunny toward him, her face brightening after he takes it. There's a yellow cap tied around her small head. She's bald underneath.

I feel my chest start to crack right down the middle.

Cary lifts his hands. They begin to move in fluid motions, fingers forming letters and words. When he's done, the girl's face lights up and her hands move rapidly. Cary nods along. They're speaking in sign language.

Cary *knows* sign language.

My lungs swell with shock.

He signs something else. From his facial expression, it looks like he's asking her a question. The girl squeezes the duck to her chest. She nods, sadness brimming her eyes.

He gives her another smile, this one warmer, reassuring. His gaze never leaves hers as he makes the bunny hop around the floor. Tiny hands fly to her mouth as she laughs.

I fight off my own chuckle.

Soon, Cary is signing again, his eyebrows climbing his forehead. Another question, I think. She replies a little slower, her lower lip poked out. A long moment passes before he reaches out to her. There's still slight hesitation in her pretty brown eyes.

With an exhale, she takes his hand.

Every nerve in me screams. I want to yell at him. She's too young for this to be happening. But the second he looks at me, my voice evaporates. Dust on the wind.

"I will not be long," Cary repeats from earlier.

He smiles at the girl. She's pink-cheeked, even while glowing white. Slowly, he escorts her into a dark room, disappearing.

I stumble to the spot they just were. Where her stuffed animals still sit. My legs give out. I slump down the wall. Shaking, I grab the tiny duck, then pull my knees to my chest.

It's so quiet here. So cold and empty. A house built for

sadness. For grief. How can my dad stand to be in a place like this?

It's not long before I hear footfalls. I smell the sweet earthiness of Cary. He kneels in front of me, hands resting on my knees.

I force my voice to work. "What was her name?"

"Yuri."

"How old was she?"

"Nine."

"How did it happen?"

He pauses. His other answers came so clinically, plainly. This time, he falters, lips almost pulled into a frown. "Brain cancer. She battled for the last three years."

His fingers tighten on my knees.

"She loved animals. Good food. And her mom. She told me—" His voice catches. "She did not want her mom to be alone. To miss her."

I press the duck to my chest. "What did you say to her?"

He smiles to himself. "That they will be together again."

A numbness runs through me. From my feet to my ribs.

How does Cary know if they'll see each other again? He's only the ferrier. He guides souls to Aides, but Milos decides where they go after. Whether they end up in the Meadows, Elysium, or the Abyss. What happens to children like Yuri?

How much in their short life tips the scales one way or the other?

After a beat, I ask, "Could you have saved her?"

It's crossed my mind more than once. The power he must

hold as a Deathless. But the resigned look on his face says it's not enough.

"What about Death?"

He exhales a long breath. "Unfortunately, it does not work that way. No one can change what Fate decides."

My jaw stiffens. I stop myself from screaming. From begging him to find a way. All that power in him—in all the Deathless—and nothing can bring the dead back to life.

I put Yuri's duck down. "How do you do it?"

"August," he says, voice scratchy, "I do not have a choice. This is who I am."

"She was a *child*, Cary."

"I know. But it is not always like that."

A rough laugh shakes me. "Oh, I'm sure it's all sunshine and rainbows."

"Sometimes," Cary tries with a sad smile. "Not often."

"So, you never fight back? You just do this because you have to?"

"At first," he confesses. His thumb brushes along the goose bumps on my forearm. "But not anymore."

"Then why?"

Something unreadable flickers in his eyes. "Let me show you."

For a solid minute, I retch into someone's rosebushes. Thankfully, no one's home. Nothing but hot, sour saliva comes up anyway. Cary's hand runs along my back. His strong fingers press the tension from between my shoulder blades.

I drag the back of my hand across my mouth. "Is it always that bad?"

"Only for mortals."

He leads me over a bluestone walkway to a single-story house. The brick exterior is painted white with peeling black accents.

Sucking in a clean breath, I say, "And how many mortals have you done this with?"

"Why? Are you jealous?"

I scowl at him.

He grins. "Only you." With a hint of shyness, he adds, "You are my first for many things."

A soft smile blooms unexpectedly across my face. "Where are we now?"

"Macon. In Georgia."

The porch steps creak under our feet. Dense humidity forms a coat of sweat on my skin. My T-shirt sticks to my back.

Cary doesn't bother knocking on the peacock blue door. He walks right in.

Music fills the small foyer. Something old and bluesy.

We move through a living room. Splayed on the coffee table is an unfinished knit sweater. A framed painting of a Black man playing the trumpet hangs above the fireplace. Age leaches the color from all the furniture. Walking canes lean against one wall near the kitchen, where a teacup sits next to a bowl of waxy decorative peaches.

Cary's mouth opens. I cut him off with a wry grin.

"Stay here. I know."

Again, his fingers ghost over my knuckles. Tender heat dances up my forearm. I hide in the entryway's shadows to watch him.

"You're late."

Inside the sunroom is an old woman with deep brown skin, big silver curls, and a stern smile. She sits like a queen in a cozy lounge chair.

Across from her is an identical woman. Except, her eyes are closed, posture slack. She looks peaceful. Like she's sleeping. But I know better now.

Cary does a half bow. "My apologies, Bernice."

"My friends call me Bernie." Her accent is thick, Southern. "My grandbabies call me Grammy. Everyone else calls me Mrs. Woods."

"And what shall I call you?"

She sizes him up. "I don't know yet. But not Bernice. Only my parents and my late husband called me that."

"Very well." Cary smiles. "Do you know who I am?"

Her tongue clucks dismissively. "Of course I do. Been waiting on you forever."

"Have you, now?"

Bernice's gaze cheats to the other chair. Where her mortal body is. "My Joseph died eight years ago. Our kids are all grown. They got their own families now."

She points a wrinkled finger toward the far wall. Wood-framed photographs take up almost every inch. A tapestry of life through decades. Bernice with her husband, her children, then grandchildren. So much joy and laughter caught on film.

Sadly, she admits, "Been just me. For too long. I'm—I'm tired."

Empathy flashes in Cary's eyes.

I bite the inside of my cheek while studying the pictures. In her youth, Bernice looked so much like my mom. Cold dread spears me. I don't want to imagine Mom's life ending like this. In a house I never visit.

Alone, without Dad.

I don't want to think about my parents dying at all.

My gaze snags on a photo of Bernice from a different era. Her early twenties, maybe. She's red-lipped and bright-eyed. The camera caught her mid-performance in a sparkly dress, the audience fawning over her. She was a *singer.*

From her chair, Bernice admires the same picture. "I was belting in nightclubs before I was old enough to drink." It's as if she's talking to me, not Cary. "That's how I met my Joseph. In a jazz band."

He steps over for a closer look. "How long were you a performer?"

"Two decades." She laughs, big and brassy. Like her voice was meant to take up space. Pack rooms. "Best time of my life. Until my kids came along."

There's a flutter in my chest that feels like hope but disappears too quickly.

Cary's finger draws an invisible map over the other rows of pictures. Bernice with one, two, finally five children.

"And them?" He looks at Bernice, but it's like his gaze is pointed at me.

"What about them?" Bernice says.

He pauses. As if his next question is something he's never thought to ask a soul before. "Are you worried about them?"

Bernice sighs. "Nope. My kids will be fine. That was my job as a mother. To love them fiercely. Unconditionally. And to pour so much of my own heart into them that when I died, I'd still be with them."

My fingers pluck restlessly at my bracelet.

"It's gonna hurt," she continues. "But they'll survive. And go on. That's what we all do, whether we want to or not. Everyone is given time. It's never enough." A smirk plays like a steady progression of major chords on her face. "But I sure as hell made the most of mine!"

Another laugh, this one echoing through the whole house.

I wonder if these halls will miss that sound. Do more than just the people we meet and love miss us when we're gone?

Cautiously, Cary touches her shoulder. "Are you ready for what is next?"

Bernice wrings her hands. "Will my Joseph be there?"

"I cannot answer that for you."

"Figures." She squints at him. "You can never trust the pretty ones."

I bury my own laugh in my shoulder so Bernice doesn't notice me.

Cary doesn't hide his snort. "Whenever you are ready."

Bernice stares wistfully at the wall of photographs. She takes her time scanning every frame. As if she can take them with her.

"Okay. Let's go."

A gossamer of white falls over her. A stardust queen. She meets Cary's smile with one of her own.

Once they leave, I sit in the lounge chair Bernice's soul just occupied. I stare at her sweet-faced corpse. My mind drifts to Yuri, Hasan. How they were each afraid in their own way. But Cary was there for them.

He was kind. Comforting. Even a little teasing.

He is the first real smile they see once this life is over.

Cary isn't just the ferrier of souls. A Deathless relentlessly dedicated to his role. He's something more.

I just never got to see it until now.

Jazz continues to hum throughout the house. My hands itch for a pen. To pluck notes from the song and scribble words into lyrics. I settle for letting the music run through me. In my head, I compose a ballad that will never be heard.

Cary steps back into the sunroom. He's not alone.

A blue-eyed Siberian husky comes charging in. My eyebrows shoot up my forehead. Cary shrugs weakly.

"She followed me."

The dog turns in quick circles before she flops on the

ground, whimpering. Instantly, Cary kneels to scratch behind her ears. He doesn't jerk away when her long pink tongue swipes at his cheek.

"Good girl," he whispers smiling as he strokes her nose.

"You like animals," I observe.

I remember how he was with Diana. How, despite his stiff shoulders and flat tone, he's always let Cerby be affectionate with him.

"I care about a lot of things," Cary says frankly.

"You look like you want to take her home."

Under his breath, he whispers, "I wish." Then, more clearly, he says, "Cerby would not approve."

"I can take him off your hands," I offer with a wide grin.

His glare has very little heat behind it. "Stop trying to steal my dog."

"Is she—" I stop, wincing. I'd forgotten the harshest part of death. "*Was* she Bernice's?"

"No. Someone else's."

A small relief relaxes my jaw. I look out the window. Dappled rays of sunlight break through patches of gum tree leaves. "Are there more souls waiting?"

"Always."

"For you?" My eyes flit back to him.

Gently, he brushes a hand over the dog's thick fur. "Not in this realm. They wait for the others."

My memory jumps to all the faces Henri told me about in the ballroom. Deathless of dreams and nightmares and vengeance.

"So, we're done?"

"Depends." Cary studies me. "Am I still cold to you? Nothing more than a ferrier?"

I rub my chin, considering. "Maybe?" There's humor in my voice. A smile I can't fight.

"I am not who you think I am, August."

"I know." My answer comes without hesitation.

For a long minute, his eyes search mine. A question circles his black irises: *Do you?*

I stand and offer him my hand. "Take me back to Santa Barbara. There's something I want to show you."

"And what is that?"

My smile widens. "You ask too many questions, Cary."

15

IT'S AFTER SUNSET when I punch in the code to unlock my mom's greenhouse.

Sorbet skies stream rose and tangerine through the glass dome roof. Dreamy floral notes tickle my nose. The flowers and plants seem so alive at this hour. I look over my shoulder. Cary is close behind, eyeing everything.

I spread my arms out wide. "Welcome to another one of my favorite places!"

Cary wanders down an aisle. "It is beautiful."

"Yeah," I exhale, a quiet laugh chasing my words. We were just in Soho. Tokyo. Georgia. The farthest I'd ever been before today was Anaheim for a family trip to Disneyland when I was eight.

But this greenhouse stands up to all those places. Reverie held safe behind glass.

When I look again, Cary's stare is centered on me. Unwavering. Does he find me beautiful too?

A blush streaks up my neck. Hot and distracting. I refocus to tell him about my mom's love for plants. The history behind her family and the greenhouse. Everything I can remember.

"I'm terrible at growing things," I confess, fingering the petals of a red larkspur.

A look dances on his face. Amusement? Surprise?

"I'm serious. I kill every houseplant my mom gives me." I giggle. "It's pretty tragic."

"Like your dancing," Cary suggests, that wicked curve to his mouth making it hard to scowl back at him.

We meet in the middle of another aisle. Near a raised bed of fiery poppies. Smiling, I whisper, "I love it here because it's quiet."

His gaze drops to my mouth. My heart skitters.

"It's also magical," I say.

"Is it?" His eyes finally lift.

"Obviously. I mean, I can't believe my mom does all of this! She turns the smallest seed into the prettiest things." I lower my chin, frowning. "Even when this world is ugly to her. Or to me."

Cary's thumb strokes my jawline. "You make this realm prettier too."

I roll my eyes and say, "Shut up." But he doesn't.

"I have seen it, August." His touch slides delicately along

my lower lip. I'm helpless to the way my name sounds on his tongue, in his assured voice.

"Where is your favorite place?"

In the half-light, his eyes go dark. Slightly dimmer. "I am not allowed one," he says.

"Not allowed?" My face scrunches.

He shakes his head. "I am never anywhere long enough to call it my favorite."

Cary has been to every corner of this earth. Guiding souls to Aides. But how much time does he get to spend in his own world? Death never rests. Which means he probably doesn't either.

"What about home?" I ask.

He looks away. My stomach coils.

"At the ball, Milos said something."

His jaw tenses. Hard as stone. "What did he say this time?"

Warily, I reply, "That he can't leave Aides. And that being who he is wasn't his choice."

Cary steps away. His fingers flex at his sides. He drifts over to a bed of island snapdragons. Their petals sway under his touch. Blood red against fair gold skin.

Moments pass before he speaks again.

"I was young like Yuri when my mother came to me with a choice: Grow to become the ferrier. Help souls find their way past our gates. Or stay in Aides. Become the prince who protects our world by balancing where those souls go next." He inhales deeply. "The other role would go to Milos."

A sharp exhale leaves my lips.

His thumb traces the veins of a leaf. "We were so small. Not yet ready. But my brother loved Aides. He would run in the Meadows and hide in the grand rooms. We would sit on the shores together."

I try to picture it: Tiny versions of them. A less scowly Cary and a bright-eyed Milos, being kids. Creating chaos everywhere they went.

"Giving that up would have been unfair to him."

"So you gave up your own life in Aides for him," I say.

He turns to face me. "My mother trusted me. She knew what I could handle. Besides, I could still be around her."

I piece together his words. "Your mom is Death."

He nods.

There's a softness in his expression. The same fondness I wear anytime I look at my own mom, no matter what oceans are rippling inside me.

"Did you even know what it meant to be the ferrier?"

He nods again. I watch him move over to a couple of potted flowers. *Cymbidiums*, boat orchids. Their fleshy, thin magenta petals shiver under his tender touch.

"I had watched other ferriers," Cary explains. "The ones before me."

My brows knit. "Before . . . you?"

In the falling sunlight, his eyes grow blacker. The deepest parts of the ocean. He looks at me. "I am not the first, August. None of us are. Except my mother."

The revelation jolts me. I lean on a workbench. So many questions crowd my brain. I don't know where to start. But Cary does.

"Deathless have existed for as long as your realm. We are chosen. And we can choose to carry this power"—he turns his palm over and I swear I can see rivers of gold along his palms, brightening the shape of his veins—"for as long as we want."

"Then what?"

He sighs up at the sky. "We give up the power. To someone else worthy. We leave behind who we are for Elysium."

My breath catches. It's like the room is spinning. There's so much I still don't understand. But I see the somberness around Cary's eyes. Pulling at his mouth.

He didn't fully understand the role he was taking. What he'd committed to. Or what he'd condemned Milos to.

Cary was a *child*.

I move closer to him. "You love being the ferrier, though."

His lips twitch. "Can you tell?"

Nodding, I say, "You're so good with them. The souls. You're . . . gentle." My hands fidget, desperate to touch him. I stop myself.

"The last ferrier was"—he pauses, chewing his lip—"*tragic*."

Now I'm grinning.

"He did not care for their fears," Cary continues. "For him, it was just a role. Like with . . ."

He trails off. But I know what he wants to say: *Milos*.

There's a weight behind his stare. My pinkie skims the

back of his hand, coaxing him on. To tell me more.

"Over time, my brother has changed. He makes his own rules." He frowns. "I blame myself. I made him who he is."

The sun tucks behind the trees surrounding the greenhouse. In its afterglow, we burn pink and violet.

"Is this the life you want?" I ask.

He can give it up. Stop being the ferrier. That's what he said, right?

The skin between his eyebrows pinches. "I do not trust anyone else to do what I have to."

I shake my head. "That doesn't answer my question. Is this what *you* want, Cary?"

"Is this the life *you* wanted, August?"

The suddenness of his own question makes me pause. Bright orange petals draw my eye. *Marigolds.* On Mom's workbench. A wave curls in my belly, splashing its way up my chest.

"No," I whisper. "It's not."

He watches me, expectant.

The truth, I remind myself.

"It was a car accident," I say. "Almost two years ago. That's what killed him."

With an unsteady voice, I piece together that night for him. Being nervous behind the wheel. The casual drive around London's quiet neighborhood.

Then London himself. Hair damp from a day at the beach. His weird smile as he went on and on about UCSB. He'd planned a visit for us. It was three weeks away.

My voice goes high, breaking at the part about the red light. Tom Petty bleeding through the speakers. London had something to tell me. An unfinished discussion. But all I saw was the boy I loved, eyes as green as the traffic light.

All I saw was the other car's headlights before the blackness swallowed me whole.

Now my vision clouds. Hot, stinging tears turn Cary into a blurred shape. "I had the green light," I croak. "That's the rule. I go on green. I had just passed my driver's test. I knew *the rules.*"

It didn't matter. The other driver was texting and driving. Not paying attention.

An echo of pain reverberates through my left shoulder. I stretch it out, then continue. "I'm the reason he's dead. He should be here."

Not me clogs the back of my throat.

On my worst days, that's my first thought. It should be him here. Still breathing. Living his life. Not wasting away like I am.

London's dreams burned so brightly, while all of mine flickered out the moment he died.

I drag my arm over my eyes. "Sorry," I say with a hiccup. "I don't know why I'm crying. It's been so long—"

Cary catches my jaw between his fingers. His other hand brushes curls off my forehead. He stares into my eyes and says, "You have nothing to apologize for, August."

"I can't help it." I blink free more tears. "I'm sorry it hurts. I'm sorry it hasn't stopped hurting." I inhale shakily.

"Sometimes, I'm drowning. Sometimes, I'm fine. But the tide keeps coming. It won't stop."

My eyes squeeze shut. I don't open them until there are no more tears to fall.

"And I'm sorry I stole everything from him."

I've never told anyone any of this. To be honest, the only person I've wanted to tell is London. I keep waiting for Cary to agree. Or for him to give me a pitying look like everyone does.

Poor August, he can't get it together. He can't move on. He'll never be okay.

That look never comes.

Tenderly, Cary pulls me into him. He holds me. His scent is a tangle of fruity snapdragons and pomegranate in my nose. He's warm, solid. His hand presses to my spine.

He keeps me close.

Against my ear, he whispers, "It was not your fault."

It's not the first time I've heard that. My parents. Max. The school counselor who sat me in her office to talk about what happened. They've all said it.

But coming from him, it's different. Truthful.

"You have no control over what Fate decides."

I sob-laugh into his shoulder. "I have no control over *anything*."

His fingers slide across the back of my neck. Goose bumps rise in their wake. My pulse flutters. When I draw back to look at him, it's as if I'm finally seeing him.

His thoughtful features. The care in his gaze. He's a god. And a boy. And something much more.

Unthinking, I say, "I have no control over how I feel about you."

"Is that good or bad?"

"I don't know," I say, voice rough.

His smile is playful. "Maybe we both ask too many questions."

One of my hands finds the back of his head. Soft curls loop around my fingers. I lean forward and he meets me halfway.

Our mouths melt together. That awkward hesitation from before is gone. Cary's tongue explores my mouth, fearless. I tip into the kiss. Grin at the shocked gasp rattling in his throat when I bite gently on his lower lip.

Too quickly, he breaks away.

Wild dark eyes roam my face. Dread sits between my shoulder blades. Was that too much? Is he regretting it?

His thumb sweeps over the corner of my mouth. Breathless, he says, "I need to go. The souls . . ." His words fall away. But the want pulses like a gilded heartbeat in his eyes.

That same want spreads through me, an eagle stretching out its wings. High on adrenaline, I blurt, "Take me with you."

His features twist. "August, come on. You know I cannot—"

"Take me with you," I repeat, stubbornly insistent.

The gold brightens around his irises. A flash, then gone. He grabs my other hand, nodding.

I almost forget to lock the greenhouse on the way out.

Cary's room isn't what I expected. In a good way.

Dark wood floors shift into cream walls. Light twinkles from a cluster of small globes that drip from the ceiling like falling stars. Thick bouquets of asphodels spring from clay vases decorated in vibrant blue art.

And there are books all over.

Stacked on rustic furniture. Piled in a high-backed chair. Open on the gray area rug.

Gauzy curtains dance in front of an open window. I breathe in briny sea spray. Underneath, an earthy sugariness from a bowl of fresh pomegranate on the small table nearby.

I try not to stare at his wide—and appealing—platform bed. It's perfectly made. Dressed in onyx. Not a single dent in any of the pillows. As if he never really sleeps here.

"Because he's a vampire," I whisper, amused.

A coffin is probably tucked away somewhere.

"Sorry for the mess."

I spin around. Cary smiles from the doorway. A blush roses his cheeks. Grains of sand stick to his clothes. The undone buttons of his Henley show off smooth skin and muscle.

Shrugging, I say, "Mine is worse."

"Are you inviting me to your bedroom again?"

Now it's my turn to flush. "You like to read?"

"I do. When I can."

His fingers trail over spine after spine. From here, I can

see some of the titles: *Giovanni's Room*, *The Picture of Dorian Gray*, *Beloved, I'll Give You the Sun*, *Pride and Prejudice*. They're from my world. I wonder how he got them here. Did he steal them? Can Deathless get library cards?

There are other books, thick tomes, with titles in a language I can't read. The same one from the garden's maze.

I can imagine him sitting on the shore. His curious face tucked between the pages. Forgetting the world exists. At least a dozen books lie cracked open around the room. I wonder which is his favorite.

"Do you ever finish any of them?" I ask.

"Of course. Time moves slower here," he reminds me. "One page at a time, August."

My eyes stray to an oddly shaped guitar on a tufted ottoman. It's long necked, the round wooden body polished. I almost reach for it.

"My mother loves music," Cary says.

"What is it?"

"A bouzouki."

"Do you play?"

Instantly, my skin prickles. I want to launch myself into the sea. It's a ridiculous question. Why else would it be here?

His mouth stretches. "Sit."

I look around. The options are sparse. I could knock some books off his chair. Or flop onto the floor. Instead, I gently lower myself onto the very edge of his bed.

He takes the ottoman. Holds the bouzouki like a practiced performer. He plucks a string. The note is like honey. Rich and thick and soothing.

I lean in to watch.

Eyes closed, Cary plays. His fingers move smoothly along the fretboard. I don't recognize the song, but it's beautiful. Haunting. The melody buries itself in my bones.

It's not until Cary lifts his head, threads of hair in his eyes, that I realize my hands have been moving along with his.

My body tightens as I stare at my blue-and-yellow bracelet. A memory springs free: London explaining why he gave it to me. To control my anxious nerves.

So he wouldn't be embarrassed by my silly composing gestures.

Shame rises feverishly into my cheeks. But Cary doesn't look at me the way London would. He mouths, *Keep going*, giving me permission.

And I obey.

When he plays again, my hands follow his melody. Sound for sound. For a second, I picture a piano in front of me. I hum, low but freely. A smile tucks into the corners of his mouth.

Our eye contact doesn't break until the song fades.

"Why didn't you tell me?" It's not accusatory. It's just that . . . Cary *keeps* surprising me.

"Like you told me you play piano?" he retorts.

I scratch the back of my head. It's a fair point.

He grins wryly at me. "Is it my fault you are as bad as Henri when it comes to secrets?"

I lean back on my hands, lips pursed. "Since when did you get a sense of humor?"

"A very, very, *very* long time ago." He smirks. "Since, you know, I am so old."

"Ancient," I agree. "Prehistoric. I didn't even think I was into older men until—"

I stop short. Cary's mouth widens. "No, please. Continue. Until . . . ?"

Glaring half-heartedly, I mumble, "Never mind."

Cary rests the bouzouki delicately on the rug. He sits next to me on the bed. This close, his lashes are fine and feathery. His eyebrows thick, lips full. He takes my hand.

"Wanting things is dangerous," he says, finally answering my question from earlier.

I inhale.

His thumb presses to the pulse point on my wrist. "Especially when it is something I cannot have."

Heat races underneath my skin. "You can't?"

He sighs. His fingers skim up my arm. Light and warm against my collarbone. Every nerve in me chases the touch.

"But I want you, August," he confesses. "I have wanted you for longer than you know." The urgency in his voice trembles through my spine. "And I fear I will never stop."

Silence wraps around us. Everything but the sea outside.

I can't think of what to say. How to tell him I want him too. Constantly.

In ways that are terrifying and thrilling.

I settle for leaning forward. Kissing him, slow and purposeful. My lips tell him what my voice can't. He listens, then complies. His soft mouth opens against mine.

Strong, confident hands find my waist, the back of my neck, pulling. I go, like being dragged by the tide.

We fall to our sides. Impatient fingers slide beneath my shirt. I tug at his Henley, at anything between us. Our inexperience is exposed in tremoring hands. In jerky, uncoordinated movements.

But then we're free of barriers.

He crushes me to him, skin hot and aching. I kiss his neck, the muscles of his chest. He smells like salty shores and ripe fruit. He swells against my bare belly.

I'm hard against his thigh.

His strength overwhelms me. Soon, I'm on my back. His teeth are against my throat. He presses my name to my skin. Over and over.

I look up at him. The globes of light form a crown of stars around his head. He's panting, wide-eyed. Simultaneously nervous and starved.

"This all right? Can we—"

I snuff out his hesitation before it can spark a flame. My hands clasp around the back of his neck. "Yes."

He's everywhere. Gasps under my jaw. Fingers strumming

my ribs. Hands along my thighs. My hard-on flush against his stomach.

A newness washes over me. Like this is the first time.

Cary stares into my eyes. He moves to the tempo of my inhales, exhales. When I slip away, he brings me back with a gentle kiss. When I tense, he pauses and waits. Then begins again.

My fingers tangle in his hair. He lets me guide us to a place we both want.

And I can't stop wanting more.

He is the earth, solid and grounding. He is air, filling and necessary. He is fire, hot against my skin and melting my anxiousness. He is water, refreshing and I drink him in.

I'm overwhelmed. He is too. It twists us until everything and nothing meet.

Until we're still and breathless and *here*, together.

After, Cary kisses my naked shoulder. I feel hazy. Those long seconds when waking from a dream. But it's not one. This happened.

I turn my head to admire his soft expression. Sunrise gold splashing through his black eyes. With swollen lips, he smiles.

"Are you still scared to want?" I ask him.

"Yes." Before my body tightens, retreats, he brushes a hand over my cheek. "But life without fear is pointless. Fear is what gives flight to risks. To the moments we remember most."

A smirk pushes at my cheeks. "Where'd you steal that from? Jane Austen? Another one of your boo—"

He quiets me with a deep, hungry kiss.

"I need to go soon," he whispers.

"When can I see you again?"

His face stills, then relaxes. He closes the gap between us to kiss me again. "Too many questions," he says against my grinning mouth.

The Before

"YOU DID IT!"

London throws his arms around my neck. His damp hair brushes my cheek. I breathe him in. He smells of chocolate and sea spray. The way he always does after going to Hendry's Beach.

He squeezes me tighter. Like it's been more than hours since we last saw each other. We're standing in his driveway. It's night and his neighborhood is gradually slipping into that drowsy stillness. Lukewarm early October air slides over my shoulders as London finally releases me.

"You got your license! Can you believe it?"

I smile goofily. "No." I haven't been able to shake the surprise since the instructor told me.

He huffs a breath. "I knew you would. You worked too hard for this."

My lips curl higher. It's because of him I even decided to try. He made me study. And practice. Recite every step of each skill to him over late-night video calls.

I would've done it, eventually. When I felt like it. But London's extra push made this happen.

Leaning forward, I kiss him, quick and fleeting. No one can see us. His parents are inside. Dim lamplight glows fill the windows of neighbors' houses. Yet, a curl of nervousness still grips me.

"What was that for?"

"Because," I say.

He chuckles. "That's not a real answer."

But it's mine. For now. London doesn't fight me on it. Instead, his fingers tiptoe over my white T-shirt. "You know what this means? You can drive us to school now. And to the beach. Prom next year—"

"*Prom?*" I say with a laugh that echoes. "Let me guess. You already planned out what we're gonna wear."

His face lights up. The sun bursting through storm clouds. "Well, now that you mention it . . ."

Naturally, he's already created a list on his phone. He scrolls through it. Everything from tux styles down to the boutonnieres. Marigold for himself. Orchid for me.

I arch an eyebrow, confused.

"You look amazing in purple," he explains. I wouldn't know. I don't wear it often. Also, orchids aren't one of my favorite flowers. But I trust him.

Excitement illuminates his eyes. "What do you think?"

His energy is contagious. A feeling that burns you from the inside out. It's like the day he gave me the UCSB sweatshirt. Or that night a few weeks ago, in his bedroom. After we had sex.

I want nothing more than his happiness. Nothing more than him.

"It's great," I tell him.

A light breeze rustles through his hair. The house's floodlights cast his face in cool ivory. He's quiet. Studying me. As if my answer wasn't what he expected.

What he wanted.

Instinctively, my fingers twine around my bracelet, tugging. When he catches me, I abruptly stop.

A glint flashes across his expression. "You know what you need?"

I blink, shaking my head.

"To practice."

"Practice?" I repeat. "Prom?"

He shakes his head, then gestures behind me. A gleaming obsidian black Mercedes-Benz sits in the driveway. His dad's car.

My eyes widen. London cuts off my protest before it fully forms. He grabs my hand.

"You're nervous. It happens to everyone. This will help."

"London," I start.

"Just a quick loop around the neighborhood. Me and you."

Groaning, I say, "I didn't even drive myself over here."

My mom did. She'll be back in an hour.

"Which is all the more reason for us to do this," London insists.

I pause to consider him. The electricity in his smile, a wildness behind his lashes. This spontaneity that's so unlike him. London *plans.* He doesn't do anything without thinking it through at least twice.

He gives my hand a squeeze. "Auggie, come on."

"Will your dad be okay with it?"

His gaze flits back to the house. Up to the second floor. Shadows move behind gauzy curtains. The window is open. Tense voices drift down.

His parents.

A muscle in London's jaw jumps. "He won't mind."

I wait until he turns to me. "Are they fighting again?"

Silence stretches. This is a part of himself he still hides. From everyone at school. Even from me, on occasion. I try not to pressure him.

There are things I should tell him that I don't.

He licks his lips like he might talk about it this time. Then he grins and says, "Tonight's not about them. It's about *you*. You got your license! Let's go for a drive."

A desperation grows in his stare. "Okay," I whisper, threading my fingers through his.

His mouth loosens into a genuine smile. It fills me. Washes away my own doubt.

"I'll go grab his keys," he says.

I nod, not wanting to let him go. But I do. Only for a moment.

London doesn't get far before spinning around. He runs back to me. Drags me in for a hug that I relax into, squeezing him back.

His forehead rests against mine. Green eyes holding me.

"I love you, Auggie. Always."

That last word strikes me. There's a strange weight to the way he says it. But it beats like oxygen in my blood, sings like the mockingbirds hidden in the trees.

"I love you too," I say, beaming. "Always."

His kiss is enticing and too short. Ivory light frames him as he moves toward the house. The shadows can't touch him. He is a sun. He is mine.

At the door, he watches me for a long moment. "Can you stay a little longer? After we get back? To"—he fidgets—"talk more?"

He beams at me, but it's not the weird smile I'm used to. The one he had just a second ago. I hear more strained voices from the open window. London looks like he's fighting a frown or a scowl. Is this about his parents or something else?

I nod for him. "Yeah. Of course."

I want him happy, I remind myself. *Always.*

16

GOLDEN LIGHT PASSES through the white petal pinched between my thumb and index finger.

Narcissus.

Like the flower on the inside of my forearm. The one I misidentified before letting the tattoo artist ink it onto my skin.

I smile, thinking about Cary tracing its shape with his finger. The soft kiss he pressed to it while in his bed. The way he called it *sacred.*

I've been doing this for minutes . . . hours? The sun is up, but time is suspended. Frozen in a snow globe, waiting for someone to shake it up. Every thought in my brain is murky, blurred. As if nothing before yesterday ever happened.

Cary is the only crisp thing I can focus on.

The apartment is strangely quiet. No noise from the kitchen, no Max yelling at appliances. Just me, sighing dreamily.

Oh, and Diana. She's busy cleaning herself in a corner of my bedroom.

I twist the velvety soft petal a second longer. Wishing it could make Cary appear again. Take me back to Aides.

A buzzing noise bursts my daydream. I find my phone on the floor. When I read the screen, my eyebrows scrunch.

It's a FaceTime call.

"Mom?"

"Auggie!" She's breathless, eyes wild. The background behind her is hard to make out. But she's somewhere outside. "Are you okay?"

"Yeah. Why wouldn't I be?"

"Where are you?"

"At"—I almost say *home* but stop short—"my apartment."

"Why aren't you *here*?"

"Here?" Confusion drags my lips into a frown. In her video, I see bright green grass. Chunks of gray I don't recognize. "Are you at the greenhouse?"

"No. Why would I be there today?"

Because you're always there sits unsaid on my tongue.

I pinch the bridge of my nose. A throb begins just behind my temples. It hurts to think. "Mom, what's wrong?"

Surprise flashes over her face. Then anguish. "Auggie, are you serious? We were supposed to meet an hour ago."

Her words confuse me more. After an exasperated breath, I say, "We weren't—"

A series of messages cuts me off. One by one, notifications drop down on my screen. All from Max.

> WHERE ARE YOU???
>
> Your mom is worried I'm worried WTF August?!
>
> are you OK? upset? is it because of the anniversary?
>
> I CAN'T BELIEVE YOU'RE NOT HERE

The ache spreads through my skull. I can't make sense of anything Max texts. Why would I be upset? What anniversary? My parents got married in the summer.

"Auggie."

My mom's voice rips me from the depths of fog. My breaths come fast, harsh. I stare at the screen.

In a calm voice, she says, "Focus."

I can't. The haze thickens. "What the hell is happening, Mom?"

"August." Her eyes command me to look at her. "Do you know what today is?"

I force myself to think. "Sunday."

"No." She exhales, losing patience. "*The date.* What anniversary is today?"

"It's—" I blink away the sting behind my eyes. "Today is—"

"The day of the accident," Mom finishes for me.

Her words blow through me like the wind. The phone almost slides from my weak grip. Suddenly, the fog fades.

Reality seeps in, giving the memories root:

Driving through a sleepy neighborhood. Tom Petty's gruff voice. The flash of another car's headlights. Glass shattering into a million stars. The hospital.

Standing over London's dead body.

Gasping, I jolt to my feet. Mom's voice reaches me, tinny and distant. "Auggie, stay with me."

"I forgot," I wheeze out, shivering.

It's the anniversary. I was supposed to meet my mom and Max at the cemetery. We were going to visit his grave together.

Today's the day London died, and I forgot.

Mom's still talking. But my ears are crowded with white noise. The thud of my heart slamming into my sternum.

Two years have passed. There hasn't been a single day when he wasn't on my mind. His beachy brown hair. Weird smile. The light behind his green eyes. How he liked his coffee. That moment he was wrenched away from me.

Now it feels like chunks of him are missing. Floated away on the tide.

The thump grows louder. It's not in my chest. It's the front door.

I'm not sure how I get there so fast. Or when I drop my phone. Guilt and nausea churn relentlessly in my stomach as I grip the knob.

Cary is on the other side.

Swallowing roughly, I say, "I forgot."

"I know."

"No. I forgot *him*." My entire body trembles. "I couldn't remember that today was . . . *is*. Today is the anniversary of the car accident."

Mouth flattened in a grim line, Cary says, "August, I know. You forgot because of me."

"Because of you?"

His face is serious. Closed off like the boy I met in Viva Catalina's. Not the one who held me in the greenhouse. Who pressed delicate kisses to my cheek in his bed.

"You"—the words stick to my throat—"did this."

He walks inside, fingers flexing at his sides.

Absently, I close the door. I don't want to ask my next question. It comes out anyway.

"How?"

Cary's brow pinches. "Lethe. The water I use to bring you back. It is for souls, not mortals. It takes your memories, so you forget what you left behind. That is how souls move on."

"It takes m-memories?" I stammer.

His eyes lower before he nods.

I tug at my curls. That doesn't make sense. We've gone through those waters more than once. Nothing changed before. I haven't forgotten anything else.

Except . . . I did.

Lake, the girl Max was dating. And Hal. I couldn't remember how I got the day off from work. Or what today was.

Anger spreads like an unattended flame. My hands turn

to fists. "You knew this would happen," I bite out.

"No, not at first. I swear. You were the first mortal—"

"I don't care," I snap. "That's all I have left of him. *Memories.* And you took them from me. Without asking. Without telling me!"

His dark eyes follow as I pace the room. He doesn't say anything. Offers no explanation or apology.

My eyes squeeze shut, disgusted. Every moment I was with him, he was gentle and careful. Even when his tone was cool and distant. He stood between me and Cerby. Took me to the Meadows. He played music for me. Let me inside his world.

And I let him in *mine.*

Bitterness burns like acid on my tongue. "You could've told me. At any point. When we were—" My voice cracks. I'm not going to cry in front of him again. "You could've told me the truth. The *whole* truth."

I blink my eyes open. Gold coils around his irises. A snake ready to strike.

"Just like you could have told me the real reason you kept coming back to Aides."

The surprise knocks the air from me. "What?"

"All of your questions," he says, venom in his voice. "If I remember every soul. Where they go. Asking me to take you to Elysium. If Death can bring back the dead."

He moves closer. Every soft line I saw in his face yesterday hardens.

"I thought you came back for me," he growls. "Until yesterday. When you finally talked about him. London, the boy you love."

"*Don't*," I warn through clenched teeth. "Don't say his name."

Hollow eyes meet mine. "You want to see him again. You wanted *me* to take you to him."

I don't answer him. Absently, my fingers twist around the blue-and-yellow bracelet on my wrist, yanking.

"You have made your entire existence about him," Cary says. A fact so cold, my skin stings.

"Don't pretend you know me."

He laughs indignantly. "Oh, how could I not? You let his death stop your life. His wants destroyed your needs. You have been given time that so many are not. What have you done with it, August? *Nothing.*"

I surge toward him. Stand tall beneath his gilded glare.

"What do you know about loss, Cary? You're a Deathless. You have power. You're immortal." Rage thunders in my every word. "You collect souls and leave behind the ashes. You're clueless about what it's like after you're gone."

"My role is to—"

"Fuck your role," I seethe, eyes wet. I tug harder on the string around my wrist. "I didn't ask for this. To constantly feel this pain. To never know how to be okay again. To look at you and—"

He waits silently.

But whatever words I have disappear. I look down. There's a limp thread of blue and yellow in my hand, snapped where it was once tied around my wrist.

I broke London's bracelet. Now it's another part of him I won't have anymore.

My eyes lift. "Of course I want to see him. Talk to him. But you'll never understand why."

His gaze runs over me. The gold recedes. All that's left is something I can't quite name.

Because I've never truly seen it on him.

"Yes, you are right. I was a fool." He steps around me. "I have nothing but moments. In this realm and mine."

I blink, clutching the bracelet.

His eyes turn glassy, somber. "I can never stay. Or belong." He stills, holding his breath. On his next exhale, he says, "Who wants that? Who could ever love the ferrier of souls?"

My lips part. Nothing comes out. It doesn't need to.

"No one," he whispers.

The raw sadness on his face slams into me like a fist.

This is who he is. Why he keeps a distance. Never allows anyone in. But it's no excuse to lie to me. To steal one of the only things I have left.

At the door, he commands, "Never look for me again, August Clarke. Do not return to Aides. Until it is your time."

The door closes.

London's bracelet slips from my fingers. I fall to my knees and try my best not to throw up.

"Order fifteen for Adib!"

I nudge sluggishly through Viva Catalina's door. It's slow inside. Customers here and there. The Sunday-evening dinner crowd hasn't arrived yet.

I'm twenty-three minutes late, my previous record shattered. No one notices. Junie and Tonia are busy in the kitchen. Kennedy takes orders at a table of four. I don't see Angela anywhere.

A clatter of metal catches my attention. Max stands behind the front counter, so surprised, she dropped a handful of silverware.

"What are you doing here?"

I hoist my drawstring bag higher on my shoulders. "What does it look like? I have a shift."

She bristles at my tone. "Are you serious?"

I give her a blank stare.

"Auggie, this is ridiculous. Today is—"

"I know what today is," I grunt while beelining through the kitchen toward the employee restroom. Max's stomping footsteps follow.

"So that's it?"

"Pretty much," I say, hiding the exhaustion weighing me down.

"Did you at least talk to your mom?"

Briefly, I falter. My mom is the one who found me on the apartment floor. Not crying. Trembling on my knees, desperately trying—and failing—to fix London's bracelet. It took almost an hour to convince her I was fine enough to go to work.

Distractions are needed. So I won't think. Or finally break down.

"I talked to her," I say. "And my dad." That wasn't a fun conversation. At least I had an excuse to make it short: the bus arriving.

My hand reaches for the restroom door. Max is quicker. She squirms around me, blocking it.

"Talk to me. Now."

I sigh, almost resigned. "I'm fine."

"You're lying to yourself *and* me," Max argues. Her arms cross over her chest, brows knotting. "You're never around anymore."

"Says the girl who's so busy with all her college friends," I say, scoffing.

Max's nose wrinkles with anger. "That's not fair. I can't just—"

Her voice cuts off abruptly. It's not the first time she's swallowed words around me. I hate it as much as the commiserative looks people give me. Like they'll ever know how I feel.

"Can't what?" I challenge her.

"You keep disappearing, Auggie. You don't talk to me. You never answer my texts or calls."

Something clicks in my brain. In Aides, I never have my phone. It's always in my room when I come back. But not while I'm there. Of course I miss Max's calls.

But I've never explained to her why. "Listen, Max, there's—"

"And you keep forgetting things," she cuts in. "Like Hal. The girl I was dating—"

"Wait . . . *was* dating?"

"Yes. I told you it was over the other day!"

My face falls. Everything in my head is still shadowy. Thanks to Lethe.

Thanks to Cary.

"Sorry, I know," I try. "There's a reason—"

Max's cheeks redden. She doesn't let me finish. "We promised each other we wouldn't do this. That we'd stay in contact. You said you needed time and space. I gave you that." Hurt curls across her features. "But you're not getting better. You're giving up. Your life didn't end when London died."

Hearing his name—how similar her words are to Cary's—ignites a smoking fire inside me. For months, years, I've been trying to blow it out. Contain it.

What for?

At the start of senior year, I had a mandatory meeting with my school counselor. I'd barely survived junior year. My parents wanted to ensure I graduated.

The entire time, I sat quietly in her office. Nodding as she went over the stages of grief. All I wanted was to leave. Escape. But as she talked, I could identify the stages I'd already experienced, even if they weren't in order:

Denial, which lasted about thirty seconds after standing over London's corpse.

Depression, the unending swell of it.

I was a long way from bargaining and acceptance, but the feeling I was avoiding most was anger.

Before the accident, I was hopeful. Nice. Reasonable. Patient. I was who I thought people wanted me to be.

I kept whatever else brewed beneath that silent.

Not anymore. I'm too drained, too hurt, too broken to be Before August.

"I made a lot of promises," I spit. "To you. My parents. Myself. *Him.*" My shaking hands ball into tight fists. "Guess what? Not everything in life goes the way we want. Sometimes, the choice isn't ours."

She blinks, stunned.

"You haven't given me space or time, Max," I continue. "You're always pushing me. What? My grief isn't moving fast enough for you? For anyone?"

Her teeth clench. "We're trying to help you."

"I didn't ask for anyone's help, Dr. Cho!"

She recoils. That look is in her eyes again: *Who are you?*

But it's more than that. There's rage and betrayal. Her voice comes low and uneven. "I miss my best friend."

The flame inside me burns away the edges of Before. "I miss him too," I say hoarsely. "But he's not here anymore."

Max pushes off the door and storms past me.

I wait for a beat, then turn around. I think she might be there. The Max who came to visit me every day. When I couldn't get out of bed. Who made sure I finished high school.

Who asked me to move in with her and carried a mattress up three flights of stairs so I'd have a new home.

It's not Max, though.

It's Angela. A mix of concern and pity scrunches her expression.

I reach for a bracelet that's not there. Shame tenses my spine. To my feet, I say, "Sorry. I swear I'm not like this."

Another lie. This *is* who I am, isn't it? This is what I've let grief make me.

"August." Angela's in front of me now. She squeezes my biceps, forcing me to look her in the eyes. "Go home. Take the day off."

"But my shift."

"We've got it covered."

Panic floods my throat. "Angela, I need my job."

I can't go back to my parents. To that house. I don't know where I stand with Max. If she's already mentally started packing what little I have into cheap cardboard boxes. But if I have a job, I can at least find somewhere else to live.

"No one's firing you. It's okay," Angela promises with a sad smile. "Whatever it is you're dealing with is bigger than pizza. And I can't have you feeling this way in front of my customers."

I want to tell her I always feel like this. That it's not going anywhere.

Instead, I nod.

On my way out, I pause at the front counter. Max refuses

to meet my eyes. She pretends to be busy wrapping napkins around silverware.

I shoulder through the front door without looking back.

Sunbeams cascade through branches thick with green leaves as I walk to the bus stop. State Street Promenade is shaped by the appetite of tourists. Shops are alive with browsers. Diners fill restaurant patios. Noises spill like waterfalls from the gelato shop onto the sidewalk.

When a faded blue beanbag lands at my feet, I look up.

A girl around my age smiles. She's freckle-faced and fawn-skinned, billowy bronze curls hanging past her shoulders. She picks up the beanbag, then runs back to her boyfriend. A gasp scratches my throat.

He's tall, narrow-waisted. Salt-crusted brown hair that comes to his chin. Eyes as green as ivy. Skin browned by the sun. But it's not him.

It will never, ever be him, a haunting voice in my head says.

They kiss, then continue their game of cornhole.

People move around me. But I'm frozen, alone. I could walk the promenade with my eyes closed and not fall. I've spent my life here and it has never felt like this. Like I've lost my place in its arms.

I did this. To myself. To the ones I love.

Everywhere I turn, the ghost of my life with London follows me. Nothing in Santa Barbara is *mine* anymore. I have nowhere to go to escape.

Nowhere but—

I plunge my hand deep into my drawstring bag, searching. Blindly, I brush a phone charger, earbuds, my work shirt . . .

"Shit!"

Something pricks my finger. The sharp edge of a card. I pull it free.

Just like when Henri gave it to me, the card is blank. Black and glittery in the sunlight. A thin trail of my blood runs down the surface.

My breath hitches.

Something else is there. Embossed text so slight it's unnoticeable at first glance. A trick card you find at a novelty magic shop.

Grimacing, I smear my blood over it until I can fully read what it says.

HENRI OF AIDES
DEATHLESS & WORLD TRAVELER
1028 STATE STREET
SANTA BARBARA, CA

17

"YOU'RE HERE!"

Here is a squat, pearl white building wedged between an office supply store and a high-end vintage store. *On State Street.*

SANTA BARBARA TRAVEL is spelled out in Arial font. The window display has posters of island getaways and mountain destinations, lush city landscapes and whales breaching crystal blue waves. I've passed this agency a hundred times before but have never stepped inside.

Beige walls are layered in maps. The carpet is a dull green. Fake palm trees stand tall in the corners. It's all very unremarkable. Except for the boy emerging from one of the cubicles in a floral-print silk shirt and pinstripe slacks.

Henri smiles roguishly. "It took you long enough."

I gape. "You . . . *work* here?"

Two older women peek from behind their cubicles, blatantly eavesdropping.

"*Work* is such a misleading word," Henri says. "I prefer *influence. Inspire.* I liven this place up. Right, Carol and Betty?"

Both women give unconvincing hums before disappearing again.

Henri leans in with a conspiratorial gleam in his eyes. "It's a glamour. They can't see my true form. To them, I look like an overly tanned white man with blond hair and the brightest teeth they've ever seen." He flashes a winning grin. "I have places like this all over the mortal realm."

"You do?"

"Hello! Deathless of travelers. Did you not read my Wikipedia page?"

My eyes narrow. "You told me not to!"

"Exactly!" He fixes his shirt cuffs. "So, what's wrong?"

"I never said anything was wrong."

"No, but this"—he flaps a hand at my tense posture—"*did.*"

I sigh, then tell him what happened. From leaving the masquerade ball to discovering the truth about Lethe to my fallout with Max. I omit the parts about kissing Cary. And all the details that followed. But, for whatever reason, I confess to feeling like I don't belong anywhere.

"I just . . ." I trail off.

I need someone to talk to. Who isn't Max. Or Cary.

For his part, Henri rubs his chin, nodding. "Have you considered—" He halts. "Never mind."

"What is it?"

He smiles sympathetically. "You never felt like that while in Aides."

I hesitate, scratching the back of my neck.

"Think about it, August—there's a reason you kept coming back. Maybe something's waiting for you? Something you can't find in this realm."

My fingers tug on the straps of my bag. The ruined blue-and-yellow bracelet sits at the bottom. There *was* a reason I kept going back. One that I didn't mean to forget. Another aftereffect of Lethe.

I wanted to find London. Tell him everything I couldn't two years ago. Everything I've felt since.

A cold emptiness shifts through my sternum. "There is a reason." I glance at the tattoo on my forearm. "But I don't know how to get back to Aides without Cary."

"Well, there might be a way."

My head snaps up.

Henri frowns. "It's not exactly easy. And it comes with a heavy price."

Images flood my mind: Sunlit skin. Aloe green eyes. Wavy brown hair. Warm hands on my face. That weird, contagious smile on his lips.

Quickly, I say, "I don't care. Get me away from here."

Henri claps his hands. "Fantastic!" He hooks his arm with mine. "But first, we need something very important. Or the ritual won't work."

"What?"

"A peppermint latte."

I jerk to a stop. "Is there a magical coffee shop nearby run by another Deathless?"

His laugh is like the start of thunder. "No! Don't be silly. There *is* a lovely café just down the promenade."

"You're not serious," I say, glaring.

"Shockingly, we don't have bespoke gourmet coffee roasters in Aides."

At the door, he waves to Carol and Betty, who don't seem to care that he's leaving in the middle of the day without a reason.

"Voilà!"

Henri spreads his arms wide like he's unveiling a buried treasure.

We're in front of the Great Arch at the Santa Barbara County Courthouse. It's a short walk from State Street Promenade. We came immediately after I bought Henri his precious latte.

I look around, lost. "This can't be it."

There's no way these grounds are a hidden doorway to Aides. It's just a historical courthouse. A tourist pit stop. When I came here with Cary, he didn't mention anything. But of course he didn't.

Secrets are the only thing the ferrier loves.

Henri smirks. "Oh, you poor mortals. You know nothing."

Irritated, I turn in a slow circle. "So, what do we do? Walk through the arch? Is there an invisible door somewhere? A camouflaged stairwell?"

I hope this isn't one of those rituals that requires a blood sacrifice.

"That silly thing?" A laugh erupts from him as he gestures to the arch. "It's a decoration. We need *that.*" He points to the Spirit of the Ocean.

"The fountain?"

"*Enchanted* fountain." He extends his hand, as if he's politely offering to help me climb in.

My eyes bulge. "No. Absolutely not."

He sighs. "I've already told you. I can't take you to Aides." His other hand rubs at his charm. The serpent and wings. "Unless you're dead."

When I shiver, Henri adds, "Trust me, August."

That's my problem. I've put way too much trust in Deathless. But I don't have any other choice.

Henri wiggles his fingers at me. There are no guided tours on Sundays. Still, weekend guards patrol the grounds. For trespassers or unhoused people who want somewhere warm and quiet to sleep.

Another beat passes before I whisper, "Okay. Fine."

With his assistance, I climb over the wide stone ledge. The water's cool, but not uncomfortable. It stops just above my knees.

I hug myself, feeling silly when nothing happens. "Now what?"

"You must submerge yourself in it."

Right. That's how it works with Cary.

I frown at the rippling blue water. "And then?"

"Think of your favorite place."

"Should I close my eyes and chant *there's no place like home* too?" I ask dryly.

Henri beams. "Ha! You're funny. I see why he likes you."

A blush flares against my cheeks. I almost correct him. Because Cary hates me. And that feeling is very mutual at this point. But that's a discussion I don't want or plan to have with Henri.

I ease down. The water soaks my waist, then my chest. I lean back. Within seconds, my spine and shoulders are wet. The breeze flutters over the water's surface as I stare up at Henri.

"Your favorite place," he says again, reaching to press a hand on my chest. "Close your eyes."

I do.

He pushes down. I sink, fighting every instinct to kick out. Gasp for another breath.

Underwater, I let my mind drift to the clock tower. Sitting on the stone ledge beneath the teal-accented window. My fingers wiggle as I imagine a pen between them, scribbling lyrics. A song about London. Something about the sun against his evergreen eyes.

The water moves around me, but nothing else happens. I'm still here. Lungs tightening as Henri holds me under.

Fear begins to claw at my chest. Sharp and wild as mountain lions. It's been too long. It never takes this long with Cary.

My eyes shoot open. Through the bleary blue, I see Henri. His mouth opens and closes in a chant I can't hear. His hand remains firm against my sternum. He's not going to let me go.

I try closing my eyes again. My favorite place. I just need to think of it.

Think, think, think.

Shoreline Steps. The torii gate leading down a narrow staircase. Listening to the Pacific serenade the shore from a wooden rail. Somewhere I can be alone. Far from the weight of everyone else's grief.

Another few seconds go by. Nothing.

I'm still here.

My fight-or-flight initiates. Feet kicking, I shake and twist. I need to get out of the water. Henri presses harder. I almost scream, but then I'll definitely drown.

Is this what he meant? That he can't take me to Aides unless I'm dead? Does he need to kill me? Is this the only way to London?

I stare up at Henri, pleading. His lips slow enough for me to read what he's saying: *Your favorite place, August.*

Through the panic, clarity sinks in. Behind my closed eyes, an image unfolds like a flower in bloom. It's not the clock tower. Or Shoreline Park. And despite what I said to Cary, this isn't just *one* of my favorite places.

It's the only one.

My mom's greenhouse.

I see lush leaves, green stems. A burst of vibrant colors: cotton-candy pinks, candied crimsons, bright tangerines. Golden rays stream through a domed glass ceiling.

Rich floral scents in my nose. Dirt underneath my fingernails. Seeds growing into something untamed and beautiful.

My whole life, that's where I've felt safest.

The pull is instant. Cool water takes me in its arms, cradling me. Relieves the pressure on my lungs. Whisper its song. The one it always writes just for me.

My body finally relaxes as I sink.

Sink.

Sink.

My eyes open. The blue water is gone. In its place is a high ceiling. Ivory with gold accents. Floating globes of light wink like starlight.

Aides.

"You're alive?"

The surprise in Henri's voice isn't very comforting. He stands over me, eyebrows lifted. That playful grin of his is half its normal size.

Groaning, I choke out, "Why wouldn't I be?"

"Well . . . I wasn't sure that would work."

"You *what*?!"

I sit up, even as my muscles scream to stay down. There's a

plush carpet underneath my palms. The spacious room glows warmly from the matching floor-to-ceiling windows on either side. At the center, an oil black throne embellished with gold leaves sits empty.

"He has never helped someone like you cross over."

A sharp breath cracks my lips. Milos steps into my eyeline. I scan his strong square jaw, those elegant cheekbones. The cypress crown is bright against his dark hair. His mouth curves into an enigmatic grin.

"Hello, beautiful August."

Henri reaches a hand down. I take it and stumble to my feet.

"Milos," I whisper, unsure what else to say.

"It has been too long since you visited me." He tilts his head, his honey eyes glinting. "But not since you have been *here*."

My spine goes rigid. He knows I came back to Aides. With Cary.

Before I can ask how, he says, "This is my realm. Secrets cannot hide from me here." There's no anger in his tone. Only annoyance. A child whose favorite toy was stolen by their older sibling.

Embarrassment heats my face. "I'm sorry."

"No need to be." Milos strides closer. His halfway-undone shirt reveals clean lines of a defined chest. "But why are you here . . . now?"

I don't know how much to tell him. If any of it will matter.

"I'm looking for someone," I say, throat tight. "A soul. Someone who meant a lot to me in my world."

One of Milos's thick eyebrows flexes, intrigued.

"I haven't been able to find him here." My tongue feels thick, heavy with uncertainty on whether confessing will hurt or help me. I push on. "I've tried."

"Have you?" He studies me more closely. "Aides is big. There are so many souls. Ones that you cannot reach."

"But you could help," I hedge. "You're the prince. You decide where they all go."

His eyes narrow, considering.

I hold my breath. My blunt fingernails dig into my palms. Hope is high in my chest, though I know it shouldn't be. I gave up on hope and wishes a long time ago. But it feels like I don't have much else left.

Finally, Milos lifts his chin. The light cuts along his smooth smile.

"And what of my brother?"

Fighting a wince, I say, "What about him?"

"Does he know you used him? To get here? To get closer to me?"

The truth of his words sinks sharp teeth into my skin. Shame runs cold in my veins. I used Cary. For his knowledge, his powers. For anything that could bring me closer to London again.

I knew what I was doing every step of the way.

But I didn't expect him to be more than just a hard, uncaring face. To *like* him in a way I haven't in a long time. For it to ache so deeply when he figured it all out and wanted nothing more to do with me.

Milos clears his throat.

"Yes," I say, a sourness filling my mouth. "He knows."

His smile is a blade. "You know, Deathless are not supposed to bargain. It's a silly, archaic rule. My mother believes what happens to mortals is Fate's decision. We are not meant to make deals to change destiny."

I watch as his gaze drops to his hands.

"But what good is this power if we do nothing with it? If we do not decide our own destiny?"

In my periphery, Henri tenses. He's not close enough to read his face. But his breaths are tight, short.

"Fate does not control me." A quiet, bitter laugh passes through Milos's lips. "However, the curse of who I am does."

He touches my bicep. I force myself to stay still.

"I will make a deal with you, August."

My eyes lift, eager.

"I will find this soul for you. You can be with him. Whenever you are in Aides." His fingers drag down my forearm, tickling my knuckles. "He is yours."

That hope I'm not supposed to have throbs against my temples. "What do I have to do?"

His eyes flicker. A viper trapping its prey. "Commit your soul to me. For eternity."

Milos's words strike like lightning. I could be with London.

Anytime I'm in Aides. He would be mine again. That's what I wanted, right? It's why I kept coming back here, isn't it?

But there is a price. *For eternity.* I start to step back.

He grips my hand, bones shifting the wrong way. "It is a small exchange," Milos promises. "His freedom for mine."

"What do you mean commit my soul to you? I have to . . . be, like, your—" I can't find the right word. "Husband?"

He snorts dramatically. "August, please. I do not want your heart."

My eyes fan over him. Faint red smudges climb up his neck. The aftermath of careless kisses.

Milos leans in. "I want your power."

A haze falls over my brain as I look down at my free hand. Mellow brown skin, protruding veins. The nail beds rough from lack of attention. I don't see anything spectacular. Not like I do in Cary.

What is Milos talking about? I don't have any power. I'm normal.

Just a . . . mortal.

"My power?"

Henri won't meet my eyes when I stare at him. There's a *ding* behind me at the other side of the room. I whirl around.

Cary steps off the elevator, then stops abruptly. Before I knew him, the expression on his face was unreadable. A blank canvas. But now I can pick out all the vague tells: a small muscle in his jaw shifting, the quiet flare of his nostrils, dimmed light behind his eyes.

Milos barks out a laugh. "No one told you?"

A blend of frustration and humiliation surges through me. As hot as a newborn flame.

This isn't the first time Milos has said something like this. Mocked my ignorance about their world. As if I should be aware of every secret and understand a place that didn't exist to me a month ago. I never said anything before. Out of respect, out of need.

But I'm done being his joke.

My glare shifts over each of them. "Tell me *what*?"

Predictably, Cary doesn't answer. Neither does Henri.

Milos drops my hand. "How do you think you can come and go from Aides? Or see the souls? Did you not wonder why my brother's pathetic beast does not harm you?"

I thought it was because Cary told him not to. Because Cerby liked me.

There's a spark in Milos's eyes. Gold, twinkling. "You saw my brother in the mortal realm even when his power should have hidden him. *How*, August?"

I look past him. To Cary's hardened face. The face that told me so much—his sadness and regret and wants—in my mom's greenhouse but gives nothing away now.

"I don't know," I say quietly.

"Because you are not one of them," Milos announces. His fingers tip my chin toward him. "Not entirely."

I blink. *Not one of them.* How could I not be? My dad is a nurse. My mom works in gardens and sells flowers at farmers markets.

I'm just a boy from Santa Barbara.

Not entirely, he said. Frigid fear wraps around my lungs.

"What am I?"

Somewhere, slightly out of focus, I see Cary step farther into the room, his mouth opened in protest. Henri rests a hand on Milos's shoulder, speaking first. "He's not ready—"

Milos jerks free, still holding my chin.

Gleefully, he says, "One of us."

18

MY REALITY IS SHATTERED.

In the broken shards, I see so many versions of myself:

The August who loved following his mom around her greenhouse. Another August, who wrote songs about a boy who left the world too soon. The August who no longer knew how to get out of bed. And the August who met the ferrier of souls. Another August, who accidentally fell into the underworld and discovered powerful immortals.

Finally, the August who is one of them.

Breathless, I whisper, "It can't be true."

I search the room. Three faces tell me everything: Henri's twisted and guilty. Milos's arrogant and elated. Cary's defeated and apologetic.

Resentment burns wild and merciless underneath my skin. It leaves my blood scalding. Steals the oxygen from my lungs.

"How is this possible?" I hiss at Cary.

His mouth pinches. "I told you. Deathless have existed forever. Generations and generations. Our power is given. And then passed on to another when we are done."

Milos makes a disapproving noise.

I ignore him. "What does any of that have to do with *me*?"

Cary lets out a soft breath. "Most times, we step into our role because a previous Deathless is ready for their next journey." His eyes roam over me. "But there was once a Deathless who chose something else."

"What did they choose . . . ?"

His dark gaze slides away from me. He looks at the floor. That one curl droops farther down his brow.

"The mortal realm," he says.

My forehead wrinkles. This doesn't make sense. I would know if I was one of them, wouldn't I? I try my best to process everything. It's too much.

Milos steps between Cary and me.

"The short version: She abandoned us for your world. Left behind all that makes her immortal." His thumb smooths over the inside of my forearm. "Yet, somehow, her power lives. Faint but here. In you."

He studies my tattoo as if seeing it for the first time.

"*Narcissus.* Favorite of the Deathless of life."

I falter. "Deathless of . . . life?"

"Of children and the young," Cary supplies, looking at me again. "She took care of them. Built the gardens for them."

"And gave it all up for the love of a mortal." Milos steps away, twirling his hand carelessly above his head, bored. "At least, that is what the old stories say."

"And I'm . . ." Words catch on the roof of my mouth like taffy.

"A descendant of hers," Henri finishes.

I'm dizzy. Nausea roils in my stomach. Me, a descendant of a Deathless. The one who cared for children. Who loved flowers and gardens.

Cary starts toward me. "August—"

"Did you know?" I ask, furious.

Remorse crowds his face. "I suspected."

"When?"

"That first time you followed me here. On the shore."

When I was trapped under him. A blush warms my face, but I refuse to let it distract me.

Cary watches me like the memory is playing out in his own head too. "You felt—" His hand reaches for me.

I retreat, my anger too untamed to be near him. He grimaces, then says, "You felt different."

"I felt different," I repeat dully.

He nods. "Then, in the great hall below. The flowers, they . . . they brightened for you."

I remember. At the time, it was strange. But everything about Aides is strange to me.

"They wanted to be near you. Just like I want—" Cary stops again, eyes closing.

"You never said anything."

Blinking, he says, "I wanted to. So many times. But . . ." His voice trails off.

"But *what*?!" I shout. Hurt flows river-deep in my voice. "Why didn't you say anything? Why did you keep another secret from me?"

His silence stretches longer than the distance I've put between us.

"Because that is who he is," Milos posits. "My brother is selfish. Comes and goes as he pleases. Never thinks about what his decisions mean to anyone else."

Gold pops like oil from a heated pan in Cary's eyes.

Milos grins. "This is about us, not him."

"Us?" I rasp out.

Milos angles himself until Cary is blocked from my view. "My offer still stands. Think about it: You can finally have what *you* want."

London's name almost spills from my parted lips.

"I know about loneliness, August." Milos rests his hand on my chest. "Being left in a world without a choice. Everyone around you doing as they desire while you are"—his eyes soften—"stuck. Waiting."

That's exactly what it's like living with grief. Loneliness, even while you're surrounded by people. Forced to watch them carry on. Death doesn't stop the world from spinning. But it freezes you in that same singular moment, day after day.

All you can do is wait. For the wave to pass. For the ache to dull. For things to feel normal. Then it starts all over again.

"We can have what we want," Milos whispers.

I look down at his hand still on my sternum. "And how do you get what you want?"

His smile briefly slips. He recovers.

"Through you. Descendant of the Deathless of life. The first Deathless to exist among mortals, permanently. We thought her power lost. Then you showed up." His fingers skim delicately up my chest. Like I'm a treasure he fears losing again. "When you commit to me, I can leave too. Only temporarily, but it is . . . something."

I consider his words. My heart kicks anxiously. "What about my parents? Will I be stuck here?"

"No, no. You come and go too. We *both* can." Milos gestures toward Cary. "Because of his decision, I have been trapped here. Just like you have been trapped."

Past his shoulder, I can see Cary watching me. A hawk eyeing the rabbit.

In a soft, genuine tone, Milos adds, "You are powerful, August. *We* are. Together."

Powerful.

It's a word I've never associated with myself. Someone has always protected me. My mom and dad, since I was born. Max, in high school and after. London, with all his plans.

Cary, from a world that isn't mine. But maybe it is.

This is my chance to finally protect myself. To have what Fate or destiny stole from me. To be free of grief and guilt's crushing weight.

"Do not do this."

Cary's voice cuts through my thoughts. I glare at him. "Why not?"

"He is not telling you everything," he answers. "You will lose more than you think."

An acidic laugh bubbles up my chest. I repeat the question I asked him in my apartment: "What do you know about loss, Cary?"

"Not enough before." His expression turns somber. "Too much now."

It's hard to escape the honesty, the care in those black eyes. But I do. "Can I have some time to think about this?" I ask Milos.

For a long moment, he stares at me. Then he nods.

"Anything for you, August."

With an easy flick of his wrist, a thick cloud of smoke hovers between us. It solidifies into an elegant hourglass. His index finger twirls. The hourglass flips over. Grains of pink sand pour steadily from one end into the other.

Milos smiles darkly. "Until the sand runs out."

It's not Henri or Cary who escorts me away from the throne room.

It's Aminta.

We don't take the elevator. Instead, she leads me through a bronze door hidden at the back of the room. The winding halls are lined with burgundy wallpaper. Filigreed damask patterns shimmer under elaborately crafted lanterns. Cinnamon and smoke scent the air.

Aminta's silent as we walk. My eyes dance to the tablet by her side. On instinct, my hand wants to snatch it. Run away with it. Find London on my own.

But do I still need the tablet?

Descendant of the Deathless of life.

Milos's voice echoes in my head. I'm still unsure what power I have. If I have any.

The hall changes again. "Where are we?"

Aminta ignores me, her steps quickening. Soon enough, we're cast in an amber haze outside a pair of doors I recognize. It's the room where I put on my suit for the ball.

Where Cary danced with me.

You will lose more than you think.

His words stick to me like honey. I don't trust Milos. At least, not completely. But he hasn't kept any secrets from me. Not the way Cary has.

Aminta unlocks the crimson doors with her tablet, then turns to leave. "Aminta, wait," I blurt.

Her ivy eyes narrow like she can't believe I said her name.

"You used to be a soul, right?" I ask.

She doesn't answer.

"And you made a deal with Milos."

Again, she's quiet. Her arms fold protectively around the tablet, pulling it to her chest. She's hard to read. There's obvious irritation pinching her features. But her cheeks suck in as she thinks.

I hold her gaze. "You know who I am, don't you?"

Slowly, she nods.

"Can I trust Milos? Will he give me what I want?"

Something familiar flares across her face, small but noticeable. She was human once. I wonder who she left behind after dying. Are any of her loved ones here now? Have they faced Milos yet?

Would he bargain with them like he did with her?

"Tell me what to do."

Please, I say with my eyes.

Aminta examines me. I stare back, open and honest. Finally, she steps aside, motioning toward the room.

"Wait here."

I walk inside. "Will you help me?"

"No."

It comes out so fast, so final, I stumble. "N-no?"

Her teeth clench. "Why would I ever help you?"

"Because . . ." My pulse pounds in my ears. "Because you were like me once."

"I was *never* like you."

Disgust rolls down her face. Or is it envy? I never find out. With one click, the doors close. Locking me in.

My fists pound against the doors. They're heavy and thick, but for a split second, I think I can shatter the wood. Like maybe I really am part Deathless. That I have the same strength Cary and Milos have. But the only thing that comes is a throbbing ache in my knuckles.

"She doesn't remember her life before becoming what she is now."

The voice comes from behind me.

It's Poppy leaning against the mirrored wall. She's in a fitted black suit, glittery red petals waterfalling down one side. *Poppies.*

I raise my eyebrows at her, looking for more.

She shrugs. "That's part of the deal. In order to live here, by Milos's side, souls must first drink from Lethe. Forget everything and everyone they've known."

My jaw drops. Poppy smiles sorrowfully.

"Nothing comes without a cost. Even in the afterlife."

I step back, taking in what she's said. Every soul who's bargained with Milos, who's been given a different fate, has no memory of who they were before. Of course Aminta wouldn't help me. What for? Her life as a mortal doesn't exist anymore.

Poppy eases off the wall. "Don't worry. He can't do that to you. Not unless you ask him to."

My face tightens into a scowl. "How long have you known about me?"

"Not very long. I knew you were different from the

beginning." A playful smile unfurls on her gold-stained lips. "Other than that cute face and those curls."

I don't return her smile.

"But I should've known sooner. Because of Cary."

My eyebrows shoot up.

Poppy laughs, bright and airy. "He's talked about you for a long time now." At my confused face, she goes quiet. "He hasn't told you, then."

"No," I grind out. "No one around here tells me anything. It's getting really old."

"Sorry about that. But he has his reasons."

I scoff. "Yeah. Selfish ones."

Mirth sways through Poppy's near-black eyes. She drifts closer. "I can't speak for the ferrier or his actions. However, I can show you something. Close your eyes."

I flinch back toward the doors.

She gives me a tender look. "I won't hurt you, August. You know that."

It takes a moment for my body to agree. As much as I distrust every Deathless now, Poppy's warm in a way that feels familiar. The same way you wake up from a dream, unable to remember it, but somewhere in your bones, you know it was good.

I flutter my eyes shut.

"Now breathe in."

Smoky earthiness fills my nose. An almondy taste coats the back of my throat.

When I blink, the room with its mirrored wall and blue-sky ceiling dissolves into a long hallway. The potent odor of ammonia hangs in the air. Harsh white lights burn my vision.

I know this place, intimately: Santa Barbara Cottage Hospital.

My knees turn to jelly. Why did Poppy send me here?

When I reach for a door to leave, my hand passes right through it. Shocked, I yank my arm back. My whole body is translucent. Swathed in a moonlight blue glow. Panic rockets into my throat.

Am I . . . dead?

Voices echo down the hall where two boys stand. One is in all-black, his skin a light gold, hair slicked back except for a single lock curling against his forehead.

Cary.

The other boy is shorter. Built like a surfer. His wavy brown hair stops just past his chin. He's in a T-shirt and board shorts, slides with socks. There's a gauzy white shimmer to his sun-bronzed skin.

"London," I half sob.

He doesn't hear me. They don't see me either as they approach. Cary holds London's hand the same way he held Yuri's and Hasan's and Bernice's. With care and gentleness.

"Wait, wait," London pleads.

"We cannot. It is time." Cary gives him a soft smile. "This is not your end."

I can't breathe. London's so close, a few feet away. My heart cracks just like his voice when he says, "*Please.* Just this one thing."

Cary pauses. His delicate features begin to harden.

"I do not make bargains."

"It's not, I promise." London drags anxious fingers through his hair. The dried trail of blood at his temple is gone. "I know I can't stay. But you can. I just . . . I need you to watch over him. The other boy who was in the accident with me. His name's August. He's—"

My breath hitches in rhythm with London's.

"That is not my role," Cary says coolly.

"Please," London repeats. "Something awful happened tonight." He shakes his head. "I didn't get to tell him so many things. Things that would've changed a lot. For him and me."

I take a wobbly step forward, then another. My hand stretches toward him. "What did you want to tell me?" I say, my voice thin.

He doesn't answer me. Those aloe green eyes stay fixed on Cary.

"I cannot speak to him for you," Cary warns.

"You don't have to." London's nose wrinkles like it does when he's stressed or overwhelmed. "Just check on him."

I'm right here. Next to them. My fingers slip through London's shoulder like smoke. I can't touch him, hold him, comfort him.

Only watch helplessly as everything happens in front of me.

A second slips by. Cary's furrowed brow relaxes. Softly, he says, "I will."

"You will?" London looks ready to cry.

I am. Slick, hot tears that evaporate a second after kissing my cheeks.

Cary nods once. "Now, we must go."

They pass through me. I try to follow, but my feet are stuck to the floor. Sinking *through* it. Before I can yell London's name, beg Cary to bring him back, everything melts away. The hospital fades back to the room in Aides.

I slide down the doors. Pull my knees to my chest. "He was there," I whimper. "London. I saw him."

Poppy crouches in front of me. "I know."

"Was that a dream?"

"A memory. From Cary."

When I don't immediately respond, she continues. "He doesn't dream often. But when he does, it's always a memory." She smiles gently. "Cary is far from perfect, but he is much more than just the ferrier of souls now. Thanks to you."

I blink hard. "Me?"

She catches one of my tears. It sits fat as morning dew on her fingertip.

"He's watched you ever since that night," Poppy says. "Cary never goes back after collecting a soul. Never stays to see what mortals go through after. Until you."

I inhale an achy breath. Reality falls like a stone in a fountain. The splash sends me reeling.

Cary is always in Santa Barbara when I need him. Even though there are souls all over the world waiting for him. He's known things about me without me telling him. Like Shoreline Steps being the place I go to escape. My favorite bakery on State Street. Where I live.

Poppy sees the questions forming in my eyes. "He promised London he'd check on you *that night.*" Her mouth curves higher, deeper. "But, August, he kept returning to you."

She touches the back of my hand.

"You changed him. He feels something for you—for mortals—he's never felt before . . . compassion."

My laugh comes out deflated. "I can't tell."

Poppy grins. "Did I mention he's not perfect? Or great with words? He's used to being alone. That doesn't mean he *wants* to be that way." Her eyes twinkle. "And I doubt you want the life you've been living either."

I don't. But nothing has felt in my control for so long, I'm not sure how to get it back.

When she stands, I look up at her. "What about Milos's offer?"

This is my chance to talk to London. To apologize. To hear what he wanted to tell me.

"It's your decision, August. I can't tell you what to choose."

It's not the answer I was hoping for.

Poppy offers me a hand. "But I promise you, moving forward doesn't mean we forget the past. It's part of the path that got us where we are. It stays with us, always. What you decide to do with it is up to you."

Behind me, the doors click, unlocking.

"I have to go," she whispers. "There's a gorgeous girl with green skin waiting for me."

My eyes grow. "Leu?"

Poppy winks. "You and the ferrier aren't the only ones who get to have fun around here."

She steps into the mirror, disappears. All that's left behind is a dusting of red petals on the carpet. Like the remnants of an unfinished dream on a pillow.

19

MILOS CLAPS AS Aminta leads me back into the throne room. He sits lazily on the throne. Not far away, Henri stands, shoulders stiff, while Cary refuses to make eye contact as he waits by the elevator.

I focus on Milos. His grin cuts like a razor. The floating hourglass has run out of sand.

I've run out of time.

Milos leans forward. "Beautiful August, are you ready to make a deal?"

My gaze flits to his neck. The faded rouge climbing the side. Aminta wears a matching shade on her lips.

I do not want your heart. I want your power.

"No," I say.

His head tilts. "No, you are not ready? Or no, you do not want to make a deal?"

I lift my chin, clinging to whatever bravery I can find. "The second one."

A relieved sigh comes from somewhere in the room. Henri, maybe. In the corner of my eye, Cary is as still as a statue.

Milos slides a finger over his mouth, considering me. "Are you sure?"

"I wish things would've ended differently for me and London," I answer. "There's so much I want to tell him. But I'm done chasing the what-ifs. I can't change what happened."

Carefully, my eyes cheat back to Cary. He doesn't react. Not out loud. But that muscle in his jaw moves. Just slightly.

"I trust London is safe," I say to Milos. "And one day I'll see him again. Tell him everything. Now I'd like to go home. Give my life another chance."

Silence descends on the room. Milos's stare is unwavering. I do my best to look like I'm confident in my decision.

He licks out a smooth smile. "How very sentimental. So mature. I knew you were special." He stands. It only takes five steps to reach me. "It is also too late."

My face falls.

Was I supposed to be here sooner? How long ago did the sand run out?

Milos's grin turns cruel. "This is your fifth trip to Aides. You know what that means."

I pull in a painful breath. Cary warned me. Right after Milos invited me to the ball. My head snaps in Henri's direction. "Why didn't you say anything?"

Henri tries to respond, but Milos cuts him off.

"How could he possibly know you had already visited a fourth time? That you snuck here with my brother for some"—his eyebrows wiggle suggestively—"*private time*?"

A pit opens up in my stomach.

Milos circles me, snorting. "Hmm. Our dear ferrier is not the only one who loves secrets."

In the half light, Cary's eyes are hollow. His lips flat. I hear his voice in my head, the last thing he said to me in my apartment:

Do not return to Aides. Until it is your time.

He was trying to stop me. To keep me safe from this fate. And, like a fool, I didn't listen.

"I can't stay here," I rush out. What about my parents? Max?

"You had a choice," Milos notes. "You turned down my offer, remember?"

His offer. Of course. He said it himself, right here in this room.

My *power.*

I square my shoulders. "I'm the descendant of a Deathless, right? That means I can still come and go. I'm not bound to Aides. Like you are. I have her power."

Milos's lip curls. "That you do."

Pride vibrates through me, my chest puffed. Milos treats everything and everyone like a game that he always wins. But I can play too.

"I'm leaving," I declare.

Stepping backward, Milos throws his arms wide dramatically. "Please, show us your power! Leave! You are free to go." Gold slithers around his eyes. "If you can do it on your own, that is."

On my own . . . How do I do that?

Two hours ago, I didn't even know any power existed somewhere in my bloodline. That it was passed down from a Deathless. Now I'm just supposed to use it?

I look around for help. Henri lowers his eyes. Aminta turns away. Cary offers me a long, unyielding stare. I've only seen him travel between my world and Aides through water.

But there's none of that here and I'm not him. I'm not a ferrier.

I don't know *what* I am.

Closing my eyes, I take a deep breath. My fingers spread. I reach for a thread of something I've never knowingly had access to. An outlet. A well waiting to be filled.

Seconds drift by. Then a minute.

Finally . . . nothing. I'm as empty as when I came here. There's no buried power inside me.

And I'm never going home.

Next to me, I hear Milos snort arrogantly. "Pathetic. You will make a nice addition to my collection of—"

"There is another way."

My eyes fly open. It takes me a moment to recognize where the voice comes from. But I know it as sure as my heartbeat.

Cary strides forward, his stare pointed at Milos. "The labyrinth."

"The labyrinth," he echoes, incredulous.

"What if he solves it? He can leave Aides, right?" Cary proposes. "Is that not one of the bargains you make with souls who want a second chance?"

Milos glares at him, then lets out another short laugh. "No one has ever escaped *my* labyrinth."

I look between them. A moment slips by before recognition sets in. They're talking about the garden's maze.

"He can do it," Cary announces. He avoids my eyes while adding, "August is so much more than any of us thinks he is. Including you, brother."

A burst of warmth spreads unexpectedly through my chest. It radiates with the same bright confidence in Cary's voice. He *believes* in me.

The feeling is short-lived. Milos waves a dismissive hand above his head.

"Fine. Let him try." His wolfish smile is all teeth. "Either way, he is never leaving Aides."

"How does it work?"

Henri flinches, surprised I'm speaking to him. I am too. His betrayal still stings. But I'm alone here, minutes from doing something I'm not even sure I can. And he's the closest I've had to a friend in Aides.

Eventually, he asks, "How does *what* work?"

I gesture widely at the elevator. It's only us inside. Milos insisted on a personal escort to the labyrinth. Someone other than him. I wasn't shocked when Aminta didn't volunteer.

Cary didn't either, which both relieved and amplified my anxiety.

"Oh." Henri leans against one of the brass walls. "It's ma—"

"Don't you *dare* say magic."

"Would you prefer I lie?"

I thump the back of my head against the opposite wall. There's so much unexplainable power running through Aides. Running through me too, apparently, even though I can't feel it.

My mind drifts back to the throne room. When I thought I could just call upon something that was never there before. The delight in Milos's eyes after I failed.

I examine the inside of my forearm. Right under my tattoo. I search for a trail of gold. Something sparkling in my veins. Maybe a hint of fire or the tingle of strength.

Anything to help me get out of here.

"The elevator is enchanted," Henri explains. "It takes you where you need to go."

"Can it take me home?" I tease.

He smiles sadly. "Where you need to go *within* Aides."

I remember the masquerade ball. When I ran out of the ballroom to look for London. But the elevator took me to the gardens instead. Was it trying to keep me safe? Out of trouble?

Did it know Cary would find me there? That we'd end up kissing?

That he was what I nee—

The doors glide open. I push aside any more thoughts of Cary.

Guards wait inside the great hall for us. Henri gives them a brief nod. I don't make eye contact. They trail at a short distance as we walk. My lungs fill with bright floral notes.

It's not long before Henri breaks our silence. "I was like you once."

"What, a prisoner?"

"No." He pauses. "A mortal."

Those two words bring me to a cold stop. I scan his face for the lie. But it's not there. Henri smiles as he always does—carefree, bold as the moon.

"I don't remember much," he continues. The skin between his brows pinches. "It was so long ago."

I squint at him. It's hard to imagine a mortal Henri. What was he like? Still loud and spectacular? Did he look the same then?

"Then how did you become a Deathless?" Soon after, another question bubbles up, hope singing in my marrow. "Are you also a descendant?"

Tell me I'm not alone.

With sympathetic eyes, he says, "No. I was a soul. Chosen by the last messenger Deathless." He motions grandly at himself. "Obviously, she was not as fashionable as I am."

My heart skips. Henri was a soul. Which means he died. I trace the boyishness in his cheeks, those adorable dimples. How young was he when it happened?

Something he said at the pizzeria comes back to me:

We are chosen. But some are born from other Deathless. The rest . . . come from elsewhere.

Henri was talking about himself. *Elsewhere* is the mortal realm.

"How many Deathless used to be souls?"

"Not many," he replies.

I run through all the faces from the masquerade ball. Gorgeous, breathtaking. The kind of beauty I rarely see in Santa Barbara. How much of that is the power of Aides? And at what price?

Now Poppy's in my head: *Nothing comes without a cost. Even in the afterlife.*

Henri stops in front of the two statues at the room's center. The ones I admired before. The woman with a crown of asphodels and the other holding a bouquet of daffodils.

"Narcissus," I whisper.

"Cora," Henri says of the one cradling the flowers. He gives me a sidelong stare. "Deathless of—"

"Life," I finish for him.

I couldn't see it before. Didn't *know* what to look for. But something about her pulls ever so slightly on my chest. A thin string tied between us.

I wonder which of my parents she's related to. We don't look alike. Mostly because she's a statue. But is that where my dad gets his intense love of helping kids from? Or is she the reason my mom is so gifted with plants and flowers?

My gaze shifts to the other woman. "And she is?"

"Death."

"Cary's mom," I breathe out.

"And Milos's," Henri reminds me. I don't want to think about him. Either of them.

Turning away, I follow Henri toward the end of the hall. "Why are you telling me this?"

Henri's face smooths into soft lines. "I'm loyal to Aides and Milos. But I haven't forgotten who I was before. There's still a part of me that"—he exhales, touching his chest—"feels a connection to mortals. I help where I can."

The soaring walls of the labyrinth loom over us. Tangled foliage hides the stone beneath. The entrance is an open mouth. Waiting to swallow me. Heady spice from the saffron crocus scents the breeze.

Smiling fondly, Henri thumbs one of the red threads. In a low voice, he says, "Trust your instincts, August. Watch your surroundings. Listen carefully. And try not to go backward."

His eyes glance over his shoulder. The guards watch us.

I lean closer. "Are you *helping* me?"

He clucks his tongue. "Clearly." Turning to me, he adds, "Look, Milos built the labyrinth to entertain himself. It's dangerous and difficult. Stay alert and *don't* look in the mirrors."

I shudder, remembering that mistake last time.

"What do they do?"

"Reveal your worst fears and nightmares," Henri answers. "Milos had Meli create them."

Careful. She'll give you nightmares.

Henri said that at the ball like it was a joke. Now the playfulness is gone from his eyes. Serious, he says, "They're meant to distract you. Avoid them."

I nod. "Is it true? That no one's ever escaped?"

"You're not 'no one.' You're *August*." He takes my cheeks in his hands, pinching. "And this face is way too pretty to be trapped where no one can see it."

I laugh, elbowing him away.

After a final smile, Henri steps over to the guards. I inhale deeply, then walk through the maze's entrance. I haven't even made it ten steps before Henri calls, "Look for what you need the most and it will be there!"

"What the hell does that m—"

A rumbling noise cuts me off. It sounds like gears turning. Suddenly, a stone wall shoots up from the floor. It closes the labyrinth off from anyone else entering. Or exiting.

I'm sealed inside.

"It's fine," I mutter to the flower-covered walls. "I can do this."

I have to, I remind myself.

In front of me, the narrow passageway is lit by streams of gold light. They cascade through thick leaves overhead. For a few feet, nothing changes. Sculpted shrubs carved into mythical creatures. Vibrant blooms blossom along the ivy.

Around the first turn, a gilded thorn mirror taunts me. I ignore it, navigating until I reach the end of a corridor. Two choices await:

Left or right.

The landscape is identical both ways. The stone floor is clean and level, no footsteps. Not a single indication of what path others chose before me.

Trust your instincts, August.

"Yeah, thanks, Henri," I mumble.

After a breath, I choose left.

It goes like that for what seems minutes. The passageways shift from short to long. Some have mirrors, others don't. Flowers burst along the walls in sugary colors: pink amaryllis, orangey hibiscus, lavender aster, yellowy tulips. I alternate between going left, then right.

The light follows me like a gleaming shadow.

Around another corner, I stop. Against the wall is a gilded thorn mirror.

"No." I spin in a circle. "This can't be the same spot."

But I can't tell. Nothing's changed. No matter how many steps I've walked, it all looks the same—clean and untouched.

Sweat prickles against my forehead. Erratic heartbeats fill my ears, loud as the buzzing. The . . . *voices.* I hear them everywhere. Behind me, in front, through the walls.

Quickly, I run past the mirror.

Around every turn, I lose track if I've gone left or right. Or right, then left. I pass winged lions and six-headed snakes and men with bull heads. The mirrors' frames change from leaves to roses to feathers to serpents. I never dare look into their reflections.

My footsteps aren't heavy enough to hide whatever's chasing or leading me.

AugustAugustAugust.

Dots swirl in my vision as I cut another corner. A harsh exhale of voices brushes the back of my neck. I look over my shoulder.

Nothing's there.

My foot catches on something. A loose stone, maybe? I tumble forward, palms braced for the fall. The sting of my hands scraping the floor is not nearly as bad as the impact. Or what I see at the other end of the passage.

It's a man. But not exactly.

He's half-hunched over, his feet dragging. Limp dark hair droops into his unfocused eyes. His jaw is cracked open, but the only thing that comes out is a constant buzzing. Clothes hang off his frail body. A dull gray film covers him.

He's a soul like from the beach. And he's staggering closer. Hunger fills his every broken step.

Get up, my mind screams.

"G-get up," I stammer to myself. But I don't. My bones feel heavy. The only thing that works is my arms. I throw them in front of me as if that might keep me safe.

Nearby, I hear a wisping noise. Through my fingers, I spot movement behind the soul. Vines slither like vipers along the floor.

They coil around the soul's ankles. He struggles against them. It's useless. He's jerked to the ground. In a blink, the vines tug him around a corner, gone.

The noise goes with him.

It takes forever before my breaths calm. For the shivers to fade. I lower my arms, but it's another mistake.

On the wall in front of me is a mirror. Gilded thorns circle smoked glass. Ice flows down my skin. It can't be the same mirror from before, right? Have I really been going in circles this entire time?

Pain thrums from my scratched palms as I pull my legs to my chest. I don't know where to go. How to start again. Definitely not in the direction that soul was just yanked. But the other way is just another left or right that will lead me back here.

The voices are louder in my head.

AugustAugustAugust.

Helpless, I look into the mirror. The reflection ripples like the tide at dawn. I'm too exhausted to prepare myself for what I'm about to see.

Will it be me from the car accident again? Maybe my parents in the hospital waiting room? Or London's parents the moment the doctors tell them their son is dead?

Maybe it'll be something worse:

Max in a coffin. Mom as she sobs over Dad's headstone. Me, kneeling in front of my parents' graves.

Every possible outcome swirls in my brain before the reflection even takes shape. Meli's power seeps into my throat like smoke, choking me.

Still, I can't look away.

When the glass solidifies again, a gasp rattles my entire body. It's my worst nightmare come true:

A boy with wavy brown hair. Sunlit tan skin. White T-shirt and board shorts and slides with socks.

It's London before a car smashed into us. Before I killed him.

He steps right through the glass to stand over me.

20

LONDON IS *HERE*.

He blinks those aloe green eyes, staring at me, head tilted curiously.

The only thing my shuddering lips can say is "I'm sorry. I'm so sorry, London."

His weird smile slips into a disappointed frown.

I'm frozen on the ground. My wet eyes blink over and over. As if this might be an illusion. A dream that I'll wake from at any moment and he'll be gone again. Ripped from my life before I get to say goodbye.

But it's not.

London kneels in front of me. He's haloed in a pale white shimmer. The same Hasan and Yuri and Bernice were blanketed in.

"How?" I croak.

His nose scrunches, thinking. It's absurd how much I've missed that one little gesture.

"I'm not completely sure," he says. "A boy with dimples and really pretty hair brought me here."

A piece clicks into place. It was Henri. He found London.

Look for what you need the most and it will be there.

My mouth slides into a wobbly, tear-soaked smile.

Tentatively, London reaches for my forearm. His hand doesn't pass through me like it did in that memory Poppy showed me. This time, his palm rests coolly against my skin.

A sob racks my throat. "I'm so sor—"

"Don't!"

I flinch at the intensity in his voice. His face crumples the way it did whenever he was fighting with himself about something. "August, please don't say that again."

"But what happened to you is my fault."

He sighs. "It *wasn't.* You do this all the time. If something's wrong in the world, it's because, somehow, you're the problem. You let everyone in your life tell you how to feel and who to be." Regret sits heavy in the corners of his eyes. "Including me."

I blink away more tears, shocked.

London rubs my forearm. "I've had a lot of time to think here."

My mind races to one thing: He still has his memories. He hasn't sipped from Lethe. Which means he hasn't been judged by Milos yet.

"I loved you, August," London goes on. "You were my first

boyfriend. My first everything. And I wanted so much for myself and you."

"I did too."

He smiles sadly. "Let me finish." When I nod, he adds, "If that accident never happened, you wouldn't have been my last boyfriend. Just like I shouldn't be yours."

I can't stop my face from falling.

Briskly, he says, "No. It's okay. You know it's true."

To my surprise, I don't disagree. I *want* to. Everything inside my knotted cold belly does. But I know he's right.

Since I was fifteen and London raced up the clock tower's stairwell wearing that UCSB hoodie, I wanted to see what was next. For *him*. All his plans. His dreams. Becoming that version of himself he constantly talked about.

And I wanted to be there. Right by his side. I didn't care how. As his boyfriend. His friend. I just wanted to see it.

I wanted to see . . . *us*.

That was my plan. The only thing I cared about. Then the accident happened and I never got the chance. *He* never got it.

That's what hurts the most. What keeps me drowning beneath the surface. All the unanswered what-ifs.

Our love, our story together never got a *the end*. We never got a true goodbye.

How do you just move on from that?

How do you let go of someone when you were never given the choice to?

London squeezes my arm. "We wanted different things. I

tried to make you fit into all *my* big dreams. Even when I could tell they weren't what you wanted." He grimaces. "But you never challenged me either, August. You always let me have my way."

"I wanted to make you happy."

I've never said that aloud. I barely admitted it to myself. When we were together, I didn't complain. Or fight for my way. I went along with everything.

Because I loved him.

Because he was the first boy to love me. To hold my hand and kiss me. To touch me like he wanted me, wholly.

That kind of love was all I'd ever known. It was enough. At least I thought it was.

Until I let Cary in.

London brushes my cheek. The coolness makes me shiver.

"I know why you did it, August," he tells me. "But that's not how relationships work. How *love* works. And it's not how I want you to live your life."

A frustrated breath slides past my lips. "I don't know how I'm supposed to live my life."

Without you is so close to my tongue, I taste the sad honesty in it.

"Yes, you do. You're just scared everyone else won't approve."

I mock-scowl at him. "Are you calling me a people pleaser?"

"Fuck yeah."

He laughs. It's not as warm as I remember, but it's still nice.

I watch him for a long moment. "You told Cary to look after me."

"I was so scared when I realized it wasn't just a bad dream." Fondness fills his eyes. "But he took my hand. Told me his name. He calmed me down."

I remember the smile Cary gave Hasan. How he played with Yuri's stuffed bunny. The genuine amusement on his face while listening to Bernice's stories.

I fit all these pieces of the Cary I know now together. Not just the ferrier. Cary the giver. The boy who smirks and remembers all the little details and listens. Who looks after souls before himself.

Who looks after me, even when I'm difficult.

"You know, the internet never mentions how nice Death is," London jokes. "And kind of hot."

A blush rushes my cheeks. "He's not Death."

London quirks an eyebrow in that *but you agree he's hot?* way. I don't comment.

"That night, I needed you to be okay," he admits. "I knew you'd blame yourself for the accident. That you'd feel guilty."

"I did," I whisper. "I do. All the time."

"No way," he says in mock-surprise, then flashes me that weird smile.

I kick his foot, grinning back.

He goes quiet, considering. His nose wrinkles again. "I didn't think Cary would go back for you."

I smile to myself. "He doesn't make bargains. He also doesn't break promises."

Behind London's stare is something I can't quite make out. At least, not at first. He knows what I feel for Cary. He can see it but is choosing not to comment. I'm grateful.

Softly, I say, "Sometimes, I—" My chest pinches. But I need to tell him. I've waited too long for this moment. "I think it should have been me. That night."

London studies me, the corners of his mouth drooping. I keep going.

"You had everything planned. Your whole future. And I didn't. I still don't. You deserve to be there." I point up. "And I'm really sorry you're not."

London sighs, shaking his head. He touches my cheek again. "Time to stop blaming yourself, Auggie," he insists.

"Easier said than done."

His fingers wrap around my wrist. Where his bracelet used to be. "I know. But you can do it. You're incredible and talented and I was so lucky to have you while I did, so . . . you have to carry on. You need to live your life. *You* deserve it."

I lift a teasing eyebrow even while another tear slides over my lips. "Is this where I finally disagree with you instead of letting you get your way again?"

"No. I mean, yes." He laughs. "Don't do this for me. Or anyone else. Do this for August Clarke. The boy I'll always love."

My heart squeezes too tightly. "I'll always love you too, London."

"I know." He stands. "Now love yourself. And let others love you too."

Inhaling raggedly, I say the other thing I've needed to tell him for too long: "Goodbye, London."

His face brightens. A jeweled sun in my darkest moment.

"Goodbye, August."

Then he backs away. Toward the mirror. The glass takes him like a wave swallowing a sandcastle.

And I'm alone again. On the floor of a labyrinth I still don't know how to escape. But the emptiness I've carried in my chest for two years slowly begins to fill.

A wound finally beginning to heal.

I stay there for minutes. Maybe longer. I will myself to do what London asked me to: Carry on. I need to get to my feet. Run.

The voices are getting closer again.

"August."

I hear them. Like they're right above me. Floating down from the thick roof of leaves overhead. Their footsteps echo. Dread pools in my gut when I realize I'm too late.

Whatever souls that have been following me are already here.

When I look up, it's not the gray-faced man from before. The bloodstained woman who Milos banished with a flick of his wrist.

It's Cary, hair falling around his face. Dark eyes shadowed. His mouth pulled into a stubborn pout.

He reaches a hand down to me. "Come on. This is not your end."

After helping me to my feet, Cary starts determinedly down a passageway. He barely glances over his shoulder to make sure I'm behind him.

I am. Open-mouthed, confused. Ignoring the burn in my thighs as I try to keep up with his long strides.

"How are you in the labyrinth?"

"My brother cannot resist a bargain," he says, eyes forward.

"*You* made a deal? You never make deals!"

"This was an exception."

"This or"—I swallow—"me?"

He doesn't answer. That little flex in his jaw does. My stomach tangles in a knot of shock and relief.

Cary came to find me.

But this is Milos. Nothing with him is ever simple. We turn down a corridor, and I ask, "What did you bargain?"

At a fork, Cary examines the options. He lands on going right. "I gave up . . . something," he replies through clenched teeth.

"What?"

"It does not matter." The way he says it . . . Cary gave up something valuable, important. Just to save me.

I hide my smile from him.

Down the passage is a mirror against one wall. Its gilded thorns wink in the light. Cary exhales loudly, striding past it.

I jog after him. "Do you know where you're going?"

"No."

"Shouldn't you ask me, then? Being that I've been trapped in here since—I don't know—the dinosaurs were alive?"

Cary spins on his heel, glaring. "And how far did *you* get?"

I jut my chin, defiant. "Obviously farther than you're getting us."

"You were sitting in that very spot"—he points back the way we came—"when I found you. At the labyrinth's *beginning*."

"After being in this spot"—I stomp a foot—"multiple times."

His scowl deepens.

I let out a long-suffering sigh. "I've tried this path. It doesn't go anywhere." I look around. "Is there even a way out of here?"

"Of course there is," Cary says confidently. "My brother is cruel, manipulative. But he also sees no fun in watching anyone instantly fail. He wants someone to rise to his challenges. Fight back."

A small smile twitches against his mouth. Like he's remembering a different Milos. Maybe the one he ran through the Meadows with. Hid in dark corners with. The brother Cary had before he made a choice that changed them.

Empathy crowds into my chest.

I made a choice too, that changed everything. That left

me alone, even when I was surrounded by people.

We're not so different, Cary and me.

Idly picking at a vine, he asks, "What should we do?"

I fall back against the wall, rubbing my temples. The leaves shift around me. Flower petals brush my cheek in a gentle kiss.

"August, staying here is not an option."

"I know," I snap. In the distance, I hear the whispers, chants. Hollowed voices growing. Cary's face says he hears them too.

Grimly, he says, "The souls who made a deal with Milos. For a second chance. They will do anything to escape."

My shoulders quiver. "Can we help them?"

He shakes his head. "They are not who they once were. They have been here too long."

Anger builds in me. How could anyone be loyal to Milos? All that charm and unnerving beauty is hiding how insidious he really is.

"Come on. We need to keep going."

I hesitate. Underneath the buzzing, there's a faint, almost recognizable noise. I close my eyes, concentrating.

Listen carefully. That's what Henri told me.

I hear a song. The rhythmic sway of waves.

Water.

It was too quiet before. Buried by the blood roaring in my ears while running. My feet pounding the stone floor. Every thought in my head, incessantly loud. But it's here now. As constant as my heartbeat.

"Down here."

This time, it's Cary who has to move fast to keep up. He's sure-footed behind me. I lead us through a windier path, different from the previous one.

Fear made all my decisions before. Every left or right was influenced by anxiety. But now I'm clearheaded. Moving on instinct.

We slip past shrubs sculpted into animals I can't even recognize. The mirrors change too. Gilded snowflakes. Crescent moons. Spiky asphodels. Their reflections call our names, demand our gaze.

We don't look.

Something else changes in the maze. Or I hadn't noticed it before. When I lean in the wrong direction, the flower petals on the walls close tight like fists. If I turn the other way, they bloom. Full and beautiful.

They're directing me. Composing a song in step with the water.

At some point, Cary finds his way back to my side. He smells nice. Clean sweat and salt water. Our knuckles brush—steel meeting flint. The fire spreads to my lips.

"What do you know about Cora?"

His head turns a little. Shock briefly rings his eyes. "Only what I have read."

Right. Cary, ferrier of souls and part-time bookworm. It makes me smile. Knowing more about him now.

"It was long ago. She loved what she did for souls." His

eyes lower. "But she did not have a love of her own."

I guide us through another passage, listening.

"Then she fell for a mortal." Cary keeps his gaze from mine. "And he fell for her too."

We take a left. Then a right. It's another two passages before Cary speaks again.

"Love is not promised to Deathless. We cannot neglect our obligations."

He stops again. The tightness in his jaw tells me he's fighting with himself. Deciding whether to reveal more.

I cautiously brush the back of his hand. His fingers flex. Finally, his dark gaze levels with mine.

"What happened?"

"She hated being away from him." Behind his lashes, gold licks at the black. "So, she brought him to Aides."

I slow my steps as reality catches up. "He was the last mortal to come here, wasn't he? Before me."

Reluctantly, Cary nods. "She broke the rules for him. Over and over. Until she was given a choice: our world or yours."

Another piece falls into place. The rule of five visits. Cora is the reason it exists. Not to protect mortals. To protect the underworld's secrets, its existence.

"She chose love," I say.

"She chose mortality," Cary counters. "To lose who she was."

"For love," I reiterate. His mouth purses.

The flowers direct us to a narrower corridor. Our shoulders

graze. I say, "Then a Deathless can *choose* to be mortal."

Cary looks up. "Yes. I mean, no one has since her. From what I read, it is . . . well, complicated."

He doesn't elaborate. We fall back into silence. Heavy, suffocating silence.

"I'm sorry," I blurt. "That I used you."

Despite the anger still churning in me, I have to say this. I kept secrets from him too. He deserves to hear why.

"I was so desperate to talk to London again. Tell him—" I catch my bottom lip between my teeth, hesitating.

Time to stop blaming yourself, Auggie.

London's in my head. In my chest. He always has been.

"I needed closure. To say goodbye to him. The right way. And I let that desperation turn me into something I'm not."

Cary gives me a blank stare, unresponsive.

My face scrunches. "I should've told you the truth from the beginning. I shouldn't . . . You deserved better."

After a beat, Cary looks away. The flowers and serenading water take us left. Then left again. Out of nowhere, he says, "You were right."

When I stumble, his hand catches my elbow. Fast as lightning. He steadies me, then adds, "I did not understand mortals. I did not understand you, August."

His gaze is back on me. I open my mouth, but I'm unsure what to say. So I listen instead.

"There are millions who will never know that kind of love.

Who will never experience what it means to be loved in that way."

I swallow, struggling to keep eye contact. His intense stare refuses to let me look away.

"Grief needs to be *felt*," he says. "It is not a burden. It is a reminder. You were given the choice to love. To be loved. And you took it. You let it grow and become bigger than even you imagined."

My eyes burn with fresh tears. I don't blink.

Softly, seriously, he says, "That is a *gift*, August."

I lose the war with tears. Only a couple fall. Cary's fingers catch them.

He smiles. "But I did not understand how heavy that gift was until you. Until I saw the pain and guilt and loneliness that comes with it."

We stop somewhere in the middle of a passageway. His thumbs brush my cheeks dry.

"Sorry I never stuck around to see what happens after." He studies me. "I wish I had. I wish I had known sooner how that pain changes who you become."

Cary stays like that. Gentle hands cupping my cheeks. His attentive stare following my reactions, reluctant to look anywhere else.

Feverish want gnaws at my heart.

I want him in ways that are dangerous. That *hurt*. Because I know what it means to lose someone.

Because I can't have him.

Cary can never be mine, fully. He's the ferrier of souls. They need him and he won't leave them for . . . me.

I know it. In every bone. That doesn't stop my heart from slamming into my sternum, begging me to say something.

Tell him.

We've kept too many secrets from each other. Left too many words unsaid in our silence. His mouth quirks like he's reading my mind.

"Say it, Auggie."

My breath catches when he says my name. When he calls me *Auggie.* It's a new collection of notes, a forte that echoes through my head.

I reach up. My hands rest just under his ribs. He leans forward, exhales lowly. All I can think about is how that noise has unraveled me time after time.

"You give to all of them," I manage, voice shaking. "Every single soul. Let me give to you, Cary."

"Give what?"

I lick my lips.

"Wait." His fingers freeze on my jaw, thumb to my lips. "Listen."

It's hard not to. The buzzing is hauntingly loud. A swarm of bees cutting across a field.

Cary grabs my hand. "We need to go. Which way?"

It's hard to focus on the low ripple of water above the voices coming closer. I tune my ears. Pretend I'm on a crowded city bus with some kid dribbling his soccer ball. A baby crying. Some finance bro shouting into his phone.

I listen for the thing that calms me in the worst moments:

Music.

We run.

Around corners. Sliding through rights and lefts. The mirrors seem to glow brighter, reflecting light right into our eyes. I tug Cary with me, terror in my throat. Nightmares at our backs.

My hand tightens around his.

All Fate does is take from me. First London, which then snatched being able to call the house I grew up in my home. The city I love wasn't mine anymore. Losing him meant losing my love for music. It frayed my friendship with Max to loose threads I can't tie back together.

I know I can't have Cary. But I'll be damned if Fate yanks him from me too.

The light intensifies. It's almost unbearable, especially with sweat falling into my eyes. Eventually the glare melts. Rays of gold soften into pinks and oranges. The stench of dread fades to the fresh scent of shore and water.

An opening. An exit.

"Come on!"

I pull and Cary trips without falling. He meets my every stride. We stumble through the wide mouth at the end of the passageway.

Free from the labyrinth's jaws.

21

SILENCE.

The buzzing is gone. In its place, I hear the satisfying lap of water. A light breeze rustling cypress tree branches.

I'm bent over, hands on my knees. At some point, I lost Cary's grip. I don't know where. A knifing pain stabs my side. But I can't take my stare away from the labyrinth.

Nothing else emerges after us. Slowly, the vines stretch and twine. They form a gate that seals the maze.

We're safe.

As my breaths start to calm, I hear a slow clap from behind me.

My spine goes rigid. Sand kicks up as I hastily turn, panic cold in my belly.

Milos stands on Lethe's shore. His smirk taunts me. Cary kneels at his side, face crumpled in agony. Milos's fingers dig carelessly into his shoulder. The hiss he lets out vibrates through my body.

"Impressive," Milos says. "No one has ever found their way out of my labyrinth. Though I had hoped you would." Amusement glints in his eyes. "You truly are special, beautiful August."

I ignore his sneer. Concentrate on Cary. His half-bowed head. The way he struggles against Milos's grip, unable to shake him. He looks helpless.

No . . . *powerless.*

"The bargain," I say roughly.

Milos's mouth curves, sharp as a scythe. "My brother and his wants," he tuts.

He watches me. Waits for every little dot to connect. It doesn't take me long.

Of course Cary wouldn't tell me what he gave up. What he offered Milos to get inside the labyrinth. It was too big. He didn't want to put any more pressure on me to solve the maze.

He didn't want to burden me.

"His power," I say.

The light around Milos's irises is the purest gold. "Only temporarily."

He says it like it's a consolation. A prize for surviving his game. His fingers push deeper into the space between Cary's neck and shoulder. The skin purples in a way I've seen before. *On a human.*

"He was so worried about you," Milos huffs. "I do not know why. Clearly you are more than capable."

A low groan breaks past Cary's clenched teeth.

"Why his power?" I seethe.

"To make sure the challenge was still fair," Milos tells me, his lips pursed innocently.

I start toward him.

"Ah-*ah*." Milos shakes a finger while gripping Cary's tendons harder. His knees sink deeper into the sand.

"Let him go!"

Milos grins, teeth bared. "Soon. But first tell me—how did you two escape?"

My brows furrow. Irritation cuts across his features. My eyes fall to Cary. Through his strained expression, I see a warning in his gaze.

Do not tell him.

"The music," I reply.

Milos balks. "What music?"

"I heard a melody," I say, then smile. "And I wrote a song to it."

It's not a lie. Lethe gave me the notes. I simply composed my own lyrics over them: *right, left, right again, three lefts, two rights.* Not my best work. But it's finished, something I haven't done since London's death.

"Liar," Milos snarls. "You could not have solved my labyrinth with . . . music."

"I did," I say. "I beat your little maze. And now I can leave."

"It is true, brother," Cary adds, ragged breaths between his words. "You made a bargain. Now honor it."

Snidely, Milos says, "Always the rule follower. Mother's favorite. Her good, disciplined, obedient lapdog." He snatches his hand away from Cary. Nudges him into the sand with his foot.

Cary catches himself, but only just. His muscles quiver. My pulse beats thickly against my throat.

"Are you sure you want to leave, August?" My name is a dissonant note on Milos's tongue. So different from the way Cary says it. He grins kindly. "What about London?"

I flinch, eyes wide.

I hate that Milos knows who London is now. But I keep the fact that I saw London from him. That he's no longer the reason I'm still here in Aides, rooted to this place.

When Milos realizes his words have no effect on me, his tone changes. "Think of what you could have here. Never having to say goodbye to those you love ever again."

A cold sweat breaks out along my hairline.

I can't control Death. I can't stop who she comes for. *When* she comes. But if I accept Milos's deal—a life in Aides for him to have access to whatever power he believes I have—then I could at least still see the people Death takes.

I'd never feel the waves of grief. Drown in my heartache.

Cary's voice drifts through my head like the softest ballad.

Grief needs to be felt. *It is not a burden. It is a reminder. You were given the choice to love. To be loved. And you took it.*

I'm tired of fearing grief. Of thinking it'll destroy me instead of remembering what it gave to me in the first place.

I raise my chin. "No."

A deep shadow folds around Milos's face. "No?"

"No," I repeat, unflinching. Bold.

He throws his arms wide. "You would give all this up? If you leave, you cannot return."

The reminder strikes like lightning:

A mortal can only cross over five times. After that, they are forced to make a choice.

"Remain here, for eternity," I recite to myself. "Or never return. Not until death."

"Look around, August," Milos says in a syrupy tone. "This can be your kingdom. Your home."

For a moment, my eyes scan around. Aides is beautiful. Alluring, unpredictable. Veiled in a power that still leaves me breathless. There's a whisper-quiet part of me that feels a belonging.

I'm *welcome* here.

Santa Barbara is haunted by ghosts. By incomplete dreams of the August I *was*. Reminders of the August I never became. I wanted so badly to run from it. To escape.

But my parents are there. Max is too.

Santa Barbara is where I fell in love for the first time.

And, unknowingly, it's where I fell in love for a second time. In a pizzeria. On the steep wooden steps above a beach. In a clock tower high above the city. Between red larkspurs and fiery poppies in my mom's greenhouse.

Santa Barbara is where the first part of my story was written.

And it's where I'm deciding to write the next chapter.

I stand as tall as Milos. On equal ground. I may not know how to call forth my power. How I made flowers bloom or vines move. But I won't let Milos feel more powerful than me.

With finality, I say, "No. I'm leaving."

From his spot in the sand, Cary smiles weakly.

Fire burns in Milos's scowl. "You think it that simple?" He raises a hand. Wisps of black snake between his long fingers.

I take a step back.

"I am the prince of Aides," he half growls. "I have a role. The one my brother gave me."

His hand touches the back of Cary's neck.

Cary stiffens, grimacing. He pulls sand between his fingers. His body trembles.

I lurch forward. "No! Stop!"

A cruel glimmer lights Milos's eyes.

I don't have time to react. Cary lets out a long, hoarse cry before Milos releases him. He pants, chest heaving. But when his head lifts, I see his eyes. Gold poured around obsidian irises.

His power is back.

"He is the ferrier of souls." Milos holds my gaze. "And you will *never* have him."

The harsh truth nearly knocks my legs from under me. No matter who I am, what power I do or don't have . . . I can't change the rules of Aides.

"When you step into the waters"—there's an unnerving calmness to Milos's voice—"you will forget this place. Forget us. Forget him."

I watch Cary's face pale.

Milos approaches me. "Are you sure you want that?"

No, I want to scream, instinctively.

I don't want to lose him. I don't want to forget him.

I look at Cary. Every hard, delicate line in his face softens. I used to believe he was unreadable. Unknowable. But that's so far from reality.

He's a nerd about reading. He loves animals. Loves sweets, music. He's careful and protective and warm once you give him a chance to talk. He loves to tease and laugh. He's made mistakes, felt guilt over them. But he survived.

Just like me.

In his expression, I see what he wants to say:

It is okay, Auggie. You will be fine. You are more than what you give yourself credit for.

"August?" Milos prompts.

I can't tear my eyes from Cary. Shuddering, I whisper, "Yes."

Waving his hand dismissively, Milos snaps, "Then *leave us.* The same way your pathetic ancestor did."

He slips past me, disappearing.

I stumble forward. My knees hit soft sand as I kneel in front of Cary. His face tips up, sweat slick against his brow. That single curl rests on his forehead. When I reach to brush grains of sand from his shoulder, he catches my hand.

I'm scared to look at him, fully. I know the next part. Just like in the hospital two years ago, the moment I touched London's cold skin.

Cary squeezes my hand. And this is the worst part. Saying goodbye to someone who's still here.

My throat tightens. "Is it true? Will I forget you?"

The gold fades from his gaze. I stare into ocean-deep black as he nods once.

"There has to be a way to keep my memories. I'm Cora's descendant, damn it," I argue, feebly.

His lips dip the tiniest amount. "There are things in Aides I cannot explain."

Tears well in my eyes. I snort despite them. "Seems like everything here is unexplainable."

"Maybe to a mortal like you."

His playful smirk keeps me from breaking down. His thumb traces my palm, then my wrist. It's as if he's trying to memorize me.

As if, after I'm gone, he'll forget too.

"You gave up your power for me."

Cary shakes his head at the shock in my voice. "It is the least I would give up for you."

My eyes flit to Lethe. "Will you take me back?"

He says the one thing I wish he wouldn't: "I cannot."

"Then how? I can't do it without you."

His fingers skim along my forearm. "You are August Clarke." His lips lift higher. "Kind, thoughtful, strong. A pain in my ass."

I let out an indignant noise. His smile goes tender.

"And you make me want things I could never have."

"Hmm. I sound like a keeper."

Cary rests his forehead against mine. "If only I could."

For a beat, we stay like that. Our eyes locked. Breaths synchronized. My hands gripping his biceps. His hand tracing the lines of my tattoo.

"I want to be yours," I tell him.

"I am the ferrier," he says, voice cracking. "I only have moments."

"Then give me those," I half growl, half sob.

"Is that enough?"

"It is for me." A tear slips over my grin. "One page at a time. Remember?"

Cary's fingers still on my skin. His lips curve up again. "You are mine, Auggie."

Questions burn inside my throat. *How long will I have to wait? When will Death bring me back to you?* I swallow them all down.

He'd never tell me, anyway.

"Get in the water," Cary instructs. "Trust her. And remember to breathe."

Reluctantly, I start to pull away.

Cary drags me back. He kisses me. Feverish and slow and with promises I can't hear but take with my tongue.

"Do not look back, Auggie. Whatever you need will be with you."

In the shallow waters, my feet are heavy. The coolness rises around my knees, my thighs. Lethe sighs happily the farther I wade.

I do exactly what Cary said: I trust her.

When the water's up to my shoulders, I breathe. It's like the first time. Like every time. She welcomes me back. One final time.

An anxious need surges through my nerves. Coils around my bones, pulsing into my muscles. Despite his demands, I look back at the shore. I can't help myself.

Cary's gone.

Before I can take my next breath, I sink.

And sink.

And sink.

I jolt awake.

A scream claws at my throat. It's too dry for anything more than a weak gasp. Sweat dampens my face. My muscles ache like I've been running. Or trying not to drown.

It takes a moment before my eyes adjust. Silvered light streams across my sheets. I'm in my bedroom. But I can't remember how I got here. My head is fuzzy, falling in and out of focus.

When I was eleven, I had my tonsils removed. My mom thought it was a just bad sore throat. A virus I caught at school. But my dad knew better. This is how I felt after the procedure and the anesthesia wore off.

Foggy. Like the world wasn't real. Walking through a thick haze and unsure of where I was going.

I blink again. My gaze snags on something. A navy blue hoodie at the end of my bed. In the night's half light, yellow letters spell out *UCSB*.

London's hoodie.

Quietly, I wait for the ache to come. Spread through my chest. Leave me curled in a ball for hours. But the feeling never arrives. Instead, a sensation I haven't felt in years blossoms bright and wild inside my veins.

Gratitude.

I hug the cottony soft material to my chest. He's not gone. I still have a piece of him here with me. In my arms. In my heart.

The door creaks open. I half expect it to be Diana.

Max's head peeks in. "Are you up?"

Weary, I nod. On the fringes of my memory, I remember fighting with her. Our harsh words in the pizzeria. Max walking away. Me storming out.

She sucks in her cheeks, also uncertain of where we stand. Her eyes fix on the hoodie. "Is that . . . London's?"

Again, I nod.

Max sits next to me. Shoulder to shoulder.

We hover in silence. I tug at a loose thread in the hoodie's hem. She glances at my naked bedroom walls. The lack of real furniture. It looks like no one lives here. Like I made myself disappear from this home Max made for me.

The corners of her mouth lift a little. "You need a dresser. And a hamper."

Diana has happily flopped onto my pile of discarded clothes on the hardwood floor.

Max taps her chin. "While we're at it, hang some photos on these boring-ass walls."

"Of you and me?" I suggest.

"No. Just me. Everyone should have a framed image of this beautiful face."

I laugh. It feels good in my chest. Missed, needed.

"Some plants too?" I propose.

Max reels back. "Plants? You?"

I give a half-hearted shrug. "Yeah. I'm not saying I'm good at it." Light warms my skin as I daydream about my mom's greenhouse. My favorite place in the city. In the world. "But I want to keep trying."

That makes Max chew on her lip.

"Auggie—" Her voice isn't as confident as it was a second ago. "I'll never know what you lost that night." She skims fingers up the sleeve of London's hoodie. "But I lost him too. We were friends. The three of us. Because of you."

She goes quiet again.

I breathe deeply. She smells of those spicy samosas from the Indian kitchen on State Street she loves. Salty from a breeze I associate with the Santa Barbara State campus.

Her hand is faintly sweaty as it closes around mine.

I turn my head to study her frown.

"What's even worse is"—she pauses to sigh—"I lost my best

friend that night. Instead of grieving over someone I'll never get back, I've had to watch you stop existing right in front of me."

I swallow a lump. "I'm sorry."

"I don't want an apology!"

The hoodie's sleeve is twisted in her fingers. The second Max realizes it, she lets go, cheeks pink.

"I know," I say. "But I need to say it anyway."

Max has never pushed me. From the moment she showed up at the hospital, letting me sob on her shoulder, to the day of the funeral, to now. She wasn't like everyone else.

That's why I owe her this.

"I kept thinking one day I'd wake up and feel better," I admit. "I'd be normal again."

"You were never normal," she teases.

My shoulder bumps hers.

"Everyone moved on." The lump swells again. I push through. "And I thought I was taking too long. That I needed to figure it out by myself."

Because everyone else did. No one else needed two years to grieve. Not London's friends from school. His parents. My parents. Only me.

Tears shine in Max's eyes. "You know that's not how grief works, right? There's no time limit."

I shrug. "It feels that way."

"Why didn't you say anything?"

Anger wrinkles my face. "Because I don't want anyone's pity."

"It's not pity," she says firmly. "It's love."

My head rests against the wall. I stare up at the ceiling. When you're drowning, it's hard to tell love from pity. Someone reaching a hand to you from someone waiting for you to save yourself. I guess I could never tell which it was.

"If you need more space," she starts, "I'll give it to you."

I try to imagine a world where I see Max less. Where she's not always right there, cracking a joke or talking about a girl she likes or complaining about a lack of coffee. Where our friendship is a flicker instead of a flame.

Exhaling through my nose, I say, "I don't want space."

Max leans against my shoulder.

"I don't want you to go away either," I continue. What she said a minute ago hangs on my thoughts like smoke. "I didn't mean to get like this. To . . . disappear."

"I know," she echoes my words from earlier.

I see her hesitation. Afraid to say what she's thinking. I give her permission with a gentle nudge.

"My mom says when someone's grieving, they just check out. It's not on purpose. They can't control it." Her finger taps the back of my hand. "*You* can't control it, Auggie."

A beat slips by as I stare at my ceiling.

"Your mom sounds like a smart woman."

An indignant laugh rattles through Max. "Never, ever tell her that."

I gaze down at my wrist. London's bracelet is gone. I can't remember where I lost it. When it fell off. But I don't think I need it the way I used to.

It was a symbol of the hold his love had on me.

Of the past I couldn't let go of.

London never lived in the past. He wanted a future. He planned for it. He planned for both of us. I owe it to him—*to me*—to do a little planning of my own.

I clear my throat. "Can you ask your mom to help me find someone? To talk to about . . . all of this?"

Moonlight accentuates the surprise around Max's eyes. "Of course. If you're ready?"

"I am," I say, confidently.

I'm done shutting the people I love out. Putting my life on pause. I trace the letters on London's hoodie. *My* hoodie now.

"He wouldn't want me to give up," I add.

Max loops her arms around me. Her face presses against my shoulder. "It's not what I want either."

Smiling, I rest my head against hers. The world isn't in full focus yet. Parts of my head are still blurred. But, for now, it's enough.

The August I am in this very moment is enough to fight the tide.

22

Three Months Later

MY FINGERS FLEX and close. Over and over.

Thankfully, the stress ball doesn't pop.

Rebecca, my therapist, watches with a kind smile. She's incredibly patient. Never seems to mind the silence. It's been minutes since I last said anything. My eyes keep flitting to the digital clock on the wall.

The slow countdown until our session is over.

Her office is nice. Whimsical, like her. Cozy furniture in bright plaid patterns. Cream shag carpet, soft as a dog's fur. Shelves stuffed with rainbow-spined books that have nothing to do with therapy.

In one corner, there's a giant scissors sculpture. On my first visit, she explained, "They represent the things you want to cut from your life."

That was six weeks ago. After Dr. Cho recommended her.

I squeeze the ball again.

"We can talk about something else," Rebecca offers.

Quickly, I say, "No." Another squeeze. "I can do this."

Rebecca nods, grinning.

Another minute goes by. The air is heavy with my hesitation. I find things to focus on until the words come.

This room always smells of candy. I can never find any. Maybe it's a candle or one of those fragrant wall plug-ins. In the distance, a dog barks. When I swallow, I taste the spearmint tea she keeps stocked in the waiting room. The sofa is worn-soft under my fingertips. Rebecca's belted navy dress has orange flowers on it.

Marigolds.

After one more squeeze, I exhale. "I saw London's parents. By accident."

Her head tilts, curious. "Around the city?"

"No." My pulse drums against the back of my jaw. "At his grave."

I visit him regularly now. At least once a week. The first time, I asked Max to come. Since then, I go alone. I like the privacy, a chance to be with just him and my ever-flowing thoughts.

I sit on the grass in front of his headstone. Talk to him as if he was there. Green-eyed, weird smile.

Rebecca nods along. "How did you feel when you saw them?"

A beat passes. I shrug weakly. "Surprised." I'm not sure

why. Of course they would visit their son's grave. But it wasn't just that.

They were together. Holding hands. The warm thrill of it caught me off guard. London had feared they would get divorced. That his leaving for college would be the breeze that swept away the last grains of their marriage.

It didn't happen.

Instead, his death kept them together. Grief is easier when there's someone with you fighting the waves. It's something I wish I'd learned earlier.

"No, I mean," I say, shaking my head, "I felt . . . good."

On every visit, I bring London marigolds. Sometimes a bouquet, sometimes just one flower. His mom noticed. She drew me into her arms, grateful tears dampening my shoulder. She didn't hate me for what happened to him. Neither of them did.

It was a relief as bright as the first rays of summer.

Now I blink away the sting in my eyes.

So far, I've only cried once in our sessions. That first appointment. It was my biggest worry. That a stranger would see me as fragile, pathetic. That I was voluntarily allowing someone to judge whether my pain was earned or not.

But Rebecca hasn't been like that. She expects nothing from me. It makes it easier to give what I want.

She makes a note in her journal. "Did they ask to see you again?"

My fingers tighten around the ball. "Yes."

"Do you want to?" Before I can answer, she says, "You don't have to. You're not on anyone's timeline, August."

"I know." Mostly.

Her dark eyebrows climb her forehead. She has pale white skin. A spill of freckles across her nose and cheeks.

"I'm not ready," I say.

"Did you tell them?"

There's no hesitation this time. I nod.

"And did they understand?"

The ball almost slips from my sweaty hand. Rebecca doesn't comment. I've done better at tempering my anger. She encourages me to let it out while we're together. To stop trying to cage the things that need to run wild.

"They came around," I confess.

"And are you okay with that?"

Our sessions have taught me something: Moving on doesn't mean forgetting. I can go forward with my life and *choose* what parts of the past I want to take with me. Like my memories of London. The things he taught me about myself. And the relationships I made because of him.

Chewing the inside of my cheek, I say, "I want to see them again. One day."

Rebecca smiles. "One day," she echoes. "When you decide to. Let's circle back to that another time. Are you still writing music?"

My face lights up. "Yeah."

It was slow in the beginning. Part of it was fear. Would I still love it? Could I write anything without thinking of London? But it happened, on a sunny morning while sitting in my mom's greenhouse.

A song I couldn't get out of my head.

I've already filled the leather journal from my dad. Lyrics inked down every page.

Songs are stories. And stories need to be told. Carried from one voice to the next. I don't want the end of my story to be what happened the night of the accident. I want it to go on.

"How does it feel?" Rebecca asks.

Tipping my head back, I breathe, "Amazing."

Her grin stretches. "Good. And college?"

I give the stress ball a half squeeze. That was the topic of our second appointment: College, my dad's expectations, the plans London created for us. What I really want for myself.

That last one took some thought. "I'm still going to apply," I finally answer.

"Do you want to talk through where?"

"No. I have a few places in mind."

UC Santa Barbara is one of them. I missed the deadline for fall semester. That's okay. I did some research. I can do a year at SB State and then transfer to UCSB. Or I can go somewhere else.

For once, I'm living in my moment rather than someone else's. I'm giving myself permission to change my mind too.

Rebecca studies me. "What do you want to talk about, then?"

Another minute ticks by on the clock. I lower my eyes.

For the last three months, I've been having recurring dreams. A place near but far. Real but not. It's never clear. When I wake up, I can't remember specific details.

Just that it's beautiful. And calling to me. A siren's song.

"August?"

My head snaps up. Gentle concern fills Rebecca's eyes. The ball is squeezed to its limit in my hand.

"Umm." I decide to pivot from the topic of dreams. I'm not ready. Smiling, I say, "I think I want to start driving again."

My parents stand when I walk out of the office. They come to every session. My dad made it a point to drive me here the first time.

His hand wraps around the back of my neck. "Okay, son?"

I grin. "Okay."

Mom sidles up to my other side. She smells of soil and fresh lemons. She looks younger too. They both do. As if worrying over me took years from the time they have.

Guilt sits as heavy as stones in my stomach. The feeling dissolves when I remember something Rebecca said:

Great parents will always worry they haven't done enough for you. It's in their nature. It's also something you can't control, so don't let it control how you feel.

Mom looks at my dad. "Should we get lunch? Do you have time?"

He puffs his chest out. "For you two? I'll make time."

"Does anyone care if I have time?" I ask with a teasing smirk.

Dad presses his hand dramatically to his chest. "Oh, Your Majesty, our apologies! Can you spare a moment for your poor *aging* parents?"

I roll my eyes. "Yeah, sure. I guess."

"Don't ruin your reputation for us," Mom says dryly, but her arms hug my waist. Like she believes I really might leave them behind one day.

Dad's phone buzzes. His coppery eyebrows knot as he reads the screen. It's obviously the hospital.

"We can get lunch tomorrow," I offer. "After my volunteer shift."

That's another thing therapy has helped me with. Twice a week, I volunteer at Santa Barbara Cottage Hospital. In the pediatric wing with my dad. It took him by surprise when I suggested the idea. Me too.

I thought I'd never be able to walk through that hospital again. Not without breaking down. Remembering every detail from that night. The memories still come. But I'm better at managing them.

Better at leaving those ghosts in the past.

The kids are great too. They're always so eager, so loud, living life as if time doesn't matter. I sing my songs for them. Sit in their rooms until they fall asleep. Anything to help them forget where they are or what they're experiencing.

Dad pockets his phone. "Nope. This is family time. We deserve this."

My face splits into a grin. "Does that mean you'll try sriracha on your burrito today?"

He pretends to consider it. "For you, Auggie? Hell no!"

Our laughter echoes through the room long after we're gone.

"You're late."

Max glares at me from the doorway of Viva Catalina's.

I grin, leaning against the front counter. I arrived an hour ago. Thirty-six minutes before my shift started, a new record.

"You'll never get promoted like this," I say, parroting the words she's used against me so many times.

Max yanks off her bag. In one easy move, she flips me a very unfriendly finger before disappearing to the back.

"Is working the register really considered a promotion around here?" Arden, the new hire, asks.

I grab the tub of dirty dishes from their hands. "Absolutely. Did you clean the restrooms yet?"

They groan, skulking away.

The pizzeria's busy today. Tables filled. Not an empty seat at the bar. January's warm weather means the patio has a nice crowd too. All customers either around my age or younger.

I box to-go orders Junie and Tonia sling out. Eventually, Max joins me.

"Remind me to never sign up for a class that's just called Shakespeare."

"That bad?" I ask.

She sighs mournfully. "Worse."

"Sorry to hear that. But you were still late." I poke her shoulder. "That's coming out of your tips. Compensation for all the extra energy I had to use."

Max smiles wryly. "Then you can use that money to pay your half of the rent. Since you're late . . . again."

I laugh. Some things in my life haven't changed. But it feels good to have my best friend back.

The flow of customers stays constant. I jump in to help Arden reset tables. Clean up the messes large families leave behind. Together, we work down the dishes piling up. Fold napkins around silverware between delivery orders.

Kennedy pops by with wild eyes. She shoves a warm plate in my hands. "August, can you take this over to table nine?"

"Why can't Max?"

She tuts. "You mean the same Max who's too busy making eyes with that pretty girl?"

I glance over my shoulder. Sure enough, Max is blatantly flirting with a Black girl who has glowing brown skin and shoulder-length locs. Her UCSB sweatshirt is cut into a cute halter top.

Before I can say anything else, Kennedy walks away, calling out, "Thanks, love you!"

Sighing, I march over to the corner booth.

The sun frames a boy's angular face. He has a warm gold complexion. Dark hair that falls in loose curls. He wears a navy-and-white-striped T-shirt. His silver chain has three red-jeweled charms in the shape of dog paws hanging from the end.

He's the kind of pretty that's almost unapproachable if not for the way he smiles. Sweet like honey.

My stomach flips. Heat stirs in my chest. A few weeks ago, I told Rebecca I was *considering* dating again. I think it's what London would've wanted. More importantly, it's what I want.

No one's caught my eye yet. I'm too busy discovering August again. But when I look at this boy, a tender lullaby starts in my ears.

The call of the sea.

I place the plate in front of him. Trying not to stare, my eyes lower to the pizza slice. His choice of toppings is . . . interesting.

"Pineapple, pepperoni, and jalapeños?"

He tilts his head. "I heard it's good."

"You heard right," I confirm.

His smile brightens. That bud in my chest blooms. A strange, almost familiar heat tingles through my limbs.

The boy leans forward. A single curl sweeps over his brow. "What's your name?"

"August."

"August," he repeats, slow and deliberate. As if he's tasting the flavor of my name. Deciding whether he likes it. I don't know why that drags a blush into my cheeks. "Are people allowed to call you Auggie?"

I cock my chin. "Only people I trust. And like."

One of his thick eyebrows curves. "Then I hope to be both one day."

My laugh is a sharp, surprised noise. "Wow. That's bold of you."

He drums long fingers on the table to the music playing. "Life's too short to be scared of rejection. We only have moments, Auggie."

I like the sound of his voice. His accent. I can't quite place where I've heard it before. He's not from around here. Probably just visiting, like so many in Santa Barbara.

I also like the way his eyes never leave my face. As if he wants to *see* me, fully.

"Who said I was rejecting you?" I tease.

The corners of his mouth soften. A new world unfolding.

"You never told me your name," I say.

His fingers stop. "Cary."

"Like Grant? Or that one guy from *The Princess Bride* movie?"

"I've never seen it."

The music transitions to something pop-like, heavy guitars and piano. My hands stir at my sides, itching to write. Maybe something about how pillowy this boy's lips look. Or the smooth hills of his biceps as he rests his elbows on the table. The sun as it dances across his dark eyes.

Cary's attention is focused on my hands, intrigued. I tuck away my usual embarrassment as his gaze lifts.

I should go, I think.

Instead, I say, "I've never seen you before," even though State Street is constantly crawling with tourists. People I will never remember.

For some reason, I know I won't forget him.

"I'm new to the city," he says.

It's my turn to cock an eyebrow. "Where are you from?"

Cary grins. It's like light cutting across a field of fog. "You ask a lot of questions, Auggie. I like that."

Epilogue

After the After

I SHOULDN'T BE here. It's not his time.

But I can't help myself.

The last time I was in this hospital, I was dead. An untethered soul. Now I'm something more. That doesn't quiet the chill that vibrates through me. The reminder that, even with its glowing white lights and cream walls, not everyone leaves this place alive.

I follow the halls to the pediatric center. A small room is gradually filling up. Doctors escort kids inside. Some are wheeled in by nurses. Their faces are bright as sunlight on the ocean despite the tubes or machines or caps hiding bald heads.

They're eager for what's next. I am too. And our wait isn't very long.

An older girl whoops when, from the other side of the

room, *he* walks in. A smile flows like a wave over my lips. My pulse leaps.

He's older now. Twenty. He still has the same crown of tight bronze curls. Warm brown skin and vibrant eyes. A faint shadow around his round jaw from facial hair he can't quite grow right, just like his dad.

"August," I whisper, though no one can hear me. Or see me.

Still, his head turns for the briefest second before he refocuses on the cheering kids.

He goes around the room giving hugs. High fives. It's cool in the hospital, and he wears a navy hoodie.

My grin arcs higher. It was once mine. He hasn't forgotten me. Our dreams. But he's also made space in his life, in his world, for new things.

Soon, another boy joins him. He's just as tall, with pale gold skin. Loose curls fall around fine bone structure. His hugs last longer. His attention lingers on anyone who calls him.

"Cary! Cary!"

He's careful with each of them. Cracks terrible jokes to make them laugh. Kind with his almost-black eyes. He holds their hands. Just as he held mine.

A memory wisps like smoke in my head:

We stood in Aides's great hall. Cary and me. Surrounded by flowers and statues and power I couldn't wrap my brain around.

"Wh-what do you mean you *choose* me?" I stammered.

He smiled patiently. Then he explained to me his time as the ferrier was done. He was ready to move on. He finally *could*. He told me why he stayed for so long in the first place.

"To care for them." Gold glittered in his eyes. "So they did not feel alone or scared after their mortal time ended."

The souls, like me.

"But why me?"

It made no sense. This was the underworld. There were so many others he could pick.

Again, the corners of his lips lifted. "Because you *care*, London."

He reminded me of that night. When he came to me in the hospital. Of the one thing I asked him to do:

Look after August.

"You wanted nothing else of me," Cary said, relieved. "I know you will do the same for them. Just like I did."

It was a lot. What he was asking of me. I knew of the Deathless. I had been in Aides for two years. Well, longer in their time.

That didn't mean I fully understood them. What it meant to *be* one.

I had so many questions. How long had Cary been a Deathless? How long would *I* be one? What if I said no? I'd been waiting my turn to be judged by the prince. Was there something greater waiting for me in Aides?

Something . . . worse?

Was I good enough to carry the weight and power of the ferrier?

"London."

His hand grabbed mine. I remembered the comfort in his touch. And I saw the certainty in his eyes. It was the same way August used to look at me.

Like I was a flame that couldn't be put out.

I'd needed that Cary in the hospital. His sure grip on my hand. His smile. All my mortal life, I'd planned for what was next. And when those plans were ripped away, I had . . . nothing.

Except for his kindness.

And there were millions more who needed that. Who needed someone to understand their fear.

"Okay," I said. Helping others wasn't such a bad way to spend the afterlife.

Then another question came to me: "What happens to you?"

He stared at something in his other hand. Daffodil petals.

"I want to be with him." His gaze searched my face for understanding. I already knew. The moment I saw August again in the maze. The gentle flicker of love behind his eyes when I mentioned Cary. "Is that okay?"

I was surprised by his question. Even more shocked by how easily, how quickly I answered: "Yes."

In every second I've been away from him, all I've wanted was for August to move on. To remember me but not to be held back by those memories. To live his life.

Somehow, with Cary, I knew he'd do that.

Now I watch them sit on stools at the front of the room. A hush falls over the kids. Quiet as sunrise. Cary plays guitar. And August sings.

His voice still isn't great. To make up for it, he coaxes the kids to join in. They make up songs with silly lyrics. They laugh and laugh. And Cary grins, staring at August with fondness etched into every corner of his face.

"Them *again*?"

I don't fight my own grin when someone stands next to me. Thick, shiny black hair. Reddish-brown skin, soft as clay. Tall and lanky and impeccably dressed. The boy who found me, who brought me to August.

The messenger.

"Are you stalking me?" I ask.

Henri scoffs. "No. You're not cute enough for that kind of wasted energy." He chuckles. His attention drifts. "How are they?"

Between songs, Cary touches the inside of August's forearm. New ink maps out a flower beneath his daffodil. An asphodel. Like the ones in the Meadows. Though neither August nor Cary remembers them.

August ruffles Cary's hair. It sticks up everywhere. The children giggle. When Cary leans over to kiss August's cheek, they gag and pretend to vomit.

I finally answer Henri. "Happy."

"As they should be," he comments, yearning in his voice. He misses them. But he's not angry with Cary's decision.

My eyes study August for a moment.

We were not forever. But we were *for now*. Neither one of us knew it then. How beautiful and rare that is. To have the chance to love and be loved equally.

I do now. I think he does too.

"Come. You know the rules." Henri tugs on the sleeve of my navy Henley. He smells like coffee. My favorite scent. "They're waiting on you."

I hear them. The souls all over this realm. Death's whispered call to guide them.

Grinning, I say, "Since when do you care about rules?"

A smirk flexes his lips. "Don't stay too long." Gold flashes over his eyes. "I'm waiting on you too."

His lips brush my cheek the same way Cary's did to August. But not with sweetness. With suggestion and promise.

A blush burns against my skin. That isn't such a bad way to spend the afterlife either.

Henri disappears into the shadows. I stay a second longer. A minute. Until I don't know how much time has passed.

I take August in. Smiling, healthy, growing.

One day, I'll come back, and he'll be graduating from UCSB. One day, he'll be in the middle of Shoreline Park, on bended knee, proposing. It'll be spontaneous and completely him. He will get a dog: a Great Dane. Maybe he'll get three.

One day, he'll get married. I'll watch, smiling proudly. One day, August will have kids. He's gonna be an amazing dad. They'll live in a beachside house where August can listen, write music to the roaring waves and the laughter coming from every room.

One day, he'll be old. Gray and wrinkled, but still so in love with life. Grateful for his time.

And I will come for him. He won't recognize me, but maybe he will. Maybe Lethe's magic isn't as powerful as the one inside him.

Maybe love is its own kind of magic. One that cannot be stripped or dulled or erased. One that can never truly be forgotten.

When August returns to Aides, I'll make sure he's with Cary, wherever that may be.

But that's later. *Much* later.

For now, I watch him for one more breath.

His fearless smile. The way he lives in the moment. Every single one. His life is unplanned and . . . happy. The way it should be.

He loves Cary. And Cary loves him.

Together, they are myths made to be recited in song and stars.

Acknowledgments

For almost a decade, I have tried to write a book about my grief. Idea after idea came to me, but when I sat down to draft them, I couldn't face that ache. The tide that kept tugging me under. I didn't know *how* to. Not until I added mythology and a hint of magic and what I was truly missing: patience and grace.

Just like not every wound heals the same, not every story told can be told in the way we want. But there are plenty of people I need to thank for allowing me to go on this journey in my own time.

My thoughtful and genius editor, Dana Leydig—how lucky am I? Thank you for walking the labyrinth with me. So much of August and Cary's story exists because you believed in me. (And Henri is definitely for you!)

My wise and encouraging agent, Thao Le—thank you for taking this concept to a level I never imagined. I'm so grateful for your willingness to battle any problem that comes my way. Even the Deathless should fear you! Thank you to everyone at the Sandra Dijkstra Literary Agency for all you do to make my career what it is.

The extraordinary team at Penguin: Tamar Brazis, Jim Hoover, Marinda Valenti, Krista Ahlberg, Jessica White, Joy Hoppenot, Vanessa Robles, Lizzie Goodell, Gaby Corzo, Ginny Dominguez, Felicity Vallence, Shannon Spann, Astrid Rojas, Emily Romero, Christina Colangelo, Danielle Presley, Rebecca Waugh, Emily Parliman, Desiree Johnson, you turned a hopeful dream of mine into the most unexpected reality.

Ailee Marie (illustrator) and Kaitlin Yang (designer) for the utterly breathtaking cover—there's true magic in what you've created.

Tessa Gratton for answering all my silly questions on "how to write a fantasy." Natalie C. Parker and Lana Wood Johnson for your excitement when I was still too clumsy to explain my idea. Adib Khorram and Jen Ferguson for sitting around in a downtown LA hotel room and helping me detangle the heart of August, Cary, and London's story. Preeti Chhibber, Kate Dramis, and Vania Stoyanova for being my co-writing buddies. Dustin Thao for listening to my initial pitch years ago and being the first to DM when the cover was revealed—we really are each other's biggest fans.

Every author who has been brave enough to write a book about grief—thank you for showing me the path.

Huge thanks to the bookstores, booksellers, and online bookish communities who continue to shout about my stories. Little Shop of Stories, Brave + Kind, Charis Books & More, All the Tropes, Read It Again, Eagle Eye Books, and all the Atlanta bookstores who keep my novels on their shelves—I adore you. Sydney Wilson and Matilda McNeely for being my loudest cheerleaders every time I wanted to give up. Also, for your brilliant recs!

To the readers: This is not possible without you. You mean the world to me. I hope you continue to find yourself in my stories and know that you matter.

My family and friends—you love me at my worst. For that, I have no words. But I sincerely want you to know that it does not go unseen. I appreciate you.

Finally, to anyone who is or has struggled with grief: You are not alone. Take as much time as you need. There is no rush, no countdown. Know that what you're feeling isn't loss . . . it's *love*. And that is a rare kind of magic not many will ever have.

In the words of Laura Dooney: "What is grief, if not love persevering?"

I'm with you. Together, we will find our way.